Spawning Ground

Kevin Cockle

Spawning Ground

Kevin Cockle

TYCHE BOOKS LTD.

Spawning Ground
Published by Tyche Books Ltd.
www.TycheBooks.com

Copyright © 2016 Kevin Cockle
First Tyche Books Ltd Edition 2016

Print ISBN: 978-1-928025-57-3
Ebook ISBN: 978-1-928025-58-0

Cover Art by James F. Beveridge
Cover Layout by Lucia Starkey
Interior Layout by Ryah Deines
Editorial by M.L.D. Curelas

Author photograph by Matheisson & Hewitt Photography

This book was funded in part by a grant from the Alberta Media Fund.

Alberta
Government

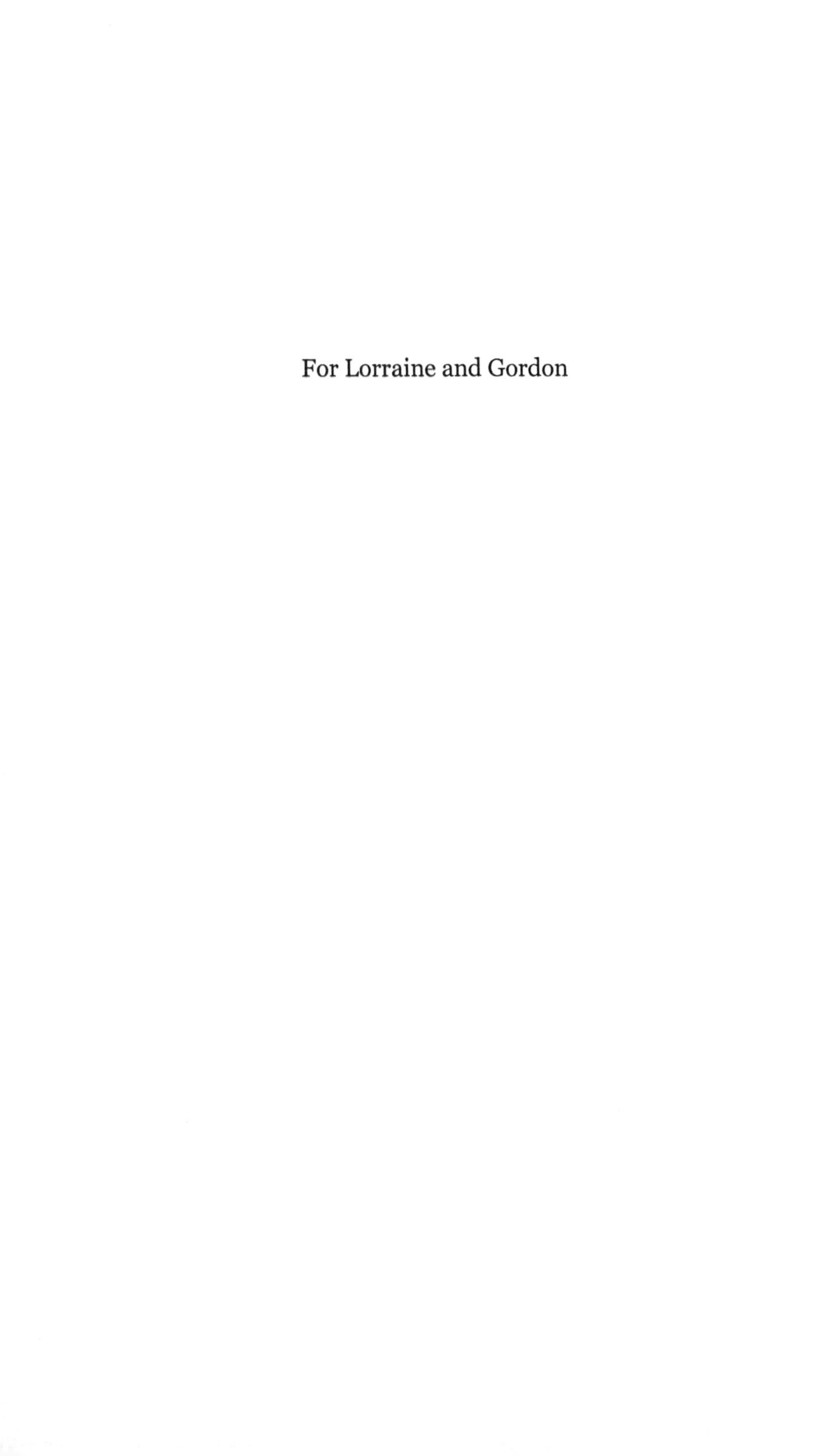

For Lorraine and Gordon

Weakness is a provocation.

— Andronicus, 89BC

Calgary, Canada

"YOU FEEL LIKE taking a break?"

John "Johnny" Johannson looked up from his present-value columns, for-ex sensitivity projections and brief-notes to see Sarah Wheeler standing there in all her glory. She was leaning her right shoulder against the doorframe of his 28th floor storage-closet-turned-office, holding a bottle of Syrah in her dangling left hand, and two wine glasses from their bases in her up-turned right. Straight, soft blonde hair trailed down behind her shoulders, framing a face of patrician cheekbones and polar-cold, silver-blue eyes that held just the hint of a Nordic taper. A crisp off-white blouse lay open to the second button, tucked into a tan power skirt that wrapped tightly about toned power-curves. Strong, heptathelete's legs ended in bare feet. It was clear that whether Johnny wanted a break or not, Sarah was ready for one.

"Umm . . . ," John began as Sarah pushed up off the doorframe with a smile, turned, and began to prowl away into the semi-lit gloom of the office after dark. He could hear the glasses tinkling in the distance, calling him to mischief.

"Jesus Christ!" John muttered as he stood to follow, then stopped, returning to lock down his various open systems with a rushed clacking of typing fingers. In India, at the Conlin, Wilhelm and Loughren (CWL) processing branch, maybe you could have gotten away with relaxed security protocols, but

1

here? In the Calgary head office? Instant dismissal for leaving your workstation open and unattended. His personal web-tv flat-screen was fine: he left that on with the sound muted—tuned to the "I-C-U" game show just as two new competitors were getting wired up.

This is it, John thought to himself as he scrambled out from behind the desk, then consciously slowed himself so as not to appear too eager. Of course, he *was* eager. He'd been three weeks at the head office on special assignment—contract only—they'd flown him and two other associates in to work the WeiTom merger. Too much security required to outsource, so he'd gotten the call-up after six long years in the sub-continental salt mines. He was twenty-eight years old: now or never country. If he wanted to make the jump from Indian boilerplate work to a full-time head office assignment, he had to make an impression.

One way—call it the "necessary" if not "sufficient" condition—of impressing the partners was to do what he was doing tonight: staying late, after getting in early. The firm had someone do the associates' laundry, had someone bring in food, anything to keep asses in saddles and riding hard. That John was good, reliable, and durable had gotten him the head-office invite, but *staying* . . . that would mean showing a bit more "compete".

In three weeks, he'd been shot down by Perry's assistant what's-her-name; struck out not once but twice with head reception; gone down in flames in one of the worst lunchroom pick-up attempts in corporate history. It was hard because they knew how badly he needed to show some swagger, and the harder he tried, the less convincing he was. CWL, like any top firm, only hired the best, most aggressive lawyers and aides. They didn't give a shit about how you handled boilerplate files in India, no matter how precise you were. They wanted to see your teeth. They wanted to know you had bite. And if you couldn't nail an assistant in damn near a month of trying, that was really all they needed to know.

And now—land o' fucking Goshan—Sarah Wheeler shows up all vixen-hot, bored, and bearing alcohol. It was a home run: she was a stunner, so that was covered, but even more important, she was a junior partner. And not just any junior partner—a woman who had articled at fourteen and billed more hours per annum than anyone in firm history. Where most young guns logged routine "all-nighters" to beat expectations, Sarah had reset the bar with her now infamous "all-weekers". Even in India, the admin grunts had heard of Sarah Wheeler. What was she now, eighteen, twenty? Something like that. Everyone knew her, everyone was impressed by her, and now, by God, John "Johnny" Johannson was going to close the deal with her, and go straight to the top of the food chain.

Stepping out of his office into a narrow aisle, passing through a maze of short-walled cubicles, John couldn't help but contrast his current surroundings with his former posting in the legal hinterland. The 28th floor here, in Calgary, was austere, grey, sterile, utilitarian, and admin-oriented, with the feel of a place that was at least partially designed to weed out those who really didn't want to be there. Like a coffee shop with ill-fitting chairs, CWL didn't want supporting players who could be comfortable on the 28th for very long. But compared to the contracts office in India, the place was Nirvana. Never mind the air conditioning that never worked, the mildew, the pre-fab walls, and the metal desks and cabinets that were just the right height for impacting careless knees or elbows, the despair in the South Asian processing branch made morale on the 28th look positively gung-ho.

John frowned when he couldn't immediately locate Sarah, but it made a kind of intuitive sense. She was a visitor to the 28th, not a resident. If she wanted a "break", it wasn't going to be down here in the 21st century equivalent of the stables. It was going to be upstairs, where they probably had actual rooms assigned for this kind of thing. Hurrying to the internal staircase that linked only the CWL floors of the tower, John ascended to the Olympian heights of the 30th floor.

The difference between the 28th and 30th floors in Calgary mirrored the difference between the 28th floor and the support hub in India. *Clients* came to the 30th after all: it was just as much a different world as India was. With its floor tiles made of Italian marble, oak paneled walls, and brass appointments, reception looked like something out of a five star hotel. It had a manorial feel, more like visiting someone's castle than an office.

"'Live' oak," Johnny muttered to himself, remembering the

orientation he'd been given by Jacob Conlin—the first and last time John had seen the senior partner. The wall paneling was not made of simple "oak": *Live oak was the preferred wood of warships in the 19th century. Twice as hard as regular oak. High tech, state of the art defence material at the time. USS Constitution was made out of it—hull so hard cannonballs would bounce right off. That's the kind of detail that matters at Conlin, Wilhelm and Loughlin. Not "oak", lad. Live oak.*

It was rah-rah bullshit, but it had the intended effect. Johnny had automatically seen the difference between CWL and other firms on the street after that talk: it was the difference between oak and live oak. He noted one other observation. CWL took itself very seriously as a weapon of war.

A door to the right of reception had been stopped-open, and John smiled. His security card wouldn't have operated the lock after hours, a fact which Sarah had thoughtfully considered. Taking the only avenue open to him, John headed down the carpeted hall feeling better about himself than he had at any time since getting off the plane at Calgary International.

There was Perry's fiefdom, then Huberman's corner-joint— each territory enclosed behind impressive double doors that would open onto further sub-suites of offices. Sarah's own office was smaller, though exquisitely decorated in a crystalline motif, but a quick head-bob past the open door revealed that she wasn't there. Through a process of elimination, Johnny hastened towards the meeting rooms along the southern wall of the floor.

Sarah was a Program chick—short for Executive Program— so in a sense her early achievement hadn't been unexpected. Still, even by Program standards, her grind had been unprecedented. They could still fail, John knew, just being Program wasn't a guarantee of success in life. But if his parents had had the cash, John would have given anything to be a Program baby.

In a sense, her Program status made his conquest tonight even sweeter. There was no goddamn way he was going back to that squalid "Little Canada" just north of Mumbai. With all the hours he'd billed, plus Sarah Wheeler in the win column? No way in hell.

Passing a couple of smaller meeting rooms, John came at last to the main boardroom, the glass walls of which had been rendered opaque. From the doorway, he saw Sarah in the dark, standing at the long, wall-length window and looking out onto the lights of the benighted city.

Relax, buddy, John thought as he entered. *Be cool.* He took a deep breath and reminded himself that he had been an all-province defensive back in high school, and had been a first-round fraternity recruit at the U of T. He needed the score tonight, but Sarah was getting lucky too. She'd come to him after all, she was needy for something. He thought hard about her net-benefit, to keep his heart from pounding itself into arrest.

Approaching from behind, he rubbed her arms gently, and muttered, "Pretty city." There was no sense in being coy: if she'd wanted to have a drink and chat, she'd have invited him to her fully-lit office and put a desk between them. John was confident in his read of the situation, as anyone would be. It's not like the woman had been sending out mixed signals.

Sarah set her wine glass down on the low sill of the window and leaned back against his chest. She was 5'10" in bare feet, only Johnny's heels gave him height on her. He nuzzled the nape of her neck and marvelled at the softness of her hair. It was almost like a pelt—thick and soft like that.

Sarah turned in the grasp, and growled deep in her throat. Johnny frowned in confusion, but she had him around the waist, lifting his hundred and ninety-three well-conditioned pounds onto his toes, walking him back and hurling him onto the boardroom table. The back of his head cracked hard on teak, and for a moment he saw sparks.

Then she was on him, straddling him with knees on either side of his ribcage.

"What the hell . . ." John struggled to sit up, but Sarah hit him a backhand across the face so hard he felt teeth loosen, tasted blood. Stunned, on his back, he felt his shirt being ripped apart, the buttons clicking across the hardwood table.

Sarah leaned into him—hands braced at his shoulders, pinning him, lips closing on his, tongue pushing into his bloodied mouth. He felt the cool softness of her hair upon his face, obscuring his vision. Struggling in her grasp, he twisted to one side, only to be slammed back down flat. He could feel her body—dense and hard with lean muscle—pressing on his chest.

And then, she was biting him, drawing blood on his clavicle.

"*OW*! Jesus Christ!" The sudden pain and rush of adrenalin gave John new strength. He pushed up off his back and nearly rolled onto his right side before she managed to shove him down again—her hands crushing his biceps hard enough to make his eyes water.

"Sarah . . ." he croaked. She looked down upon him, her hair draping his forehead and cheeks. He could hear her breathing, could feel the moist heat of her breath upon his face. In shadow, her eyes were dark, pitiless: the eyes of a mamba. Slowly he felt the pressure lessening on his arms, until finally, she pushed up off his heaving chest.

Lying there for a moment to catch his breath, he could hear her pouring herself another glass of wine, could just make out the full-bodied aroma of the Syrah in the air.

Sitting up, he saw her at the window again, hair disheveled, skirt torn, but otherwise calm. "Shit, Sarah," John said as he stood up shakily from the table. "You could have told me." He'd lost a shoe in the ruckus, looked around for a moment before locating it.

"You could have told me," John repeated as he hurried for the door, touching gingerly at his wounded collarbone with his fingertips.

SARAH DIDN'T TURN from the window until John had left. Then she sat upon the low, padded bench that ran along the base of the window, putting her back to the wall. Her face and ears felt flushed; she was breathing rapidly.

That had been stupid, she realized (*and I'm never stupid*). Part of her wanted to pursue John even now, and take him down in the hallway. She'd have him, and batter him—maybe kill him to prevent him from suing.

She shook her head to restore some semblance of sanity. The thoughts she was having! *Get a grip, girl,* she chided herself. The man would be too humiliated to sue: obviously there was no reason to kill him.

Except for the fact that she could.

That was it: that was the whole thing. Her blood was up, an expression she would not have fully understood before this very moment. Her blood wanted to do harm—to show no mercy—to lose itself in slaughter—and her brain was concocting outrageous scenarios to justify the action.

She marveled at herself almost as a third-party spectator. *This isn't me*, she told herself.

Oh yes it is, her blood answered. *Baby, this is you all over.*

All her life, Sarah Wheeler had been an icon of control. Described as "nerveless" by instructors. "Calculating". "Decisive". Run a Sosh-media algorithm on her historicals, and all you got was a near perfect plan-execute matrix, leading to preferred outcomes. Exactly the person you'd want at your firm; leading your project group; quarterbacking your football team; leading a clandestine assault squad.

Even this moment of recklessness had been plan-execute. She'd lured the man into the dark with cliché iconography she knew he'd never be able to resist. Her blood may have been driving, but Sarah Wheeler the passenger still had a say. She could have had him in his office: she had instinctively brought him to ground of her own choosing instead.

Finishing her wine, Sarah put her glass down and retrieved her phone from a nearby movable AV cabinet. She hit a pre-programmed number that was first on her list, though seldom, if ever, used. She noticed her hand was shaking, took a moment to settle herself. Sitting back down with the illuminated cityscape behind her, she waited as a stark photo of an older man with cliff's-edge cheekbones, short-cropped black hair, and a black eye patch appeared on her viewscreen. The face was the equivalent of Bauhaus architecture in bone, the same brutal economy of line and plane. He wasn't picking up.

"Hey, Dad," Sarah whispered as though slightly out of breath. She cleared her voice for more volume. "It's me, Sarah. I think it's my time, so . . . . I just thought you should know. Anyway. I'll call you after, or . . . you know. Not."

There was a long pause as she held the line open, and then: "'Bye, Daddy."

Transparency is the new identity.

— Eric Wheeler, age eight

Toronto, Canada

THE I.C.U. ("I see you") set was built on an old network soundstage and seated 500 fans in theatre-style, rising tiers. The stage itself was brightly lit, and appointed in outrageous game-show glitz, all metal and glass and neon in a modernist swirl around the two contestants. Two elaborate, high-backed chairs positioned the players face to face. Electrodes at temples, carotids, wrists, chests, and groins connected to consoles at the back of the respective chairs, recording respiration, perspiration, and cardiac biometrics. On the wall at the back of the stage, huge monitors displayed this information, along with magnified images of the respective players' right eyes. It was as though the women had been strapped into gigantic polygraph machines, with the information displayed so as to make the competitors as transparent as possible.

Separate sections of the wall displayed real-time twitter feeds—both the hashtag #ICU as well as the individual lines for Polly Walker and her opponent Janice Cromwell. It was Janice's 9,343 followers against Polly's 25,896,997, which made it a mismatch on paper, but also indicated the opportunity to be had. Taking down an internet celebrity of Polly's magnitude would make Janice a star in her own right. It was the only reason anyone ever challenged Polly at this point. She hadn't lost an I.C.U. encounter in years.

For all her well-deserved reputation, however, Polly didn't

feel right tonight. She'd felt off for the last few weeks—agitated, irritable. She knew why of course—couldn't be helped, and although the show's producers had offered to give her a pass, Polly had her fans to consider. Janice Cromwell had mounted a fairly aggressive and effective online campaign to get the match, and had done a good job of building the moment. Polly's fans had been indignant at the nerve of the upstart—the brazenness of the challenge—and the mob demanded collision. Polly hadn't gotten to where she was by disappointing her fans. They had made her, after all.

Tweets began to flow—information; deliberate misinformation; mindless abuse.

PrincessKaley: @THEpollyWALK Cut a bitch! What an ugly whore!

John316: @THEpollyWALK She's a media buyer 4 KCOM; 123k/yr; divorced; 34 yrs old

Belial: @THEpollyWALK Lookin' hot 2nite baby—sick her!

PetroGod: @THEpollyWALK OMG she's old!

Thirty-four years old, Polly mused. Janice didn't look it, which meant she'd had standard pre-emptive work done. Polly accepted the info as true: John316 was a long-time follower who routinely dropped good insights on her opposition. It was not uncommon for contestants to "seed" one another's feeds with sleeper-followers who emerged on game night with false info, so one always had to be careful. In Polly's case, her fans undertook such actions on their own initiative, which opened up an odd paradox. Polly Walker was as transparent a human being as anyone on the planet—her entire life-historical data set unencrypted, there for all to see, and yet, with thousands of operatives creating unsolicited competing narratives for who and what she was, it was actually difficult to get to the truth of her.

"You dropped out of Stanford?" Janice jabbed. She had fake-but-credible sandy-blonde hair to her shoulders, crystalline green eyes, sharp features, no wrinkles. She was dressed for the boardroom in a powder-blue power skirt and blazer, and she was taking the offensive. "Seriously? Couldn't handle the workload? Or couldn't afford tuition?"

Polly remained calm, though it was more work than usual. This was a weak opener from her foe—citing common

now. Why weren't you always?" Bull's-eye: Janice's metrics all gave a spike. Her readings were getting close to the red-zones on the far right of the graphics display. The closer they got, the more the crowd howled.

"Athletic now, but not then . . . ," Polly continued. "Aw, honey . . . can it really be that simple? Wannabe mean-girl couldn't be mean-girl because, what? You were fat? You just didn't look the part?"

Crowd chant: "CHUBS! CHUBS! CHUBS!"

Janice: holding it together, but tight, so tight. Tight always created more cracks.

Janice's pupils had grown huge and black on the over-sized monitor. Almost as if she found Polly irresistible.

"Fat then," Polly concluded: QED. She summoned her talent, her stare a bruising gaze fixing Janice's attention. "You pounded that chubby wannabe into shape with SEAL team workouts and starvation diets but she's still in there, yes? You're worse than an ugly duckling—you know that, right? You're a cliché. Lemme guess: you never believe you're pretty, even when he tells you over and over that you are. You hate other women because that's what you think Alpha Females do. You're a bitch because you're scared inside? Sweetie, I gotta tell you: you're on the wrong show. Scared is what I'm getting paid to find out. I can smell it now, oozing off your skin—the fear. Your face is shiny with it. Ugly, inside. Weak, inside. Damn, girl, listen: everybody's laughing. At you. Again."

Janice's status bars all pushed into the red zone.

A siren wailed, indicating victory for Polly.

The crowd went wild.

Snarling, Janice yanked the electrodes from her body and stalked off the set, her kitten heels clicking and skidding on the slick metallic finish of the stage. On the big screen, in real time, her follower-count began to plummet.

Polly sat back in her chair, expecting to bask in the moment as usual, but as she relaxed, she felt the colour rising in her cheeks. Quickly, she pulled the electrodes free: she'd won—decisively—and the machines had stopped recording, but perception was a good part of the game. Every result fed into the next encounter. The appearance of invulnerability was a critical advantage; intimidating opponents before they wired-in was crucial. Show-bloggers would go over the metrics and replays with a fine-tooth comb, and when they did, Polly wanted them to see her insides were as unflappable as her face. People lied all the time, but numbers never did. Polly's strength was her publicly available numerical, statistical performance, game in, game out.

She exposed her opponents with heartless curiosity, peeling back their layers with relentless, piercing intuition—men, women, and children all—and her fans lived and breathed the dominance. Nobody had ever borne the pressure of perfection as well as she had. The more she won, the more she wanted to compete, risking more and more every time out. It was unusual, special, and her people loved her for it. Winning was her brand.

Polly stood up from the chair and swooned slightly on the spot. She frowned in confusion, feeling the heat on her face and neck. Beneath her blouse, her nipples had gone pebble-hard, causing her some discomfort. *I have to get out of here*, she realized. If she fainted in the studio . . . 500 smart-phone cameras would record the event, and the whole world would know it happened before she got off the floor.

She accepted the producer's congratulations with a friendly nod, waved to the audience, and posed for photos. In the wings, the next pair of competitors waited patiently: Polly was a star, and generally took some time to vacate the stage. She stopped to sign autographs—a skill she'd actually had to learn and practice in the PIN-era—but she didn't overdo it. A few headshots signed for the kids, then she was on her phone, having her car brought around.

From the studio, down the access hallway, out to the mezzanine, down the escalator to foyer, and onto the street, every foot of the way was populated with well-wishers. Polly's ears rang with shouts and cheers as two battle-hardened private security men ushered her quickly through the route. A red-tape line on the floor told people how close they could come: some pushed their luck by reaching past that line, but no one dared step across. The studio would be fined for every injury or death caused by security, but they'd pay it like a fee, to keep Polly safe.

Polly wasn't concerned. No one was more at home in a crowd than she. On this particular occasion, however, with her head swimming as though high on accelerants, she was grateful for the escort. She allowed herself to be swept along, smiling and waving with a detached air of gratitude, and a wan sense of exultation. When she got to the limo, she collapsed into the stretch backseat, and opaqued the windows just in case.

It had been a routine win—easy in most respects. Janice Cromwell hadn't lived up to her own promotional abilities. Yet Polly couldn't stop herself from smiling—even laughing—as the car muscled its way into downtown traffic.

I'm over-reacting, Polly realized. Contentment was coming out as exuberance. And as she came to understand that, she felt a surge of alien panic.

Ignoring the car's on-board monitors, she reached for her phone, scrolling through her feeds to calm herself. A thousand messages rolled past: one-word exclamations; fawning adulation; witty/cheeky/sly come-ons. She "favourited" at random, moving rapidly through the voices, feeling the sheer volume of them.

Occasionally, there were the inevitable haters. These she retweeted to her millions of followers, many of whom were accomplished hackers—even known terrorists and criminals. God knew what they might do or not do, although occasionally, the results made headlines.

The feed had the desired effect. Polly still felt an unaccustomed giddiness, still felt slightly feverish and light-headed. But she felt more herself as she abandoned herself to the feed. She was whatever her followers said she was: an idol; a champion; an object of worship. She spread herself thinly across her network and was content to let herself be defined.

A tweet caught her attention:

MartinLayne: @THEpollyWALK You have the least bovine eyes of any human on earth.

She startled herself by tearing up as she blurted out in laughter. Thumbs suddenly animated, she typed:

:)

Replying to the one, and the many, at a stroke.

If he be not fellow with the best king, thou shalt find the best king of good fellows.

— Shakespeare, Henry V

Victoria, Canada

"THEY'RE TOTAL TEXANS," Kimchee was saying of the family on his mother's side. "It's crazy. This one time, we were at my Aunt's ranch, and Dix was talking back to my Aunt . . ."

"Sass-talkin'," Donald chimed in, affecting a Texan accent. He, Kimchee (who went by his gamer-handle, not his real name, Lucas), and Laura Wicks all shared a station-cluster—a kind of over-sized cubicle enclosing the three contract-coders who currently made up Warren Milner's software group.

"Right," Kimchee agreed, "givin' her sass, and my Aunt goes: 'Dixie, your butter done slipped off your biscuit, girl!'"

Warren had to chuckle at that one. "You're kidding." Warren out of his office and leaning on the cubicle wall was the signal for the group to rest their eyes and shoot the shit for a bit. He genuinely enjoyed Kimchee's off-the-wall anecdotes and observations. Exotic-looking Asian-Canadian kid when he wasn't talking: total suburban North American when he was.

"My dad still says 'like a chicken on a June bug' when he's enthusiastic about something," Laura ventured.

"Reminds me of my grandfather—my dad's dad," Warren smiled. "Alberta oil guy, right? He'd go, 'Son, if stupid goes to eighty bucks a barrel I want the drilling rights to your head!'"

They all cracked up. Albertans!

And then Kimchee came back with a patented change-up:

"Hey guys, lemme ask you something: do you guys shave your balls?"

Warren groaned, "Oh, man!" putting his head down on the cubicle wall. Laura threw a plastic thimble at Kimchee's shit-eating grin, missing and hitting his monitor screen. Donald just laughed and shook his head.

"I'm serious," said Kimchee, not serious at all. "I've been reading that you're supposed to be cleaning up down there—like actually shaving marbles and pillar. Shaving! I just don't know about that."

"Nair," Donald deadpanned. "You're supposed to use Nair."

"Wait, are you serious?" Kimchee was actually confused now, thinking maybe he should be using Nair on his balls. Warren started laughing at the quizzical look on the kid's face.

They'd been going hard all day, pulling extra hours to finesse the supply-chain algorithm for the new Sino-Krupp manufacturing hub. With a deadline looming, Warren liked to keep things loose. Yes, there was pressure, but if the grunts could put the overtime in, so could he. And if he wanted to talk spring baseball and bullshit a little, he knew the break would be welcomed by all. Warren had always had a light touch, whether he was managing twenty-something freelance coders, or engineers twice his age, and the fact that he led from the front generally set a good example for all. The operational results of his unit spoke for themselves.

"Hey, buddy," Daniels said as he passed in behind, tapping Warren in the back with a thin manila folder. Mitch Daniels was a slender man in his early forties, which you could tell from the grey at his temples, and the lines around his eyes, despite the work he'd had done to reduce the age-estimate to "early thirties". He was neat to the point of fastidiousness; one of the ones who wore a tie beneath a sweater-vest, even on Fridays.

"Just throw it on my desk," Warren said. He drummed his hands on the cubicle wall. "All right," he said to the group, affecting a rueful smile, "back to the grind." He turned and headed into his office across the aisle, the windows looking out onto the deepening dusk of Government Street.

"Big plans this weekend?" Warren asked as he rounded his desk. Daniels lingered by the door.

"Annual jaunt to Laughlin," Daniels said, meaning Laughlin,

Nevada. "Do a little golfing; hit the strip at night."

"Fight this weekend?"

"Should be something, sure. We'll check it out."

"Nice."

Warren sat down, opened the folder, and muttered, "Thanks for this."

"De nada," Daniels said as he turned to leave.

Warren studied the notes and cued up the schematics on his computer. His cherry-wood desk-top was eerily devoid of any non-essential objects, the space taken up instead by four freely positioning high-res monitors. Daniels was a graphic animator who in this case had put together a moving see-through diagram of one of the huge Krupp scoop-aggregators planned for the China site. In the folder was the list of component pieces for the giant machine, each specific of which had been signed-off by Daniels' initial in a column to the right. Warren double-checked the moving schematics against the notes, making certain first that all the necessary specs had been accounted for. As he mentally ticked off boxes, Warren could see that—as usual—Daniels and the visual group had followed instructions on that score.

Bringing up CAD toolbars, Warren began checking on dimensions and fittings. Despite the massive size of the machine, the tolerances would have to be exact if the projected life span of the components were to play out as promised. And it all had to fit together: an error in one part of the machine would compound throughout the entire structure, resulting in stress-failure sooner than the guarantee. That led to litigation, and Warren's name was on the list of project-heads responsible as a group for the whole contract. Which is why double and triple checking measurements was worth doing, even when the work had been done by . . .

"Daniels!" Warren bellowed, spittle hitting his screen. "Get the fuck in here!"

Engineers looked up from their stations and frowned. Most could count on one hand the number of times Warren Milner had used an expletive in the office, and you could halve that number when talking about expletives used in anger.

And Warren was angry.

His face had gone a sunburned red and his eyes were blazing.

A vein in his forehead throbbed visibly down into his eyebrow, and his jaws ground his teeth with furious intensity. It had been a matter of millimeters on the screen—not enough to inhibit the animation, which seemed to work well, but it wasn't to spec as ordered. Warren had generated the system-specs himself and had expected them to be reflected in the finished animation. He had expected his quality-check to be a routine formality. He had not expected to find Daniels with his head obviously in Las Vegas already, and not on the fucking job at hand.

Daniels appeared at the door, eyes wide, body tense. In two years of working under Warren Milner, he had never heard the man raise his voice. Behind Daniels, out in the nearby cubicles, heads and baffled faces reflected Daniels' confusion.

"Close the fucking door," Warren muttered as he rose.

Daniels closed the door, muting the scene for those who could still see through the glass walls of Warren's office.

It was the stuff of lunchroom gossip and office-lore that would be whispered about for weeks to come, and referenced at office parties for years after that. An epic chewing-out—an ass-kicking of monumental proportions for a series of errors that while uncharacteristic for Mitch Daniels, were certainly trivial and not mission-threatening.

Through the window-walls, engineers and coders gaped as Warren actually stood up and approached his senior designer, shouting apoplectically en route. Warren threw the folder at Daniels' face, causing the terrified tech to throw his hands up as he stood riveted in fear to the spot. Though muted, the shouting carried as a kind of percussion out into the office—a percussion emphasized when Warren turned and slammed his palms against the glass wall of his office.

The office adjacent to Warren's belonged to Roger Angs, a senior civil engineer who was, as far as the corporate flowchart went, Warren Milner's direct supervisor. Angs was a fit, broad-shouldered man in his forties who looked as though he could still suit up for the 49ers. He wore suspenders for fashion, not necessity, giving him more of an investment-banker vibe than an engineer look. He emerged slowly from his office, taking a few steps down the aisle towards Warren's office to get a better view of the action.

A deep scar traversed the right side of Angs' face, and part of his right ear was missing—both things that could have been corrected easily enough by the cosmeticians of the day. They were clearly the marks of some violence, and must have been shockingly painful when they had occurred. Keeping the marks intact spoke volumes about Roger Angs: he wore them as he did his suspenders.

As Angs watched the tirade, he began to smile. It wasn't a smile of amusement, as though the sight of Warren losing his shit in the office was a form of entertainment. It was more a kind of pride. It was a knowing smile; a look of recognition and approval.

Instead of barging in and putting an end to the spectacle, the floor supervisor nodded and returned to his office, leaving Mitch Daniels alone and in terror for his life.

Productive advantage begins in the cradle
— Executive Program marketing brochure

Manhattan, USA

"ARE YOU SCARED?" Richie's new friend/girl/whatever was asking through a hashish haze. Terry wanted to ignore her, but she was sitting right there, blinking at him with those dopey, glassy, vapid eyes. Where the hell was Richie with those drinks?

The penthouse had been specifically renovated for entertaining, with the high-ceilinged rooms all opening into one another to create a sinuous, high-rise footprint. At the far end, away from Terry and his friends at the moment, an expensive Belgian DJ blasted his beats—the throbbing bass of which shook the walls throughout the apartment.

Waiters wandered throughout the rooms, transporting champagne, single malt, port, and taking orders for anything else from Terry's friends and business associates. White mounds of coke lay in silver tureens about the premises; various smokes were available at one of the three bars. Twelve- and thirteen-year-old Program kids—legal adults—mixed with their elders, and set the bar for energetic partying exceedingly high. Terry remembered what he had been like at that age. It would take more than one night of narco-debauchery to slow them down.

Are you scared?

Brazilian porn played on wall monitors as backdrop, thrusting in syncopation with the music. Across from Terry in a corner of the main living room, a group of ghouls toured the "Suicide Roulette" site, clicking the "spin" button to watch in real time as desperate losers ended their worthless lives. The social aspect gave the suicide some sort of meaning: the relevance of having been witnessed. For the viewers, it was entertainment and the back-slapping validation of lives better-lived, choices better-made. Terry watched as some guy in his fifties broke down in tears, removing the unfired .38 from his mouth. The crowd of onlookers jeered in derision and hit "spin", hoping for a loser with a little more guts.

Are you scared?

There were Siamese fighting fish in one room—or there *had* been: the multi-coloured corpses now littered the ornate, circular aquariums, the crippled victors nibbling on the tattered remains of the vanquished. Terry's dad had brought in a real snake charmer from the orient for a cobra vs mongoose show, but that had been anti-climactic when the glass enclosure wound up limiting the options for the mammal. The snake lay curled in one corner of the glass cage, satisfied and deadly.

Just for kicks, Willy Bates had brought in a Pomeranian he'd illegally neuro-jacked in his own lab. Downstairs in the underground parking lot, they'd watched the little Franken-dog slaughter a normal pit bull like a blender on an avocado. Oh that Willy: such a comedian.

Are you scared?

In the sunken living room just beneath Terry and his friends, another plexiglass enclosure some 7 feet by 4 feet by 4 feet, supported by a low table with lion's claws legs, contained two ballistically proportioned young women engaged in writhing combat. Another gift from his father—the combatants in white fur bikinis, wrestling on a bed of white fur, their feet and shoulders squeaking on glass as they tumbled about. Such fighting aquariums were fairly common in New York and L.A., common enough that only a few onlookers had gathered in the cushioned seating area, and those that had were more actively engaged in their own conversations than in the competition being staged for their amusement.

Banners hung from the walls: "CONGRATULATIONS TERRY!!!", red letters loud on white. A couple of ex-girlfriends had kissed his cheek earlier in the evening; friends of his dad had stopped by to kiss the ring. Terry had been alternating between coke and booze, trying to find a happy medium, but it just wasn't taking. It was early—the night had practically just begun—but Terry was already thinking of getting some air, or bailing altogether. *Not as young as I used to be,* the twenty-year-old Terry Conlin reflected.

"Are you scared?" Richie's girlfriend repeated. Terry pursed his lips as Richie arrived, carrying tequila shots.

"Are you kidding?" Richie chimed in. In the fighting aquarium the compact blonde girl lay to the right side of what Terry guessed to be a Latina, scissoring up the latter's right leg while pushing the heel of her right hand under the brunette's chin for control. "My man's getting married, what's there to be scared of?"

Richie handed the drinks around and offered a toast. "To victory, buddy," Richie said with drunken solemnity. All three clinked glasses and shot the shots.

"Yeah, but are you?" the girl persisted. Terry couldn't remember her name, blaming the alcohol.

"No," he said. Truth was, he didn't know how he felt about things, but he knew the right answer to her question was "No".

"You feel any different?" Richie asked. He wasn't Program, couldn't know.

"No," Terry smiled. Like there'd be any difference between yesterday and today.

He glanced over at the aquarium and saw that the blonde had a full nelson from an awkward angle off the Latina's right flank while maintaining the scissor locked in around that curvy right thigh. The brunette struggled on her back, spending energy. Terry realized she wasn't trained—competing on spirit and stubbornness alone: blonde-girl had the professional sensibility and skill to carry her opponent for a while, making an appropriate show of it given the audience and the purpose of the match in the first place. The story of the bout was the blonde establishing control, attempting patient submissions, forcing the brunette to free herself at ever-greater expense. It was pure attrition, no suspense. When she was exhausted, the brunette would submit. It was simply a matter of time.

"Why aren't they punching?" Richie's girlfriend wanted to know, twirling a finger in long auburn locks as she gazed in boredom at the contest. Terry had a sudden urge to break her nose, but fought it down, congratulating himself on his uncharacteristic self-restraint.

"Those are the rules," Terry shrugged. "That's the contract." No hair-pulling, no punching, no biting, gouging, low blows, or anything useful. The terms were known in the industry as a "harem" or "soft" contract in reference to the special martial arts supposedly developed in ancient harems to avoid leaving visible marks. Just bodies and limbs and technique: actual competition, but without the messy clean up. To Terry, that's what made the spectacle provocative, even erotic: the idea that competition would be *limited* in some artificial way. It was such an alien notion that it titillated in a way that Brazilian gang-anal just couldn't.

All of a sudden, he'd had enough: of Richie; of Richie's bauble; of the noise, and the smoke-choked air. It wasn't like Terry at all to lose patience with a party. He'd been a fixture on the New York Life gossip blogs since his twelfth birthday, and could normally be counted upon to shut a room down. But he just wasn't feeling it tonight. He was edgy, and buzzed, and irritated, a combination which often led to someone needing dental work, a new nose, or both. Terry stood, smiling effortlessly, and with conviction. "Excuse me," he said.

"Something we said?" Richie asked, frowning good-naturedly.

"Bit of a headache," Terry lied. "I'll be back."

He crossed straight through the sunken area of the floor as the blonde girl took the brunette's back, pressing Latina face into white fur via the full nelson. Only a matter of time.

Terry strode towards the interior elevator and took a ride two floors up, the noise receding to a dull, thudding backdrop in the shaft. The elevator opened onto a small, dimly lit foyer that flowed towards an imposing set of leather-lined double doors. Opening these, Terry wandered into the master bedroom and kicked off his canvas loafers, feeling the bass-thump through the floor. A fire crackled in one dark wall, across from a large, low-lying bed with black silk sheets. Terry dimmed the lights, letting the fire cast its warm yellow glow about the room. A full bar along the north wall looked inviting: Terry fixed himself a cognac and took three shallow steps up to a sliding glass door, letting himself out onto the penthouse balcony.

Are you afraid?

Terry smirked. Looking out onto the lights of the city and the glittering lines of traffic far below, he felt . . . he didn't know how he felt. Hadn't known for days now. Knew only that it was time. He sipped his drink and lifted his face into the cool midnight breeze.

He drained that snifter, poured himself one more, and was out on the balcony when he heard background noise gently waxing and waning behind him: someone opening and closing the bedroom door. He turned and descended back into the room. The blonde girl stood in her fighting bikini, smiling, hands clasped behind her. She had the dense curvature of a gymnast or cheerleader: broad shoulders; boxy hips; deep thigh swells—all on a sporty 5'1" chassis. Her colour was high, skin still sweat-tacky.

Terry sipped his drink, then asked, "You the winner?"

The girl gave a demure grin, answering in a breathy voice, "Yeah."

Terry nodded. "Send the other one in," he said, and turned away.

On the balcony, Terry undid the buttons on his cerulean blue shirt, wanting to feel the night breeze on his chest. The stone balcony was cold on his feet, but he didn't mind. He enjoyed the sensation.

After a few minutes, he heard the bedroom door opening and a voice calling out: "Hello?" Terry turned and descended into the room, standing at the base of the steps to appraise his visitor.

He wasn't sure that she was a Latina, now that he looked at her full-on, and her hair wasn't strewn across her eyes, and her face wasn't pinched in grimace. With her ink-black, tangled locks and dark features, she could have been Asian, perhaps, or part thereof. Like the blonde, she had the stocky-curvy form dictated by the close-confines of the fighting aquarium—almost as if she had been genetically selected for it.

"Drink?" Terry asked, then moved towards the low-slung curve of the black leather couch that off-set the hearth. The girl seemed wary, but went to the bar anyway, dropping ice into a glass and fixing something with gin. She came slowly into view, but didn't join him on the sofa. She stood clutching her tumbler in both hands, an odd mix of muscular physicality and vulnerability.

Terry smiled. "My dad pay you both, or winner-take-all?"

"Appearance fee," the girl said. "Winner's bonus."

Terry nodded. "So," he said, eyes dancing. "D'jou lose on purpose?"

The girl flinched, a shadow of guilt clouding her eyes for just a moment before she picked up her chin. Crossing the last remaining steps, she took a seat on the far end of the couch, sitting with her knees together, her drink in her lap. "That was the plan," she admitted, fierce brown eyes holding Terry's ocean-blues, refusing to be intimidated.

"What happened?"

The girl shrugged, looking off into the fire. "I don't know," she murmured as though trying to sort it out herself. "Got in there, figured: 'I'm here, might as well win'. I don't know. Hurts either way, right?"

Terry chuckled. "I wouldn't know. What's your name?"

"Why do you care?"

"My last night as a free man. Just wanted to know. I'm Terry by the way."

"Sondra."

"What do you do, Sondra?"

"Take money from rich pervs to finance my graphic design courses."

"What, like art?"

"Yes, art school. Asshole."

"Didn't know they still had those."

"Yeah, well, you wouldn't."

Terry laughed in spite of himself: the fury of this girl! "Christ, I can't believe you lost!"

"She's like a fucking black belt! What did you expect?"

"Typical art student: always making excuses."

"Fuck you."

Terry chortled, sipped his drink, reclined, and crossed his ankles. Shadows from the firelight made the ridges of his stomach muscles look almost scalloped, like a lobster's tail. It was an intended effect.

"When do you go?" Sondra asked at last.

"My dad's sending a plane, if it's not here already. Guess I could go anytime this week. Figure I'll leave tomorrow, end the suspense."

"You don't seem too worried."

"Yeah, well, worrying ain't gonna help. Aren't you cold over there?"

Sondra laughed with practiced derision. Terry patted the seat beside him with undaunted, eye-brow wiggling lasciviousness. Pursing her lips, Sondra rose and crossed the floor, taking a seat beside him. He put an arm around her brawny bare shoulders, saying, "After all, you're here, right?"

"I am here, yes," Sondra acknowledged.

"You don't like us much, do you?"

"Does that bother you?"

"Comes with the territory, I suppose. Thanks for not bringing a bomb into the place."

"No problem."

"How much is your tuition?"

"Why?"

"I'm looking to buy your affection."

"That'd do it."

He leaned in from her right shoulder and kissed her as though tasting her. She was reluctant, but she turned her face towards his and responded. Noticing the faint bruising around her throat, Terry said: "Tell me about it."

"Tell you about what?"

"Your fight tonight."

"Serious? I fought like an art student."

Terry nodded, feeling himself stir. "You lost, right?"

"Yes," Sondra admitted, confused.

"Tell me about that," Terry insisted, hardening. "Tell me about losing."

Sondra looked into Terry's eyes and part of her shuddered. He was a man—a good-looking blonde man with a body carved in marble—but there was something else behind those eyes as well. Something hot to the touch, cruel . . . or maybe just alien. She had thought she knew what he'd wanted when he'd sent for her. Now she wasn't so certain.

She swallowed hard, and talked of humiliating defeat to a man who could scarcely imagine the concept without someone else's assistance.

The market is the morality of a disenchanted universe. Given such a universe of consistent, rational actors, morality becomes, in effect, a Nash Equilibrium. Morality is therefore derivable, quantifiable and verifiable in mathematical terms.
— Precis to "Social Media Wave Dynamics" E. Wheeler, A. Ross, K. Adams and W. Tate.

Calgary, Canada

JACOB CONLIN—THE Conlin in Conlin, Wilhelm and Loughren—fixed himself another rye and seven and eyed the wall monitor that was still in blue-screen. He was a few minutes early for the teleconference yet, and already on his third drink. *Eric Wheeler will do that to you,* Jacob thought with chagrin.

Crossing the floor to a soft leather recliner, Jacob took a seat, casting his gaze around his expensive new drawing room. The decorator had deliberately referenced the 19th century motif of the office with a Victorian library look, purchasing actual rare-edition books, going all out with live oak walls and Captain Nemo accessories like the standing globe and the brass astrolabe she had carefully situated upon the gigantic desk. The room was growing on Jacob, though he was unlikely to ever actually *read* the books, or even spend much time in the place. Still, it did convey a kind of old-world, analog gravitas. People he brought here for meetings and formal signings tended to be impressed. It was safe to say, however, that Eric Wheeler would not be one of those people.

As far as Jacob knew, he was one of Wheeler's few real friends—or at least Jacob thought of himself as such. Didn't stop him from being a little nervous prior to every meeting with the man. Even on a remote call, Wheeler's presence was . . . daunting. And it was ridiculous: Jacob Conlin was a big man—a bearish 6'4", 280, with cauliflower ears and a missing pinkie to show his credentials as a life-long scrapper—but he thought of himself as the smaller man every time Eric Wheeler was around. It was some kind of deep, creepy mojo the old man had, for he was twenty years Jacob's senior and a hundred pounds lighter— the kind of man Jacob Conlin could snap in two over one tree-trunk thigh. But Wheeler could freeze the blood in your bones with one sardonic look, and that eye of his—that one cold eye . . . it just seemed to cut through all the bullshit and look right at your real soul, no matter what you tried to do to hide it. The guy was chilling, flat out. Jacob was glad that Eric was on his side.

On top of his eerie knack for intimidation, Wheeler was one smart bastard as well. His consultation had helped turn CWL from a North American oil patch heavyweight in securities law, to a truly global powerhouse in all areas of finance. The key had been that commitment to third-world outsourcing of all low and mid-tier processing—shipping lawyers overseas just like parts of an auto-factory. Not only had that cut costs dramatically, it had allowed CWL to scale up in scope: with whole farms of admin muscle working for pennies on the dollar, the firm had finally been able to join the big boys on their own turf. And Eric being Eric, positioning CWL as a global player had been his endgame all along. Or one of his endgames, anyway.

As for tonight, Wheeler's new plan—really just an evolution of his earlier moves, Jacob now realized—was typically grand in scope and transformational in design. Man wasn't getting any younger: Jacob could see why Wheeler was locking in pieces now. At forty-two, Conlin was already thinking of easing himself onto the links, at least part time. How Eric could maintain that grinding tempo at his age, year in and year out, was anybody's guess.

Christ, I'm glad he's on our side, Jacob mused again, as the view screen finally flickered, then resolved into a head-shot.

"Evening, Jacob," Eric Wheeler smiled. His black hair was cut like a Roman general's, and that eyepatch . . . Jacob took a healthy bolt of rye, forcing himself to smile while thinking of the kind of determination a man had to have, to shake off an injury like losing a goddamn eye! Hollow cheeks, jutting cheekbones, and reptilian lips completed the raptor-like visage. Incredibly, the man had had no cosmetic work done—he wore the lines like a silent, generalized "fuck you". He wanted people to see the age.

"Evenin', Eric!" Jacob responded. From the background bulkhead and the shape of Eric's tan-coloured headrest, Jacob gathered the man was on his jet. *Never stops moving, that one. Like a fucking shark.*

And then, to Jacob's surprise, Eric gave a broad smile, showing those small, perfect teeth of his as he raised his own glass so Jacob could see it. "To Terry," Eric said.

Jacob smiled with genuine affection: it was damn good of the man to acknowledge his son. "And to Sarah!" he said, and both men drank to the other's only child.

Eric popped a pill then, drinking it down with an extra shot of whatever he was having. Jacob figured it to be an amphetamine, and asked: "You take those with booze?"

Eric offered the dry rasp that served him as a chuckle and ignored the question as he swallowed.

Jacob continued, feeling alcohol-warmed, relaxing as a result. "Time to take it easy, isn't it? Work on your short game?"

"Getting there," Eric nodded, "no doubt about it. Thanks for taking my call at this hour, Jake. I'm looking forward to having Terry on my team. Feels like finding a missing piece of the puzzle, you know?"

Jacob thought of his boy off in New York—a big swinging dick on Wall Street. He was a fine, strapping lad, no doubt about it, but . . .

"You seem pretty certain," Jacob said, voicing his own concerns with his tone, if not his words.

"Providing certainty's kind of what I do." That reptilian little half-smile. Jacob repressed a shudder.

"But how did you know . . . ," Jacob began, finally asking the question that had been on his mind for weeks now, "how could you know that Terry and Sarah would be in the same Four?"

In answer, Eric simply stared with that glacier-blue eye of his, and made the look count until the truth dawned on the younger man.

"Holy shit," Jacob breathed. "You made them code Terry?

How the hell'd you do that?"

"File that under 'the less you know'. You have Sarah's partnership papers done up?"

"Of course. Total formality really: that kid's a machine. She doesn't need your help, poppa."

"Everybody can use a little help, now and again."

"So . . . if you had them select for Terry . . . did you select his counterpart as well?"

Eric grinned until Jacob realized more of the truth.

"You're fucking scary," Jacob said, shaking his head. "You know that?"

"Leaving things to chance . . . that's just not me, you know?"

"What about Sarah? You rig it for her too?"

Eric's smile faded. Jacob was used to a limited range of emotions from his friend and mentor: seething anger; ironic secrecy; a dry joviality that was equal parts good-humour and chilling. But Jacob had never before seen the kind of veiled contemplation that was on Eric's face in that moment. Wheeler's smile was interchangeable with anger or mirth, but he wasn't smiling now. The look in Eric's eye had gone opaque, unknowable.

"Sarah can handle herself," Eric said carefully. "She's going to be just fine."

"Well, you would know." Jacob paused to drain his drink. Then he said: "Thanks for this, Eric. I mean it. My son, well . . . you know how it is. He means the world to me."

"I look forward to the family bond," Eric said, conveying sincerity. "Maybe we'll work on our short games together, before not too very much longer."

"Damn straight. Thanks for the call, Eric. It means a lot."

"You earned it," Eric grinned. "See you soon."

The screen flickered and went blue, leaving Jacob Conlin alone in his Victorian drawing room to contemplate what it must be like to play a round of golf with Eric Wheeler.

30,000 FEET HIGH, cruising north across the Gulf of Mexico, Eric disengaged his docked tablet and sat back in his chair. The amphetamine was kicking in, which was good: he had a number of operations to check in on and he wanted to do one more round of simulations before touchdown.

Sarah had called: he'd listened to the message three times. He'd heard what few others could have detected in her voice: the anxiety; the fear. Part of him had wanted to call her right away, but it would've been the wrong thing to do. *You're on your own, sweetie*, he thought. It killed him to think it, but he steeled himself, and there was no self-discipline on earth like the resolve of Eric Wheeler.

He could not afford tenderness now. He had done things that way once before, long ago, and he'd done more harm than good. Never again. He'd learned that hardest of lessons, and wore the pain of it like whip-tracks on a back that never quite heals. For Sarah to play her part, she had to earn her way. He could tweak everything else, but not that one thing. He had to hope that his preparation of her, the handling of her since birth—even going so far as to remove her mother from the picture altogether . . . it would have to be enough.

He signaled his attendant—a lovely Argentinian girl he'd picked up at auction—for another drink, and reactivated the tablet. Activating his picture files, he studiously avoided Sarah's image and brought up Samantha's instead. She'd been a charming girl—dark-featured like her mother, strong-bodied, outgoing, and tempestuous where Sarah tended to be secretive and cerebral. The attendant set a short tumbler of Ballechin on the table and offered a mechanical smile, lingering long enough to see if Eric would be taking anything extra, then leaving without interrupting him.

Fuck it, Eric thought as an impulse overtook him. People like Jacob Conlin would be shocked to know the degree to which Eric was motivated by impulse. It was not his public persona— he was held to be a kind of human computer, famous for balancing and considering every contingency before acting. But that was not exactly the way he worked. Eric knew he was driven by his passions, and if he went about satisfying himself in relentlessly methodical ways, still the passions themselves were decisive.

He selected a phone number from his personal lists—*her* number—though it had been years since they'd last spoken. She had moved around the world as her job required, but he'd always kept an eye on her. For a one-eyed man, he seemed to have a lot of eyes to spare.

It was early, early morning in San Diego. He didn't care. After several rings, a dim light illuminated a groggy face surrounded by a cloud of dark, disheveled hair. He recognized those big hazel-green eyes immediately, even if they were older and half-closed. She stared for a moment, her brow furrowed in confusion, and then: "Eric?"

A masculine voice muttered "The fuck?" off-screen. The woman ignored him, saying, "Gimme a minute." She hit pause, and Eric sipped his scotch, welcoming the mellow burn down his throat. In a couple of minutes, the picture changed to show the woman sitting at a computer, wearing a bathrobe, her hair still a tangled mess, and still lovely to behold.

They stared at one another for some time: he with great affection and sadness, she with profoundly mixed emotions—hatred among them. Finally, she broke the silence. "You called me, Eric."

"I know. I'm sorry."

"You're drinking."

"Not sorry for that. You look much the same." It was true: she was sixty playing forty with ease and grace.

"You look old, Eric. When's the last time you slept?"

"I was looking at pictures of Sam."

That rocked her. Madeline—Eric's first wife—was Samantha's mother. Her aspect softened as she saw his pain for the first time in years. And then it hit her . . .

"Oh. It's . . . it must be her time. I've forgotten her name."

"Sarah."

"Sarah. I don't know what you want me to say."

He knew what she meant. In her heart, she couldn't possibly have any generosity towards Sarah; the idea of Sarah. The replacement.

But Madeline knew what it was like to go through a Spawning as a parent. She knew in the worst way imaginable; had shared that worst way with Eric. If she could spare nothing for Sarah, still she had some sympathy for the man who had been her husband—her One. Twenty years they'd been together, when they were both young, and at their best.

She'd never forgiven him for leaving her; never understood how he could have had the superhuman will to break free of the Spawning Bond. It was commonly held that the genetically encoded predispositions between couples—and between Program parents and offspring—were non-negotiable, once activated by the Spawning. But Eric was anything but common.

"You shouldn't have called," she said at last, tears welling. It was the sight of him, the sound of his voice . . . she had spent years dulling her memory of their time together, years training her body to go on without him, to ignore the yearning of her cells. "This hurts me."

Eric nodded. "I know. I just think I needed . . ." He didn't know what he needed. This was uncharted territory.

"You're human, Eric: you're worried. I get it, even if you don't. But this is what you wanted, what you planned for."

"I know."

"You're so driven. It's wrong to be as driven as you are."

"I know."

"I know you've got the math to prove otherwise, but . . . Eric, I think you're evil, in some ways. Most ways. I don't say that to punish you: I say it because I couldn't say it before—couldn't even imagine it in so many words. I say it to make you consider that it might be true. The things you want . . . you're wrong to want them."

Eric smiled. "I don't know . . . that does seem to be an attempt at punishment."

She wouldn't take the offering, didn't even smirk. "You should delete Sam's files," she said, her voice conveying an awful finality. "You should stop spying on me."

"You're right."

"But you won't, will you?"

"Good night, Maddy. Sorry to have woken you."

She offered him one last sad smile, then disengaged because he wouldn't.

He sat unmoving at the table, staring at the blank screen, listening to the background hiss of pressurized air, letting ancient, but powerful emotions course through him. He couldn't afford to feel anything for Sarah, not yet, but he'd needed emotional release and Madeline had been the only one who could provide it.

As much as he loved Sarah—and he did love her, after his fashion—he wished that Samantha had come through. But then he realized how things would have been different—how he would have been different—how he would have been the lesser for it. The thought repelled him.

Samantha's death had given him time to position in a way he never would have done if she had lived. In a way, all that he did helped to give her death meaning. At least that's what he told himself.

I think you're evil in some ways. Most ways.

Eric's grim, thin-lipped smile returned. Maddy was wrong about that, though he appreciated her limitations. He certainly didn't blame her, or begrudge her, for thinking the way she did.

Evil as Maddy understood it was a 20th century phenomenon, ideologically constructed, meant to reinforce one worldview at the expense of others. The 20th century cast a long shadow, but the darkness had been receding for decades—due in no small part to Eric's own efforts. 20th century institutions, and the "mass" societies they once governed, were disintegrating, and with them went the notions of good and evil upon which they had been founded. Nowadays, there was only the "evil" of creating opportunities for others through one's own weakness, or the evil of not taking advantage of such opportunities when they arose. That was it; that was all there was in the new cosmology.

If anything, given those parameters, Eric Wheeler was a hero.

The body's what matters now. The material. Phys-i-cal-ity, baby. Genes, blood . . . your cells. Personality? The "self"? That's just content. Content don't mean shit.

— DJ Multiplex

Victoria, Canada

THERE WASN'T MUCH left to say.

Warren watched his parents on the monitor in his home-office, his dad on the left, mom on the right. Looking at his father was almost like looking in the mirror: the same unruly mass of brown curls; same olive skin tone that would tan dark in the summer; same wide-eyed, wide-mouthed set to the features. His dad was struggling with the news: half proud; half anxious. His mother was keeping it together better.

"You call as soon as you come through," his dad, Alf Milner, said. Warren could hear the emotion in his voice, see it in his eyes.

His mom—Kali—put her right hand over Alf's left on the table, giving him a gentle squeeze. It was as though she were transfusing strength into her husband. In her gentle Australian drawl, his mom said: "You're going to want to be alone with her after. She'll be your whole world. Let that settle first, *then* call when you're ready."

Warren nodded. He'd told them about the scene at the office; they'd told him what to expect from here. It was nothing he hadn't read about and studied for, but the Surge wasn't something you could really understand until it happened. It was the difference between being angry and being catatonic with rage. The former was something anyone could handle. The latter . . .

"I appreciate your support, guys," Warren said. "I should go."

"We've got faith in you, son," Alf said, eyes hard. "All the faith in the world."

His mom nodded.

Warren cut the feed and sank back into his chair.

He was damn lucky he hadn't killed Mitch Daniels; *Mitch* was damn lucky. Angs had promised to smooth things over with the floor. "Go on home," Angs had said, with Warren still vibrating in the aftermath of his outburst. "You may as well get to it. Take care of business, buddy. Congratulations!"

Warren's temperature stood at 99.8 degrees: he'd checked it digitally when he'd gotten home. He was a little flushed, slightly light-headed, but not feeling sick or disoriented. If anything he felt a vague sense of euphoria. Like he'd had one too many lattes.

He remembered the thing with Daniels as though he'd seen it on film, from a distance. He'd been powerless to stop the Surge. More than that, he hadn't wanted to stop it. For several minutes his body had taken over from his mind, making him a passenger inside his own head. Daniels' terror had made everything worse: the more afraid Mitch appeared to be, the more it seemed to trigger some animal instinct in Warren.

A killer instinct.

Warren switched out of his teleconference program and keyed into the Executive Program social site and spent a moment reviewing his feed. He thought about a status update, but hesitated. This seemed private to him—profoundly so. That, and he couldn't quite find the words to encapsulate things. "Almost killed a guy today". "Went batshit crazy at work today". "Went into Surge at the office. Film at 11". Instead, he went to the Program Technical page and scrolled to "personal status". He paused for a moment, but there wasn't really any doubt at this point. Activating a drop-down box, he selected "Spawning Initiated" and waited. In a moment, a video window appeared, displaying an animated Executive Program logo executing a slow clockwise rotation.

The logo dissolved, and a pretty female speaker appeared from the shoulders up, dressed in a royal blue blazer and cap that reminded Warren of old stewardess costumes from the 1960s. It was a canned message, though they'd gone to some lengths to make it look like a live video conference. The woman appeared delighted, her voice almost giddy with enthusiasm.

"Hi Warren Milner—congratulations!" the woman gushed. "By now you will have noticed several bio-metrics indicating full-cycle initiation, and you will no doubt have experienced a number of psycho-physical stresses over the last few days. There's no need to worry: elevated heart rate and core temperature; heightened aggression and increased fast-twitch response times are all perfectly natural. Your competitive envelope is now at peak performance: kindly proceed to the StandardGen facility referenced in your Spawning Instructions tab, and please read carefully the 'Rules of Engagement' protocol."

The image of the woman dissolved into a still photo of a smiling, hulking young blonde man in his twenties, while the voice-over continued. "This is your Spawning Counterpart Terry Conlin, VP Derivatives Sales at Tyler/Brock New York. Terry Conlin is . . ."

Warren had ceased to process the information, his gaze riveted to the screen. The sound of pulsing blood rushed in his ears, and he felt pressure in his sinuses and temples. On-screen footage of Conlin in an MMA gym-session showed a big man with heavy hands in hard-sparring—both standing up and on the ground. Either way, he was brutally effective. It was material worth studying if Warren were still capable of rational analysis. His blood boiled as it had in the office—his cellular response to the images on screen overriding his higher functions. He looked upon Terry Conlin as a lion might perceive a hyena on the African savannah. As bitterly irreconcilable as that.

Warren lost track of time, but gradually, he became aware of some other presence in the room. A voice cut through the fog of his seething blood, slowly drawing his attention away from the screen. He swiveled in his chair, coming back to himself enough to know how strung out he must look: like a rabid dog or something.

He heard the voice clearly then: "Warren? Honey, are you okay?"

A woman—his woman—stood in the doorway in her

bathrobe, hair matted from sleep. She was fifteen years his senior—a tall, elegant-looking person: a long neck; piano-player's hands. Gradually, thickly, he recalled her name: Ellen. He had woken her up.

"Ellie," Warren managed, his voice strained.

She nodded, the corners of her mouth flashing a small smile, there and gone. Her eyes were sad, resigned; Warren hated to see that look. She'd been with him since he was sixteen, having met him during a boardroom presentation with marketing. She'd always known this day would come. He had felt her inching away over the last few weeks, gradually disengaging: she was the wise one, after all. Now he recognized the distance in her eyes and knew it was for the best. "Come to bed," she said, and left him sitting in the office.

He changed into sweats and went to the bedroom. It was his condo-apartment, but she'd done the redecorating. The bedroom was all Ellen D'Arcy: clean lines; good honest wood; cool colours. She'd left a table-light on low, but was curled up on her left side, on the left side of the bed, facing away from him.

He sat on his side of the bed, struggling to choose words. "Ellie . . . ," he began.

"Let's talk tomorrow," she whispered, without turning around. "We'll say goodbye then."

Warren nodded. He turned the light out and got beneath the covers. He lay on his back as his eyes adjusted quickly to the dark, and he stared at the ceiling. There he'd lie, unmoving and awake, until the sun rose in the morning.

I hold strongly to this: that it is better to be impetuous than circumspect . . .

— Machiavelli, *The Prince*

Calgary, Canada

SARAH THREW HER keys onto the asymmetrical granite-topped island that dominated her kitchen, and poured herself a glass of Sapaio. She hardly tasted the velvety Italian red: she'd been drunk for hours. She changed into old jeans and a soft flannel shirt with a windproof lining, took her wine glass out onto her balcony to enjoy the view. That was the main reason she'd bought the place after all, that spectacular view of the Bow River from twenty-two floors up.

The night breeze disturbed her hair, but she barely felt it, what with the alcohol in her system, and the fact that she'd been running hot all night to begin with. The lights along the river illuminated the landscaped bike path, nicely balancing the urban view with a pastoral sensibility. She'd bought the penthouse condo with her own money—her first major purchase after the CWL dividend cheques started pouring in. The view always seemed worth it—that, and the freedom. After the condo, she'd never taken another dime from her father.

Fuck you, Daddy, for not calling me back.

She knew damn well he'd gotten her message, knew he wouldn't call her. He might position a satellite to keep watch over her or something, but he wouldn't call—that was his way. When she turned seventeen, she had announced that she would no longer be using his security personnel—partially because she felt she could take care of herself, but mostly to make things harder for him. Having James, or one of the other shooters, be her driver wasn't the same as Dad being there, and he had to be made to see that. She wouldn't let him delegate that responsibility.

She hadn't seen him in years, as a result. Petulance had no effect on him; he was a hard man to manipulate. He was out of the country for the most part anyway, for as he was fond of saying: "These little wars don't fight themselves." But he hadn't always been so neglectful.

She remembered a time when she was five or six, just after he'd sent her mother away . . . that time he'd brought the puppies. They were still living on what had once been a ranch in the interior of BC: thousands of acres of grazing land and forest, surrounding a massive mansion that was supported by state of the art security, including ground-to-air missile defence. Her various tutors lived at least part-time in the mansion, and Mrs. Loxley lived there full time, making sure Sarah was staying out of trouble, and staying focused.

She still had vivid recall of the day—warm, but heavily overcast—the clouds low and heavy across the sky. She'd heard his helicopter in her playroom and had gone to the window to watch it circling to the pad. James was with him, as were a few of Dad's other reliable shooters. She could never remember her father being outside the house without a team of four security men. He was an important man, and he made enemies throughout the world. James stayed at his side, ready to take a bullet, while the other men fanned out. She could still see their long black trench coats and neatly pressed suits, and her father carrying that big plastic box in both hands.

Mrs. Loxley was already at the door waiting when Sarah came thumping down the spiral staircase to the foyer. Her father said hello to the governess, and edged past her with that box, winking at Sarah when he got close.

"Let's go into the study," he had said. She remembered it, because normally, the study was off-limits. Now she was excited and intrigued, and she had already deduced that whatever was in that box was for her. Sarah ran ahead of her father and waited at the locked doors of his study, while he brought up the rear.

Entering the room was like going to someone else's house, so infrequently had Sarah seen the interior. A large desk was dominated by several monitors of different sizes—Dad's electronics hub—but there was also a big bay window, and bookshelves lined with both books and binders *(hard copies can't be hacked, Sarah)*. A soft, dense carpet covered the floor, cushioning Sarah's slippered feet as she stepped gingerly around the room.

Her dad placed the box down near the window, then fixed himself a drink. He was a scotch man then as he was now. He pulled his swivel chair out from behind his desk and sat down facing Sarah. She could still remember that expectant little smile, the one blue eye dancing in the natural light from the window. "Well, go on, honey," he had said. "I know you've been dying to open that box. Get in there, girl!"

Sarah approached the box cautiously, as was her nature. It wasn't cardboard, rather some kind of sturdy beige-coloured plastic. She could hear scrabbling inside—some sort of movement, and although that alarmed her, she knew nothing could happen to her with her father in the room. Emboldened, she opened the box and gasped at the contents: two golden retriever puppies blinked up at her, wagging little tails.

Sarah looked back at her father with the kind of adoration only six-year-old girls can muster for their dads. He had grinned in response; sipped his drink.

"Two puppies," Dad said then, "one girl. Choose which one you want."

Sarah looked at the box with its identical contents, glanced back at her father. She wanted both, but sensed that was the wrong answer to this puzzle. Instead she hesitated, waiting for more information.

"Gotta choose," Dad said. "One puppy or no puppies, Sarah. That's the deal."

Sarah turned back to the box, and her attention immediately galvanized the twin occupants. They were all bright eyes and trembling little bodies, making their little mewling noises. Sarah looked at them hard, trying to draw some distinction between one or the other. Finally, she reached in and picked up the one that had seemed most anxious to meet her. As if in confirmation of the fact, the puppy immediately began licking her face.

Grinning and sputtering, she turned to her father with her prize. She could still remember the smell of puppy musk pungent in her nostrils.

"Good choice," he'd said. "That's the one I would've gone with."

A puppy *and* her father's approval! Days just didn't get any better than that one. Up until that point, at least.

"What about the other one?" her father asked.

"But," Sarah said, trying to think ahead. "But I want this one."

"I know, sweetie, but the other one's your responsibility too. I mean, we could just put him outside if you want. He'll starve eventually, after a few days. You'll hear him outside your bedroom window though, whining and whimpering. He'll beg for you to let him in. That'd be just awful, Sarah. He'd suffer that way. You don't want him to suffer, do you?"

"No," Sarah had whispered, horrified at the thought.

"Well then. We've talked about this. When a thing is right to do, and necessary, and especially if it's inevitable, we do it even if it's hard."

Sarah swallowed, willing away tears. This was one of those times where he'd be watching for tears. She could recognize the signs by then.

Like when Mommy went away.

Carefully, she took her chosen puppy to her father, and handed it to him. He set his drink aside and held the dog in his lap, stroking it. Her puppy licked her dad's hand.

That one blue eye had turned marble-hard, and was on her like a spotlight. It wasn't dancing anymore: playtime was over. Sarah had been brought to the study to learn an Important Thing.

Blinking rapidly, Sarah turned, and approached the open box. The remaining puppy wriggled and yipped when it noticed her. She stooped and reached into the box, nearly breaking down when the happy little dog started licking her hand. But she hadn't broken—not right then, she hadn't. She felt the hardness within her grow, what her dad had called "tempering", and she focused on it—imagining she was a girl of stone.

Her small hands reached around the puppy's throat: she could remember the warmth of the thing in her grasp. Thumbs together she started to squeeze, and tightened her jaw as the puppy's legs pushed and scrabbled for freedom.

In all the years since—through all the things she'd done—nothing had been so awful. Oh, the noise it had made—the terrified little whinings. Those paws clicking on plastic, then clawing at her wrists. And then, the worst thing of all: the realization that she wasn't going to be able to do it. When it dawned upon her that she wasn't going to have the will necessary to break the puppy's neck, Sarah burst into wracking sobs. It all came crashing down then: failure to kill as commanded; failure to stay eyes-dry; failure to be a hard girl. Her dad had brought her a puppy and this was how she repaid him. She had actually felt guilt in that horrible moment.

And then he was there, standing over her—her chosen puppy in his hands. With a sudden convulsion, he snapped the thing's neck: a death so sudden, the puppy had never known a moment's fear, feeling itself safe in the hands of a benevolent God right up until the end.

He had dropped the lifeless bundle into the box, never taking his eye off Sarah. She released the other dog—*her* dog now, by default, and stood, staring up into her father's gaze.

"If you don't dictate to events," her father said, snarling the words because he was the kind of cold, quiet angry he got just before he went nuclear, "events will dictate to you. When you have the chance to impose your will, you take it."

The last thing she remembered was the sight of the living puppy sniffing at the dead one. How close it had come to being the other way around.

"You unbelievable bastard," Sarah muttered to herself, banishing the memories with a shake of her head. Released from her reverie, she realized she was starting to feel the cold, turning at last from the river-valley panorama to the warmth of her apartment.

Another glass of Sapaio; a quick check of her phone. Restless, Sarah went to her living room and sat down in her padded comfy chair, draping long legs over one arm. She initialized browsing on her large wall-monitor, started flipping channels at random.

News: coverage of some Open tournament in golf that day. Cameras rolled as two PGA tour golfers were having some dispute on the green. The guy in the red golf shirt grabbed the guy in yellow by his collar, and then, rushing in from off-camera, a club-wielding caddy brained the red-shirt. No charges laid, but it was another "black eye for golf"—the talking heads all rehashing the tired "is violence ruining the grand old game of golf" angle. The fact that the caddy had interfered seemed to be the unforgivable transgression.

Flip.

A late night talk show: Sarah didn't recognize the guest.

Flip.

A nature show recounting the onerous spectacle of the North BC salmon run. Fish fighting their way up-stream from the sea. Fins ragged; bodies battered—the creatures all but dead when it came time to fertilize the eggs.

Flip.

Some ancient movie—*Soylent Green.*

Flip.

A commercial for some Russian Vodka.

Flip.

Pac-Rim news: Mandarin with English subtitles. Terrorist attacks on a Sino-Krupp branch office in Tokyo.

Wait a minute. That commercial . . .

Sarah flipped back to the vodka. It was a typical booze ad: an upscale professional bar—brokers and lawyers in crowded, classy confines. Our table consists of four friends, and in particular, we see a good looking gallant rising to get drinks, kissing the cheek of his conspicuously blonde girlfriend as he leaves. Cue the vodka brand at the bar, going into a couple of martinis. Returning to the table, our hero spots a sleek brunette wearing a dramatic scarlet dress across the room—the same brunette he'd noticed on the way in, only this time, she's making hard eye-contact. Sloe-eyed, dark featured, so different from what the man already has. The ad is subversive because it's the exotic taking from the blonde, and therefore attention-grabbing. Sure enough, the man passes the table—his girlfriend's smile slowly fading as she watches him approach someone else—and not just anybody else: a superior brand. Smiling, the man presents one martini to the young exotic, and the message is clear: winners drink this vodka; its brand is supremacy.

Sarah hit freeze-frame and stared. She hadn't recognized the woman at first, the ad playing up the brunette's mysterious eyes with exaggerated cosmetics, her hair being done a different way, but it was her all the same. Polly Walker. A celebrity whose brand was winning, reinforcing the brand-claims of the vodka in the ad.

Polly Walker. Sarah's Spawning Counterpart.

It was different than seeing the woman's profile data on the EP social site. Seeing her out in the world as it were, on the web, doing what she did for a living . . . it almost seemed voyeuristic. A striking girl, was Polly Walker, oozing confidence and seductive charm. She was just Eric Wheeler's type, Sarah noted with chagrin.

The doorbell rang, making Sarah jump involuntarily. For someone to have gotten to her door, they'd have had to pass the building's various security checks and be on Sarah's approved list. Sarah rose, turning off the screen and throwing her remote onto her chair en route to the front door.

Opening the door, Sarah saw her friend and fellow CWL lawyer, Kelly Lee, standing there. Late as it was, Kelly hadn't hesitated to come when Sarah had called from the office. Kelly stood there smiling, long black hair trailing down the back of her bright royal blue coat.

Sarah gathered the smaller Asian girl into her arms and squeezed. She held onto Kelly like a drowning woman reaching for a life preserver, all the day's tension pouring out into the embrace. Pulling back, Sarah took the girl's face in both hands and kissed her desperately on the lips. When the kiss ended, Sarah looked down on a slight incline into the woman's eyes, still holding the sides of her head.

"You're trembling," Kelly said, half concerned; half astonished.

"We can do this," Sarah said, fixing her gaze on Kelly's in a way that might have reminded one of Eric Wheeler's intense stare. The same grim determination; the same iron will.

There is now no aspect of our society—no concept of the individual, no institution or epistemological structure that exists outside the competitive matrix. The market assigns all value to all things, and is the only legitimate source of value. The notion of intrinsic value as postulated by feminism, or the various progressive ideologies, is now recognized to be a species of Magical Reasoning.

— Eric Wheeler, master's thesis in Micro-Economics, age ten

Toronto, Canada

BY MIDNIGHT, POLLY was fast asleep, bathed in the pale blue light of the 360-degree monitor-wall that encompassed her bedroom. The shadowy images of news, entertainment, and social feeds from a hundred different sources flickered across her body—the touch of a thousand electronic ghosts throughout the night. Beside her on her covers, a tablet remained open, her twitter feed updating at regular intervals as followers new and old sent their warm regards.

On one part of the wall, directly in her line of sight as she lay on the bed, Polly had opened a picture file of her parents. It was a composite produced by the lab: no pictures existed of the two of them together. For Polly's father, an astrophysicist with DecTel, had died as a result of his exertions during the Spawning, and her mother, a chemical engineer with Vanguard Tech, had gone into a coma late the following day. StandardGen had honoured their commitments, keeping Polly's mother alive for the full term, then switching off life-support after the difficult birth had been successful. Polly had had to fight for life right out of the chute, but she'd come from great stock, surviving a touch-and-go incubation period. The circumstances of her birth would set the tone for the rest of her life.

Celebrity status attached itself early on, as Executive Program orphans were relatively rare. The story of the brave little girl born out of tragedy captured the hearts of a nation for a few days, and before she'd even opened her tiny eyes, the girl had attracted a bit of a following. In the course of events, this would be critically important, though in the beginning, Polly's web-footprint was largely taken for granted, its significance overlooked.

Program children cannot be placed with existing Program families, and standard adoption avenues, while theoretically possible, were deemed counter-productive. The girl represented a tremendous investment in tech and social capital: sending her out to be raised by some random family was akin to having her raised by wolves. There were grandparents, but they quickly became embroiled in costly litigation for control of the offspring, as well as the estate. Until the courts determined clear title to the child, the lab was not authorized to release the girl into the care of either party.

And yet, as always, there was the problem of money. Lab techs doted on the girl, especially when it became certain that she would survive, but it wasn't their job to provide infant care beyond incubation. The family assets had been frozen by the courts; life-insurers successfully contested the beneficiary status of the child; there were no state services as such that could take an infant, no options anywhere—it seemed as though the little girl would ultimately be doomed. And then, as if by miracle, unsolicited web-donations began to arrive at the clinic—a trickle at first, but then in torrents—enough to buy full-time nursing support, food, and other necessities.

She was named "Polly" by an on-line poll. Cameras were set up at her crib to provide viewers/donors with 24-hour viewing access. The web had a true love affair with the child who almost seemed internet-conceived, and who certainly was internet-dependent. By her first birthday, she had well over a million followers, and corporate sponsors lining up. The child who had seemed so vulnerable and tenuous at first, was financially secure before her second birthday, and by her third, she left the lab to live in a sheltered studio apartment with attendants to look after her, cameras to record her, and more fans than ever before. After that, she just went with the flow, adding sponsors, doing live gameshows, modeling, doing commercials, endorsing products. And the web adored her, adored her story. The feeling was mutual.

For Polly, the Spawning was not a thing to be feared, or at least, not a thing to be feared in advance. She had lived life moment by moment since inception, and never experienced anxiety as most people would understand the term. Though she was alone, she felt loved every day, and the thought of securing a mate intrigued her—even thrilled her when she thought it through. It was making her a truly colossal attraction: little Polly all grown up and meeting her One True Love at last. Fans couldn't get enough: she'd been adding followers at a career-high velocity over the last few months, in anticipation of the next life-event. For her part, she couldn't wait to share the experience with them.

So Polly slept soundly, while the others in her Four, unbeknownst to her, were wracked with swirling thoughts and uncontrollable emotions. Their minds tortured and vexed them throughout the night, while Polly dreamed of incomprehensible shapes, impossible angles, and unexpected connections between disparate objects. If she'd had the math, she'd have known her dreams were geometrical representations of spontaneously generated pattern-recognition algorithms. But Polly didn't need math to be what she was. Her mind was the shape of minds to come, and in that, she was as much a child of Eric Wheeler as Sarah.

There were plenty of performance enhancement alternatives at the turn of the century—many of them dating back even as far as the 1940s, and establishing formal corporate brands in the 1980s. But these alternatives didn't have the political clout of the Executive Program, so they couldn't get clearance for the survival-of-the-fittest twist that would prove to be the crucial difference. With other firms, you as a parent thought you were creating better, more competitive offspring; you were doing the engineering after all. But with the EP, you KNEW that the best were moving on. Every one of those offspring got tested in the marketplace as it were—their competitive credentials guaranteed by the fact that they had survived the ultimate test. Those were the kids everybody wanted. Because if it came down to a boardroom showdown between you and an Executive Program product, only one of you had killed to get where they were. It was a huge competitive advantage going in.

— Interview on CNN's "The Executive Program in Retrospect"

SHORN GOLDEN LOCKS lay in the sink, trailed across the countertop, heaped upon the floor. Terry stood in front of his bathroom mirror, naked, slowly scraping an old-fashioned straight razor across his scalp. Seeing no trace of hair left, he set the razor down, wet a hand towel, and washed his skull clean of shaving cream and loose stubble.

Perfection.

He stepped back from the counter to get more of himself in the mirror's frame. 6'5"; 240lbs; 7% body fat. Bald, his head sat like a bullet above a mountainous neck, his wide shoulders and dense, sculpted pecs forming Adonis-like proportions on the tapered run down to square, hard hips. His penis hung like a hog's foreleg in between massive thighs, bringing to mind his favourite, oft-used party phrase: "Shut up, or I'll beat you to death with my cock!"

Terry was surprised Sondra had been able to take all of him, but she had. She was little, but dense and brawny herself: he had enjoyed her compact, volatile energy. He doubted the feeling was mutual, but then again, what she did or didn't feel wasn't relevant. She knew what she was getting into.

After a good fifteen minutes of self-admiration, Terry strode from the bathroom back into the master bedroom—morning light streaming in through the balcony doors. Sondra lay curled up on her side, beneath the covers and facing away from him. He sat down at his desk, docked the tablet in an upright position, and booted up.

Terry headed to his online banking portal and keyed in his PVQs and PIN identifications. He stared straight ahead for the facial recognition scan which cleared him despite the new haircut, and when prompted for voice verification, Terry said: "How now . . . brown cow." With that, he was into his accounts and admin screen.

Selecting wire-transfer, Terry keyed in his own current account details, then filled in Sondra's recipient data. Last night she had told him her nine digit Student ID number as well as her social security number—both of which Terry had remembered effortlessly. Terry's facility with numbers was one of his gifts: he could recall large number strings as easily as a Normal could remember a sentence.

He did a quick query for the New York School of Graphic Arts, got their SWIFT code and transit number, and entered in the data. Then under "amount" he typed "$15,000 USD" and hit "wire funds". *Tuition as promised*, Terry thought. It amused him to keep his word when people least expected him to.

Terry logged out and selected some early-morning appropriate, easy-listening jazz, setting the volume on low. He rose from the table, crossed to the closet, and selected clothes. An aubergine silk shirt; black dress pants; Rolex; shoes imported from the house of Travoia in Italy. Pulling out a gym bag, he threw in extra clothes and under-things; toiletries; his phone. Anything else he might need, he'd buy on-site.

Mission accomplished, he looked over at the bed to see that the art student hadn't moved from her semi-fetal position near the bed's edge. He knew she was awake, listening to him. That was fine. She knew the way out. He made a mental note to have someone check in on her later, with a broom if necessary.

As Terry Conlin left the room, Sondra Jennings stared straight ahead at the ashes in the fireplace, her left eye swollen shut, lips cracked. "Harem rules" only extended to the fighting aquarium itself, apparently. Though he was intrigued by them, "soft" contracts weren't really Terry's style.

"Sarah darlin'," Jacob Conlin drawled.

The morning sun sent long skyscraper-shadows across bustling rush-hour streets in downtown Calgary. Though the air was cool, Jacob sat outside on the office's private terrace surrounded on all sides by towers of glass and steel. Sunlight reflected off windows at unpredictable intervals; the images of buildings super-imposed upon one another with a liquid, fun-house mirror effect. The terrace itself was a forest in miniature: birds sang in the boughs of blossoming May and Plum trees. The whole place somehow smelled floral, blocking out the background odor of exhausted petrol.

Sarah smiled as she approached, bearing a silver tray with two Americanos pulled by the office's in-house barista, and sugar and soy for Jacob.

"Fine morning, isn't it?" Jacob said, setting aside his tablet upon which the morning's financial news was displayed.

"Couldn't be better," Sarah agreed. She warmed her hands with her coffee and sat back into a high-backed, rococo deck chair. In the distance, and thirty stories down, traffic hummed, punctuated by car horns in a broken rhythm.

Jacob smiled like a parent, not a boss. "How you feelin', kiddo?"

"I'm good," Sarah nodded.

"You'll never forget this, Sarah," Jacob said mistily. "I envy you. You'll never be so alive again. Christ, what I'd give to do it all over again!"

Sarah summoned her inner good-old-boy: a patter she had mastered long ago. "Well, you can go if you want. I'll cover *your* cases, and . . ."

Jacob laughed his big-man laugh, genuinely charmed by her attitude. "You're a kidder. I know you: you can't wait to get at it. Listen: take your laptop, keep yourself in the loop if you have any downtime, but don't call in. Take your time—as much time as you need. Make sure you enjoy this. I'm proud of you, kiddo. You're like the daughter I never got to have."

"Your son's no slouch from what I recall," Sarah said, gently testing the water. "Big swinging Wall Street banker? He must be doing daddy proud, I imagine."

"Well, that he is," Jacob nodded, eyes sparkling, "that he is. He's gonna be a good one. So: do you have everything you need? Is there anything else I can do for you?"

Sarah shrugged. "Kelly's covering my open files; I've got my stuff all packed . . ."

"You need a driver?"

"Got that handled. No, Jacob, I'd say I'm good to go."

"Well, all right. Whyn't you finish your coffee out here, enjoy the morning. May as well let traffic die down before you head out."

Sarah smiled, sipped her coffee, and listened to the city. *Does he know I know*? Sarah mused. She couldn't tell for certain. If he did, he was being very coy about it. Didn't surprise her: Sarah was used to her father's notion of "need to know", and so, apparently, was Jacob.

POLLY SAT AT the table in her kitchen, in a pink, plush "Vengeance" brand bathrobe, her black hair lying in shower-damp coils down her back. On her left wrist, she wore a masculine, silver Rolex Submariner, which signified that she would be equally at home in the boardroom, or on the ocean's floor.

She reached across to the MediaPro laptop and actuated the camera. She smiled, letting her eyes do most of the work. Then she began: "Hey everybody, good morning. Well, wow . . . it's here, you know? It's time. I don't really know what to say—which is weird, right? I feel . . . I'm excited. I'm really excited; not scared yet, maybe I will be, but right now, I'm just anxious to get going." Polly paused, casting dark-chocolate brown eyes off to one side in contemplation, then coming back to the camera with a blinking of soot-black lashes. "I've seen her—

some video of her. She's everything I ever imagined. She's definitely going to challenge my brand: I know she'll bring the very best out of me. I'm not going to out her just yet because I don't want you guys hacking her shit and giving her grief. Afterwards, I'll tell all, you know I will, but for right now, this feels really, really private. So weird, I know, but it does. I feel so intimate towards her, towards the whole thing. If we shine a light on everything too soon, it'll be ruined, or something. That's my feeling anyway, I don't know. God, guys: I'm going to be a mom!"

A man's voice spoke in the room. "Okay: cut on rehearsal. Great work. First places in two minutes."

A make-up girl moved in from Polly's left, feather-brushing at her face as Polly tilted her chin up from habit. A wardrobe girl helped Polly out of the "Vengeance" robe and into the robe of another MMA company, this time in black. Sitting Polly down again, the wardrobe girl set a "Porsche" cap upon her head, working the long damp ringlets of hair through the hole at the back to make things cute. The Rolex was swapped out for a more elegant and feminine Cartier. Polly made a couple of passes with her wrist, practicing her nonchalance.

"Cap's a bit much, isn't it," Polly frowned at Mike, the director. Across the floor sat her agent, Willa, and publicist, Dot McKenzie.

It was Willa who chimed in. "This is your Super Bowl, honey. If you want the rate-bump, we gotta get these shots in. Your call."

Polly fidgeted with the headgear. She hated hats in real life, would never wear them on her own. It just didn't seem like something she would do.

"Fine," she relented. This was her Super Bowl after all.

Polly took a deep breath in, and smiled, letting her eyes do most of the work.

BEACON HILL PARK in Victoria was a national treasure as far as city parks went. Warren and Ellen jogged on paths alongside stoic oaks, towering redwoods, and the drooping boughs of acer trees. Early camas were in bloom in the large meadows and open fields, wet with early morning dew, and glinting in the rising sun. Running footfalls thump-thump-thumped across

Victorian footbridges, ducks made their stately procession across man-made pools lipped in stone. Warren loved this—morning runs with Ellen, Beacon Hill, the cool seaside air—all of it.

They ran cross-country style through a dense copse of shrubs and poplars, and emerged out the other side to cross Dallas Road, onto the waterfront park greens. Ellen wasn't Program, but she'd been a distance runner her whole life: she could keep up unless Warren felt he needed a serious workout. If it were a choice between breaking a real sweat, or running with Ellen, however, Warren rarely chose the former.

They came at last to an octagonal recreational building surrounded by benches, overlooking the Pacific Ocean from the cliffs of Horseshoe Bay. Their feet crunched on red-clay gravel as they sat on a bench and leaned their backs against the wall of the octagon. Overhead, rainbow-coloured parasails drifted by like an animated post card. Out to sea, a mist-obscured tanker slid out into the Juan de Fuca strait, heading south. Warren could hear Ellen recovering her breath with little "whew" sighing noises. Her hair was up, cheeks rosy, black hoodie and leggings somehow more elegant than they should have been, for running clothes.

They spent a few moments catching their breath and looking out upon the majesty of the sea. Gentle-yet-mighty swells pushed onto the rocky beach far below, the waves looking like the sinews of a giant flexing in the sun.

"Fuck," Warren said at last. "I'm sorry, Ellen."

"You can't be sorry," she said, wiping at her forehead with the cuff of her hoodie-sleeve. "I knew you were in the Program. You never lied or covered that up."

"I know, but . . . I'm sorry about us . . . this. Ending."

"It was always going to happen, Warren."

"Jesus. I'm supposed to be comforting you."

Ellen smiled a rueful little smile. "I don't want you to think that I'm being cold. I'm not."

"No, I know."

"I've been pulling back for a while now—I think you know that. For my good, and yours."

"I know. I just . . . this is happening really suddenly, from my point of view. I didn't want you to feel like I just woke up one morning and decided to abandon you. Whatever else happens from here, you were—you are—my first love. This is not easy for me."

"I'd have been hurt if you weren't hurt a little. Thanks for that, Warren. But I'll be mad if you let this hurt you too much. You're coming back; after a while, maybe you'll introduce me to the blushing bride, and I'll enjoy watching you two raise a family together. Give me some time, and I might be prepared to be a good friend to both of you, if you'll have me. But that's not going to happen if you go in distracted."

"You're not a distraction."

"You know what I mean."

"I love you, Ellie. Not as much as I could have, thanks to your fine distance-management, but still. It counts as love."

Tears formed and pushed down Ellen D'Arcy's cheeks then. There was no hysterical sobbing, no shuddering, heaving chest. Ellen sat still, her head resting against the wall of the building behind her, and let her tears go like breath.

"If you love me," she said at last, "you'll focus, and come back to me whole."

THIS IS WHERE I killed a guy, Terry realized.

The limo was slowing down as it headed for the mouth of the Midtown Tunnel. Almost three years to the day, an identical limo had been taking Terry, his driver, and his company-assigned shooter in the opposite direction, back into Manhattan. An accident up ahead hadn't set off any warning bells, but it should have. Road construction to the side, and tunnel traffic in behind had created a natural chokepoint, and when they came for Terry, they came guns blazing.

It was just a straight up assassination attempt, no kidnapping planned, not even a snatch-of-opportunity. Terry remembered bullets hitting the armored doors of the limo like stones being thrown against a metal gardening shed. Bulletproof glass held up in places, failed in others: the driver's brains splashed against the acrylic divide between the front seats and the back, and the killers had moved in from three sides.

"Stay here!" the shooter had shouted, Sig Sauer 9mm in hand. What the hell was his name, Terry reflected. Kim Thorssomething. Thorson. Something like that. Terry always remembered the "Kim" part.

Kim had thrown the door open and shot down the man who shot him—the semi-auto rifle fire driving Kim back onto the floor of the limo with his face shot away. That left the right flank of the car open, with the front and left flank covered. Terry hadn't even hesitated.

He'd pulled Kim's gun from his dead fingers out of necessity: Terry had forgotten his own damn sidearm again. Crouching behind the open, armored door, Terry heard the spackling impact of bullets, then came up firing, hitting innocent cars and earning himself a lawsuit with his first, somewhat panicky burst. Bullets banged back, causing Terry to duck, but when he rose the second time, he was in full control of himself.

Kim had fired three times: Terry had counted. Terry's first burst had been four shots, leaving nine rounds. Terry remembered being pleased at his situational awareness under fire. He'd always assumed he'd respond like a cold-blooded action hero during an attack such as this, he'd gamed it enough times with his instructors. But you never really knew. Truth was, he had exceeded his own expectations that day.

Bracing his forearms atop the door, Terry calmed his breathing and took in the situation. The frontal assailant was encroaching in a steady, creeping crouch, spitting out rounds in short, controlled bursts. Afterwards, it would be revealed that the man was ex-military, a victim of US infantry demobilization and incremental privatization: a lot of soldiers were turning up in the politicized underground, if they couldn't transition to the private sector. That accounted for the well-organized scheme and execution of the attack. In retrospect, Terry had been lucky that all three of his assailants hadn't been as thoroughly conditioned.

Terry's first shot hit the leader centre-mass, the bullet slamming to a halt on a chest protector. Terry had expected as much, and carefully walked his shooting-line up-torso. Terry's next bullet hit neck in a fine red mist, even as slugs pelted the door of the limo in response. The third shot sheared away scalp, dropping the attacker.

Six shots left. Terry rose and placed his locked arms in firing position along the roof of the limo, sighting on the third man.

He was no suicide bomber, just some white kid in his teens with no intention of driving home the assault once the wheels had fallen off. He shot high as he backpedaled, then turned to run: Terry took a breath, held it, then snapped off three more shots, two hitting the kid in the back and dropping him on his face.

Terry had drilled enough to know that he wasn't finished. Taking a fresh clip from Kim's corpse, Terry swapped out magazines and advanced from the car, checking his compass points as he worked towards the body on the right flank. A quick check of the man revealed a kill for Kim: Terry put an insurance-slug into the man's chest, obtained the assault rifle, returned to the limo, and threw the weapon into the backseat. Next, Terry moved forward to check the man he'd downed. There was no question he was dead, but Terry's body was just executing his training at this point—going through the necessary checklist. Kill confirmed, insurance shot administered, and weapon obtained, Terry retreated to the limo, the shrill bleat of crying and shouting rising in the distance. The third sortie out from the limo revealed that the kid was still alive, sliding into shock. Terry thought about administering a killing tap, but if the kid didn't bleed out, he might be worth questioning, just in case this wasn't the usual ad hoc, random, and pathetic act of domestic terror. Terry took the boy's assault rifle and did a quick pat down for other weapons before retreating to the limo.

Convinced that the attack was over, Terry called the office for additional security, medical, and investigative units. He poured himself a drink, and sat back in the plush leather seats, letting the adrenalin finally course freely though his body. He had felt elation—his body trembling with tension-release and a ferocious pride in his own decisiveness. In that moment, he knew he was what he was supposed to be. He had pulled triggers, hit what he aimed at, killed what he hit, all without flinching. He was the last man standing, and even with a faceless security man lying dead on the floor of the limo, the smell of blood thick in the close confines, Terry hadn't been able to stop himself from smiling.

In the final analysis, he was fined by his own firm for not wearing his sidearm in the city (though he was feted by his co-workers in the after-massacre party); sued by two separate families for reckless endangerment—both cases eventually settled. But most importantly for Terry, he felt he'd learned something about himself that day. When the worst-case scenario had finally materialized, he'd answered with his best. His test scores and stress-profiling hadn't just been so much econometric bullshit. Terry had made his name that day, and if single-handedly foiling an assassination attempt hadn't gotten him his next promotion, it certainly hadn't hurt, either.

Terry chuckled, causing his new shooter—Len . . . Ken . . . something—to look up from his tablet. "Forgot my fuckin' gun," Terry explained with a grin. Jesus!

Through the tunnel, onto the Long Island Expressway, turning into the Grand Central Parkway, the limo slid closer to La Guardia. Terry sent his father a text with arrival times: he'd stay at his folks' place overnight, then head up to the lake the following morning. It'd be good to see Jacob and Carol Conlin again, Terry decided. Normally, he had no sense of nostalgia, but on this occasion, he felt a distinct sense of "homecoming". He tried to latch onto the feeling, holding onto the sensation as though it were a taste, or an eye-catching colour. It faded, but the memory of it perplexed him all the same.

The limo passed through the main access checkpoint and the interior defensive screens to an exclusive road reserved for private plane passengers. Over half the old airport had been given over to private custom—the hangars and maintenance buildings all sporting various corporate logos. The CWL Gulfstream would be housed at the Tyler/Brock hangar as per prior agreement. Terry had been happy to take his own company's plane, but his father had insisted. Made no difference to Terry: every plane came stocked with the same liquor cabinet.

The limo slowed as it navigated amongst the hangars. Jets could be heard taking off or landing in the distance, the sky was overcast with the kind of rolling cloud cover that would soon burn off. Eventually, the Tyler/Brock logo came into view, and the car pulled around to the small parking area to the side of the hangar, out of the way of the main doors.

The shooter got out of the car first, checking all his compass points, satisfied the area was secure. Terry's driver of the last two years, a Haitian named Leonard Walls, met Terry at the trunk of the car, retrieving Terry's athletic bag and handing it to him with a smile.

"Good hunting, sir," Leonard said in Caribbean-accented English, showing a genuine smile. For whatever reason, Leonard didn't hate Terry, and Terry for his part had grown to prefer this particular driver to others. There weren't many non-fungible relationships in Terry's life: his driver and his barber were perhaps the only constants outside of work.

"Thank you, Leonard," Terry smiled, slinging the bag onto his shoulder. With that, he turned and strode towards the hangar doors, his heels making an impressive clacking noise against the tarmac, his open-throated shirt setting off his bull neck and newly shaved pate in dramatic fashion. He could almost imagine what he must look like, and he approved of the image. Like a football player en route to a playoff game.

Entering the hangar to echoes, Terry slowed his stride, narrowed his eyes. There was a plane in the hangar, but it wasn't from his father's firm, and it wasn't a Gulfstream. In the back of the cavernous warehouse, he could see the Tyler/Brock plane in tether, obviously not checked-out for flight today. The plane that *was* ready to go looked like one of those Russian command jobs: transcontinental range; able to handle less than ideal landing conditions, or shorter-than-usual airstrips. It was painted a dark forest green with a blue-world globe logo on the vertical tail surface: Global Conflict Management Systems Inc.

Terry hesitated, replaying in his mind the conversation he'd had with his father concerning travel arrangements. Truth was, his dad had said he'd send *a* plane, not his own corporate charter necessarily. And it was no secret that CWL did a lot of the international treaty stuff for GCM, so . . . Terry had been just about to return to the car to confirm details when a pretty South American flight attendant appeared in the open doorway to the craft. She smiled, waved: Terry shrugged and approached the metal step-ladder with a bemused expression she must have found amusing. "Señor Conlin?" the girl chuckled. "Right this way."

Terry climbed the stairs and handed his bag to the girl at her request. She led him through a small alcove and past a curtain into an expansive lounge area with a couple of work stations, cruising chairs, and chairs that would recline into sleeping cocoons.

A man sat at one of the work-stations near a window—a wiry type; close-cropped black hair; hollow cheeked, and sporting a piratical black eye patch. The man smiled a thin-lipped grin, and his one good eye seemed to dance like ice crystals in the sun.

"Good morning, Terry," Eric Wheeler said.

Who you are—who you think you are—that little voice inside your head you think is you? That doesn't matter anymore. All that matters is what you can do in a publicly verifiable way. It's productivity over being. The web says who you are now. Everything else is just cheap whiskey.

— Chthonic Sun, internet personality

THE PORSCHE'S BATTERY had gone dead over the winter. Sarah hadn't anticipated that, lost a day getting the car tuned up.

She loved the Boxster in a way that often surprised her. The sleek black chassis, the lunging road-presence . . . the aesthetics alone would have been enough to engage Sarah. The car had been customized with an old-style manual six-speed transmission, and although the power plant had been chip-optimized for fuel-injected, ultra-high mileage, the car itself was an analog throwback. Racing suspension, ABS, and corner-assist gave Sarah support, but never replaced her at the wheel. The car wasn't a shuttle for carrying Sarah's body here and there: it was an extension of Sarah's body; an amplification. She hadn't wanted to feel *safe* in that car. She had been very specific with the dealer on that score, and had happily paid the analog premium for both the necessary technical adjustments and the hefty insurance package.

Sarah traveled north on Alberta's QE2, the great highway that linked Edmonton with Calgary. The old stereotype was that Edmonton was all about housing the people who actually got the oil out of the oil sands; Calgary was where the projects got financed . . . but over the years, comparative advantage had hammered the stereotype into reality. Comparative advantage had also whittled the province down to a two-city jurisdiction, more or less. Only a handful of incorporated towns remained, and even those were under constant threat of disintegration. They were like planets orbiting either of two black holes—market-forces functioning like gravity-waves gradually breaking apart the miniature worlds, sucking the debris into the respective whirling vortices.

Change the infrastructure, Sarah, change the people. Her father's words came to her too easily, too clearly, as if the road itself had somehow summoned them. Eric and his fucking 3:00 A.M. lectures. She shook her head to clear her mind of the memory, but her dad was a tenacious one. She felt his presence like the smell of petroleum at a gas station, like the odor of warm tires in the sun.

It seemed to Sarah that she was alone in her speeding Boxster, with flat expanses of prairie wheat to either side of her, and a mercury-grey sky above. Low lying cloud cover promised a deluge, but had yet to deliver. As the day progressed, Sarah could tell that the clouds were burning off. She doubted there'd be any rain today.

Self-driving commercial trucks, labour-transit, and farm-support vehicles still used the road, but Sarah hadn't seen another soul for at least thirty minutes. Leisure travel on inter-city highways was rare outside the normal vacation-windows. Her father had told her that the highways had once been jammed—thousands of cars criss-crossing the province—but Sarah had never seen it. In point of fact, she could scarcely imagine it. Things were much more streamlined nowadays. *People aggregate to where they most need to be,* the memory of Eric Wheeler's voice said. *They stick to their most efficient patterns and routines.* The path of least resistance rarely involved the QE2 these days.

When he had been home, Eric would make a point of waking Sarah up at 3:00 A.M., just to get her used to it. He'd make them both shakes in the kitchen—he dressed for the day in dress pants, dress shirt, and tie; she in her bathrobe and PJs—and he'd use the time wisely. The windows would be black with darkness outside. Sarah's heels would bounce against the supporting rung of her stool as she drank her breakfast at the kitchen island, listening to her father's low, resonant morning-voice.

Highways are the skeleton of the Welfare State, he'd say.

They're not roads, they're the fossil remains of an ancient creature.

Infrastructure isn't bricks. It's an idea you can touch, and as you touch it, it touches you. It shapes you. It makes people the specific shape it needs them to be. People go out and make more infrastructure in their own image, and so on.

Change infrastructure, Sarah, and you change people. Change people, and you change the world.

A proximity chime brought Sarah's attention back to the present, and she changed lanes to get around a nasty-looking pothole. She had to be somewhat vigilant—the road was pitted and cracked with years of neglect; she wouldn't want to hit any faults doing 90mph. Vegetation pushed up through the pavement on the shoulders, giving the road a picturesque rather than utilitarian aspect.

Sarah asked the Porsche for a bit more speed, gunning back up to 95. She loved the illusion that she had the whole damn province to herself. The idea of the "road trip" had disappeared from the collective consciousness. The open highway held no allure in an age of digital connectivity, asset-sharing, and the seven-day work week. The only people who used the long straight-aways now were joy-riders like Sarah, people who actually owned their own German or Asian land-rockets, people who could imagine a kind of 1960's style freedom that would never again be the norm.

The car was totemic for Sarah—she knew it. It was more than an item on her asset list: it meant independence to her. She'd bought the Porsche soon after the condo, even though CWL drove her everywhere inside the city. Getting to places wasn't the point. Getting *away* from places was closer to the mark. Most people couldn't afford the luxury of escape.

It was still too early in the morning, and too cool to put the top down, but eventually that was the plan. The wind in her hair, generated by a few hundred horses of German engineering, was one of Sarah's singular delights.

The GPS beeped and a female voice with a cultured, European accent told Sarah to "Take the next exit in three hundred meters"—the car reckoning in metric, while the province had long since reverted to imperial measurements. Sarah followed instructions, accelerating in a wide, rising right hand turn to the east, which eventually curled onto an overpass heading west and north.

Sarah decelerated and came to a stop on the top of the overpass. Turning off the engine, she got out of the car, breathing in crisp, fresh prairie air, and walked over to the green-painted rail on the south side of the road. She pushed her mirrored sunglasses onto the top of her head and gazed back down the way she had come.

The QE2 stretched off on a black line to the horizon, empty as far as the eye could see. A morning breeze sent waves through wheatgrass, carrying a pleasant earthy odor to Sarah's nostrils. *It's so desolate*, Sarah thought, thrilled by the sight. Like something out of a horror movie, a zombie apocalypse. It was so easy to imagine she was the only one left in all the world, alone on that overpass. Her father was right: it was a graveyard out here. There was a sepulchral feel to the quietude, something holy about the breeze in the grass, and the awful stillness of the road, an awesome vastness to the space, as though she looked upon the ocean rather than the road to Calgary.

Change the infrastructure, change the people. How has all this changed me, then?

Sarah tried to picture hurtling automobiles drafting one another in a suicidal bumper-to-bumper configuration, like blood cells pulsing through the provincial circulatory system. She tried to imagine the devastating wreckage caused by hackerists on the first—and last—generation of civilian self-driving cars. The images simply wouldn't come. It was a thing she could know only intellectually; information she understood as a kind of data. When she tried to picture the road used as it had originally been intended, the sense of it broke down. It was the sort of thing people could only see in dreams—that weird juxtaposition of imagery that resisted conscious construction.

After a few spellbinding moments, Sarah returned to the car, satisfied with her reflections. Revving the high-stress motor and catapulting forward at speed, she resumed her progress towards the place of her birth: Sylvan Lake.

The original Sylvan Lake had been a thriving bedroom community at some point in the past, but "organic" over-development financed in no small part by clandestine toxic waste dumping in the lake had seen the place unravel in a spectacular display of self-destruction. Undaunted, the town's business owners and moneyed retirees had relocated to another town about an hour's journey northwest, and in a corporate merger between jurisdictions, a new Sylvan Lake had been christened. Part resort town nestled alongside a different, non-toxic lake, part exclusive summer-destination for weekends out of the city, and part support system for the StandardGen facility in Alberta, the new Sylvan Lake had managed to find a self-sustaining equilibrium, when dozens of other communities hadn't.

The off-ramp road was wilder, hillier than the freeway had been. Trees that formed natural windbreaks in the area crept closer and closer to the edges of the road, gradually framing the sky. Sarah reduced speed, but increased her fun as the road twisted into gentle switchback curves, making better use of the Porsche's handling and racing suspension.

She made good time regardless, clocking the distance to the town's incorporated limits from the overpass in a little under 45 minutes. Slowing down to the posted 30mph, she drove past the first of many golf courses and thought, *that does it*. Pulling over to the shoulder, she put the top down on the Boxster and smiled to smell the faint traces of putting-green must on the air.

The highway flowed naturally to the town's "Lakeshore Drive" which Sarah recognized as its main street. Following it around a sweeping right hand turn, she emerged with the marina to her left boasting a small, but inviting water park attached to a classy hotel. A leisurely stretch of wooded parkland ran along the shoreline, and along the road to her right, a number of antique storefronts punctuated the tree line.

Sarah had to smile, the town was so quaint. There were relics from the 1960s and 70s present—old signs denoting Coca-Cola and Sunoco Gas; a gas station with old-style hand pumps; bait and tackle shacks with wooden awnings that would drop down to cover the open windows at night. Fruit and produce stands sold goods from local plots—the wooden fronts of the shops painted like museum replicas from the Eisenhower era. None of these places would need to turn a profit necessarily: these were break-even joints, often maintained by retirees who had made their money, staffed by local kids maybe, or with temporary labour transferred in during ski-boat season. Sarah wouldn't want to live there, she realized, but she was surprised to find herself charmed as a visitor.

Her tummy rumbled audibly, bringing a slight frown to Sarah's brow, as she had eaten two big breakfast burritos prior to leaving the city. There was no denying it though—she was hungry again, just as she'd been warned she would be. The orientation instructions had said to eat before checking in at the lab, so Sarah kept an eye out for the first evidence of a likely restaurant.

The suspense was over in mere moments as an Art Deco diner with walls of whitewashed stucco came into view. Sarah pulled into the lot and parked beside a pole out front that supported a neon sign that said "DINER", removing all doubt as to the nature of the place. The retro-cool curves and the lake-facing roadside windows were instantly captivating. Sarah might have stopped here even if she hadn't been starving.

Turning off the ignition, Sarah glanced at the passenger seat beside her, seeing her overbuilt black laptop with the CWL logo in crimson on the top. An instinctive guilt-reflex almost caused her to check in at the office, but she fought the impulse with sheer force of will. *Fuck it*, she thought, taking the laptop and putting it in the shallow boot of the car alongside her overnight bag. The senior partner had told her to take time to enjoy the experience, and that was exactly what she was going to do.

She was the only customer as she slid into a red vinyl booth near the window, putting the lake on her left. A heavy-set middle-aged waitress approached with a smile, and Sarah assumed she might also be the proprietress. "Menu?" the woman asked as she automatically poured Sarah an unsolicited coffee.

"Please," Sarah nodded, relaxing in spite of herself. She never drank restaurant-brew: she drank it now, somehow feeling that it might be part of the ambience. It was thin and weak, and virtually undrinkable, but Sarah sipped at it regardless.

She went with a classic greasy-spoon breakfast: two real eggs; actual pork-product bacon; short stack. It was wildly over-priced, but it was good in a brawny, unsubtle way—the quality greatly magnified by the hungry-traveler multiplier. Sarah enjoyed it for what it was—the food being as much a museum item as the diner itself. When the waitress/owner asked her, "Are you staying in town?" Sarah replied: "I'm heading to the lab," and earned a respectful smile along with some solitude. She imagined that it was easier for townies to chat up Program candidates after the Spawning, rather than before, for obvious reasons. Sarah didn't resent the silence; she wasn't much for small talk.

Sipping at her second cup of wretched coffee, Sarah took out her phone and hit Kelly Lee's number. In a moment, Kelly's face filled the screen, and she scrunched her eyes and nose in greeting.

"Heyyy," Kelly said. "You there yet?"

"I'm at the town," Sarah replied.

"You okay?"

"Yeah. Miss you."

"Wow. Wish I were recording this."

"Shut up," Sarah smiled. "Anything going on?"

"As if you want to know. You picked a busy fucking week to pull a stunt like this."

"They're all busy weeks," Sarah smiled.

"Yeah. So what's the scoop? Just wanted to see my face?"

"Something like that."

"I wish I could be there, but, you know: who'd do your job for you then?"

"I think you're breaking up!"

"What? You miss me? Say again?"

"Fine. Sarah, OUT!"

"Okay," Kelly laughed, hung up. Sarah grinned and put her phone away.

Sarah's core sexual identification wasn't bi or lesbian, but being Program, and knowing what was in store for her—that she was basically "coded" for a particular market-selected mate from birth—she had tended to date women as a basic precaution. It felt less complicated on all fronts, more satisfying emotionally, and left her free for dalliances like she'd had with the associate the other night . . . although the violence of that encounter had come as something of a shock. Her body was revving—seething—despite her outward calm. Johnny

Johannson had been the right guy at the wrong time: on another night, that would have gone exactly the way he had hoped. As it was, he'd been very lucky she'd been able to rein herself in, before . . . well. Before something irreversible had happened.

Kelly had used the code-phrase "Wish I were recording this," indicating that the communications were being monitored. Sarah smiled ruefully at the thought that although her father couldn't be bothered to contact her directly, he had no problem bugging her devices. Evidently, it was as close to caring as he was going to get.

Sarah finished her coffee and paid the cheque with her phone. It was almost noon, and warm out now: perfect convertible weather. Backing out of the gravel lot in front of the diner, Sarah headed down the lakefront, leaving the built up area of the town for the curving bend of the north-shore drive.

The road merged into a narrow two-lane blacktop outside of the town, and tree boughs often reached across from either side to form an arboreal arch overhead. Sunlight strobed through newly green leaves, and the woods became thicker and more unruly, though occasionally, the bright blue of the lake's surface could be glimpsed to Sarah's left.

At the northern-most point of the lake, the road forked. A large green sign with the word "CLINIC" printed upon it in white indicated that the right hand option should be taken for the StandardGen facility. A checkpoint booth dominated the intersection, operating a gate that blocked the left hand fork in the road. There was a gate apparatus on the right hand fork of the road as well, but it lay open during regular business hours. Electrified fencing pushed into the woods on either side of the fork, neatly delineating the StandardGen property line. It wasn't really intended to be a high-security area—such measures weren't necessary in Alberta—but casual visitors would be discouraged all the same.

Sarah came to a halt beneath the window of the booth and watched as the armed guard descended from his post. He was heavyset, in his early thirties, and looked to be more tollbooth attendant than ex-military, though Sarah knew better. He smiled once he got a good look at Sarah, and affected a pose of bored authority.

"Name?" the guard asked.

"Sarah Wheeler," Sarah said, electing not to return the smile. The guard handed her a small blood-diagnostic akin to a diabetic blood monitor: she pressed it to her thumb and barely registered the automatic pin-prick. Returning the monitor, Sarah watched as the man verified her identity on his tablet. When he began his routine inspection of the vehicle, Sarah stared straight ahead, obviously and deliberately ignoring him.

"Pop the trunk please, ma'am?" the guard asked. Sarah complied without compunction. She hadn't brought her gun, or any other weapons: none would be allowed on the Spawning Grounds anyway, so it would have been an extra hassle.

Eventually satisfied, the guard retreated to his booth, recording the arrival of an expected guest. He waved through the window, smiling and hoping to catch Sarah's eye. Sarah accelerated down the road towards the clinic without so much as a glance in the man's direction.

In moments, she cleared the tree line to find a large parking lot and a medium-sized hospital facility built in 1970s-style brown-brick and concrete. Sarah curled into a spot without difficulty: the lot was all but empty.

She hesitated in the car when she turned the engine off, listening to the engine tick-down and the birdsong in the distance. Her hands were still on the ebony wheel, gripping tightly as her heart rate picked up. *This is it*, she thought. She had no choice but to go through the main doors, and once through, her life would change. She waited in the car to extend the last few moments of her life-before—like lovers embracing in an airport before parting for new, separate lives, except, of course, that Sarah was alone. The feeling persisted though, a feeling of loss, of separation. A silent goodbye.

She got out of the car, didn't bother with the top. Her footfalls seemed inordinately loud to her in the barren lot, counting out the steps to the automatic doors of "Admitting".

Entering directly into a colossal waiting room filled with rows of empty chairs, Sarah could see a receptionist at the admittance desk on the far side of the room. The building was a leftover from the era of public healthcare, of course—re-purposed by StandardGen to serve a much more exclusive clientele. Much of the bed-space had been converted to research, administrative, and processing functionality. The scale of the place was wrong, Sarah realized. She was reminded of the empty, desolate highway, only in this context, she was more chilled than thrilled by the expanse.

Once again, her footsteps seemed to echo too loudly as she approached the desk. The receptionist busied herself with a computer screen, looking up only when Sarah actually arrived and stood in one spot, waiting to be acknowledged.

"Now," the attendant said, narrowing her eyes as she regarded her visitor. The receptionist was young, of dark complexion . . . Sarah imagined she might be of Italian descent. "You must be . . . ," said the receptionist, whose nametag read "Alicia".

"Sarah," Sarah said. "Sarah Wheeler?"

"Right! Just have a seat, and a nurse will collect you shortly."

Sarah turned, dreading another walk through the cavernous space. She took a seat close to the desk, and had begun to reach for her phone when a female voice said: "Sarah?"

Sarah stood, mildly amused at the process. *Who the hell else would I be*, she didn't say. An Asian-Indian nurse whose nametag read "Gabrielle" nodded and gestured for Sarah to follow, then turned to lead the way.

A hallway to the left of reception led into what Sarah assumed would once have been emergency bedding. The space was more spa-like now, with curtained-off gurney-slots replaced by quaint little chalet-style changing rooms. A fountain splashed somewhere out of sight, soothing harp music played at very low volume over the PA system. The hard overhead hospital lighting remained though, as did the antiseptic tile on the floor. The odd patch of whitewashed cinderblock was still visible on the walls. Sarah found the odd combination of features unsettling. *Tear the place down and build what you really want*, she thought.

"Here we are," Gabrielle said with a smile, opening a door to a small cedar-wood enclosure. Her voice carried the characteristic trace of the lilting Indian-British accent. "If you could just change out of your things, I will be down the hall when you are ready."

Sarah nodded, entered the room. A padded arm chair stood in one corner, a low bench traversed three of the four walls. A heavily starched, pale blue hospital gown lay in crisp folds upon the bench, and a pair of plastic-soled slippers lay under it.

Closing the door, Sarah saw that the inside plane was covered with a floor to door-top mirror. She stopped short and was surprised to see she'd been frowning. The washed-out, arctic blue eyes were furtive, edgy, and her wind-blown hair was slightly disheveled. *Get a hold of yourself*, Sarah chided her reflection. The girl in the mirror frowned back, almost as if she knew something Sarah didn't.

Tight, but comfortable, pale blue jeans were folded and benched, joined in moments by the soft, pale blue slouchy-fitting sweat-top Sarah had worn, and her mirrored aviator's sunglasses. The attendant hadn't said anything about underthings: Sarah regarded her muscular form in white sports bra and cotton panties in the mirror and decided that was as naked as she was going to get. Presumably, if it were going to be an issue, they'd have said something. She pulled the starchy hospital gown over her head and fingered her hair into order down her back.

Exchanging her comfortable walking pumps for the slippers, Sarah completed her hospital makeover and pursed her lips in disapproval in the mirror. She put her phone into a plastic charging box on the wall and took a deep breath. With a force of will, she relaxed her brow, transforming her face from a look of pinched concern to bland stoicism. Feeling relatively composed, she pushed open the door, looked both ways, and headed off to her left in search of Gabrielle.

She found the nurse sitting behind a curved desk, located at the base of a T-intersection at the end of the hall. Gabrielle smiled, rose, and led Sarah down the right hand branch of the T to a small room with a medical bed, a few diagnostic tools on the wall, some cupboards, and what looked to be a dentist's chair. "Have a seat there," Gabrielle said, indicating the chair as she busied herself with a test-tube tray.

Sarah sat, deliberately breathing deeply through her nose and exhaling between her lips. The nurse hummed quietly to herself as she wrapped rubber tubing around Sarah's right arm, then rubbed the inner-elbow area with an antiseptic, saying, "Just a sharp poke here," prefatory to inserting a hypodermic into flesh. Sarah didn't look directly at the blood-taking, but could see via peripheral vision the nurse swapping test tubes in and out with practiced ease. In moments Gabrielle smiled and chirped: "All done. Just lie down on the bed there and Doctor Campbell will be right with you." The nurse left the room, leaving Sarah in institutionalized silence.

Sarah rose from the chair and stepped up onto the elevated bed, lying on her back to stare at a corkboard ceiling. She heard the man's footsteps moments before the tapping here-I-am knock, then a young slender figure in a white lab coat over a dark blue business suit stepped smiling into the room.

"Sarah Wheeler?"

"In the flesh."

"Okay," the man smiled, inclining his head and stopping just short of clicking his heels. "I'm Thomas Campbell. How are you feeling?"

"Great. A little cold."

"Mmm." The doctor went through a pre-arranged protocol, checking reflexes, monitoring blood pressure, flashing a light into each of Sarah's eyes. Giving Sarah a PSI disk, he asked her to squeeze as hard as she could for ten seconds. The smart device automatically recorded her results, and upon seeing them, the doctor raised his eyebrows and nodded, impressed.

Sarah closed her eyes, extended her arms to her sides and touched her nose left/right/left. The doctor tested her joints and resistance strength, muttering "Good . . . good . . ." after each exam. Satisfied at last, the doctor smiled and said, "Okay, Sarah. Ever had an MRI before?"

In point of fact, Sarah had not had an MRI before. Lying in the machine with her ears plugged, staring up into the white plastic curvature of the little tunnel into which she had been inserted, Sarah focused upon "being calm". Those were the instructions she had been given—just to relax, and not to be alarmed by the mechanical noise the thing made, which was overwhelming in the close confines.

It was all easier said than done. The first few minutes were easy, but as the novelty wore off, being "relaxed" seemed to require more and more effort. Sarah had never before experienced anything like claustrophobia, but in such a tight space, surrounded by deafening, alien noise, it was impossible to ignore her own anxiety. Ten minutes in, an electronic voice from her earplugs said: "Sarah? How are you doing?" She wasn't sure what to do. When she said "Fine", she couldn't hear her own voice, and wondered if Gabrielle—she assumed it was Gabrielle—had heard anything. She repeated her response and listened: nobody said a word. None of it made her feel any better about the situation.

After about fifteen minutes, the grinding hum was replaced by a series of mechanical knocking noises, and the bench upon which Sarah lay began to automatically extend out from the mouth of the MRI. Gabrielle helped Sarah to a seated position and smiled pleasantly, giving her wrist a reassuring squeeze. Sarah smiled wanly and retrieved her slippers, following Gabrielle to the next room and procedure.

"This is the Quickening," Gabrielle said when they had Sarah all squared away. It was another dentist's chair, this time in a larger, circular room filled with computer stations and diagnostic instruments. An IV had been inserted into the back of Sarah's right hand, and a soft blanket of tightly coiled synthetic wool covered her body as she lay at an incline on the chair. Electrodes were attached to her temples and various parts of her torso, the various diagnostic lines appearing on a nearby portable monitor. Sarah felt drowsy, and she had to admit, scared. The harsh overhead lights had been dimmed, casting Gabrielle's features in shadow.

"Just sit and relax—sleep if you wish: the process takes around two hours. This is the chemical trigger which unlocks your ability to bond with your One when he comes through. It is like a bunch of switches being thrown in your DNA, lighting up your circuit board so to speak. This ensures conception and completely engages your reproductive system in the Spawning Act. If you need anything, there is a button on the left arm of the chair you can press: I will be monitoring your progress. Do not worry about a thing, Sarah. I will be back to collect you soon."

Sarah listened to the faint, receding footfalls as Gabrielle left her side. Sarah heard the door open, saw the marginal increase in light from the outer hall, then watched as gloom descended in the room once more.

It is like a bunch of switches being thrown in your DNA . . .

Sarah closed her eyes, very much wanting to sleep, then wake up to find the ordeal completed. She was drowsy enough to lose track of time, but after a while, she felt a warmth spreading from her centre, and tingling throughout her extremities. *That would be my "circuit board"*, Sarah thought. And then she heard the music.

She recognized it immediately: Beethoven's 9th Symphony, the "Ode to Joy". She was confused, for it felt as though a full orchestra and choir were actually performing nearby, but then she realized she'd heard the music—that exact performance— one time before.

She saw the Paris Opera House again in her mind's eye— remembering the awe she had experienced at the baroque sight lines of the architecture; the deep, rich colours of the carpeting; the marble, and gilt appointments; the very sweep and scale of the place. She'd been six or seven; her father had taken her to Paris for cultural instruction and historical appreciation. She hated classical music then and hated it now, but that performance—that single, devastating performance of Beethoven's masterpiece had left an impression. She'd been captivated as she rarely had been by art before or since. The combination of events: her father sitting beside her; the majestic impact of the building; the swelling, overpowering music itself . . . it had been absolutely intoxicating. And sitting in the StandardGen lab, it wasn't as though she were recalling the music: it felt as though it was actually occurring—a fresh replay more than a memory.

In the event, her father had had to leave before the night was over. That was routine, and normally not noteworthy, but on that night, Sarah recalled how it had hurt—as though a key ingredient of what made the moment special had been displaced. The spell had been broken, for want of one particular incantation. In his place, her father had left James, his long-time lead shooter, to see Sarah safely home.

As she re-experienced her disappointment, Sarah pictured her own circulatory system as though following a tiny camera through her veins. Hemoglobin pulsed, and her cells trembled in resonance to the symphony that seemed to fill the room with sound. Coiled around her limbic system, she saw another Sarah—a woman who had always been there, sharing the same body, but hiding in the folds of helixes like a parasite. Black eyes—the eyes of a mamba—stared open and unblinking from

Sarah's twin, as corpuscles throbbed and pulsed in heart-driven torrents.

Suddenly the lights came on, filling the room with harsh white fluorescent light. Young Dr. Campbell was there in his lab coat and suit, supported by nurses Sarah didn't recognize. Above her, she could see the mirrored reflection of one-way glass from a procedural gallery encircling the room.

Sarah's feet were up in gynecological stirrups, and the good doctor was inside her, rummaging about indelicately with hands latexed to the elbow. He wore the same insipid smile he had when he had first met her. In the background, Beethoven's 9th played now as though playing through the hospital's PA system—somehow the thinner for it.

Sarah felt a tugging pressure at her groin and winced. She heard a thick squelching sound as something was pulled from her body, then smelled blood in the air as the object cleared her with a wet sucking noise. A nurse pulled a table around with shallow acrylic walls on all four sides, forming a transparent box. Into the box, the doctor sloshed the writhing, blood-and-amniotic-fluid covered body of what looked to be a puppy at first glance, though the size of a healthy human baby. It was blind, with only a grumpy wrinkle indicating an eye, and its four limbs could only scull at the plastic base—more flippers than legs at this point. As Sarah paid more attention, she realized the thing was only dog-like, not a real dog at all, with a broad gash of a mouth housing rows of needle-sharp teeth.

And then the doctor was into her again, pushing and groping.

"Gotcha!" He grinned, looking younger and more insipid than ever.

With a squelch and a suck, a second creature was taken from her body, and although Sarah felt no pain, the sound and offal smell was enough to make her cringe. The second . . . *thing* . . . was dumped into the box, sliding along plastic all slick with reproductive slime. It came to a halt and mewled, smacking its vicious lips together.

Slowly the monsters became aware of one another, wriggling horribly in orientation to one another, flipper-legs lashing at plastic for traction. Bit by bit, they closed upon one another, impossibly wide mouths gaping as blind combat was engaged.

Hard teeth sank into flabby, wriggling little bodies as one of Sarah's offspring would survive and be the stronger for having eaten its sibling. The butchery was all the more savage for the inefficiency of the combatants. Sarah watched in horror as it took minutes—*minutes*—for the death-cries of the loser to end. Even then, the visceral obscenity was not over. The smacking of those awful lips; the rending noises of teeth biting through soft bone and tissue sounded out too loudly, reminding Sarah of her footsteps ringing in the abandoned parking lot, or echoing in the cavernous waiting room.

And then the room was dim again, and silent, save for the hum of diagnostic electronics in the background.

Sarah shivered despite the blanket, sweat cold upon her body. Her heart slapped about in her chest as she slowly came to parse what was real, and what had been hallucination.

She broke down then, into great, wracking sobs of stress and tension, alone in a laboratory, in the bowels of an empty hospital, feeling more isolated and traumatized than she had since childhood.

Market-systems construct a world in which being a victim is considered to be a choice. Twentieth-century victimology is unintelligible within a market context that defines rationality as individual decision-making meant to maximize individual outcomes. Therefore, victims have no one to blame but themselves.

— Eric Wheeler, age ten

" . . . SO THAT'S THE deal. You marry my daughter; she accepts full partnership with your dad's firm; I make her head of GCM's legal counsel in North America; you come on board with me, and rule the fucking world."

"And you want the kid."

"I get the kid."

TERRY SAT IN his father's Victorian study, watching the wall monitor from a leather recliner while his father watched from behind his massive desk. Terry drank a protein shake, and was pleasantly exhausted from a hard morning workout. On the monitor, footage of Warren Milner at age fifteen played, documenting the series of tests which had earned him a black belt in jiu-jitsu. Terry had seen the footage several times by now and was bored by it, but his father had not. Jacob Conlin watched with rapt attention as his son's mind wandered, focusing instead upon the recent plane-ride with Eric Wheeler.

The man wanted his child-to-be.

"Why?" Terry had asked, affecting amusement. In truth, he was badly rattled by the thin, severe man who sat across the table from him. Any director of Global Conflict Management

Systems would have been imposing, given the power at their disposal, but Wheeler's reputation and list of accomplishments were daunting in and of themselves.

"Big picture stuff, Terry," Eric had smiled. "You and Sarah are going to help me change the world for the better, and that'll take about ten to fifteen more years. At that point, you'll both be looking to wind down—trust me, it's going to be a hell of a grind. We'll need a proper successor. So, do I leave the care and nurturing of that successor to you, or should I take the reins myself?"

Terry had had to chuckle at the notion of him nurturing anything, least of all a child. "Good point," he'd said. "What if Sarah doesn't come through?"

"The truth is, if Sarah doesn't do what I've built her to do, then I don't deserve to have the ambition I do. It would mean I've been wrong all along—about a lot of things. But I wouldn't worry about Sarah. She'll be just fine."

"And this other guy?"

Terry looked up at the monitor as the teenage Warren worked incrementally for an arm-bar. On a split-screen to the right, battle-diagnostics broke down Warren's tendencies and efficiency into algorithmic patterns. Based on the numbers, Terry at that age would have killed this kid.

Eric had more or less confirmed Terry's own analysis of the match up. "We've run ten thousand sims of the fight," he'd said. "You win eighty-eight percent of the time."

"Comforting."

"Your biometrics are better across the board. His victory scenarios boil down to fat-tail probabilities which are hard to quantify, but basically . . . stay within your performance envelope and you'll be all right."

On the screen, Warren's opponent had rolled out of the arm-bar, but had given up his back in the process. Young Warren had one hook in, and was patiently squirming to get the other. "What do you make of him, Pop?" Terry asked, respecting his father's eye for fighting talent.

Jacob Conlin considered the screen. He himself hadn't had much use for jiu-jitsu. He hadn't needed it offensively—had only studied it at all so that he'd know how to defend against it.

"He's slick," Jacob grunted. "Tireless—look at his O2

numbers. But this shit's not going to work on you."

Terry nodded. He'd come to the same conclusion. *I'm just too big*, he thought. He had more going for him than size, but sometimes, that was enough. Eighty-eight percent was a hell of a projection for a Spawning Contest. It wasn't a five-sigma deviation, but it was close. You just didn't see that kind of mismatch in Spawning Fours.

Terry thought back to the grappling match of a different kind he'd had on the plane—trying to get to the bottom of Wheeler's game. The offer was astounding, but Terry was in the investment business. He knew that if a deal looked too good . . .

"Seems to me you really only need Sarah to come through for sure," he'd said.

"But the plan is so much more beautiful with the two of you together," Eric had smiled. "Aesthetics aside, you'll be handy to have alongside Sarah—keep her in line."

"What do you mean?"

"I'm a contingency planner, Terry. Program mothers can be highly irrational where their children are concerned. Mistake prone. I think of you as a form of insurance."

"I'll be bonded to the kid too."

"True. But I think we both know that you'll be more . . . resistant to the coding than is typical. One of the reasons why I wanted you in the Four to begin with."

Terry frowned, mulling over the situation as he had done non-stop since arriving at Calgary International. He had intended to overnight at home, then head directly to the Spawning Ground. The new information had made him take an extra day to consider all the angles.

"What's wrong with this picture, Dad?" Terry said, finishing his shake.

"What, Wheeler?"

"Yeah."

"What choice do you have?"

It was a good point. His father had a way of cutting through bullshit to get at the heart of matters. What choice *did* he have? The Spawning Four was set; Warren Milner was Terry's counterpart . . . that was pretty much it. The rest of it—giving up control of the child, the family alliance, the financial ramifications . . . it was hard to see a downside. Still. It was in

Terry's nature to be suspicious.

"What if his daughter doesn't want to give the kid up?" Terry asked.

"That's where you come in," Jacob said simply. "I'm told she knows her role. It'll be difficult, but I actually think she'll come around."

Terry wasn't so certain. Program mothers were deeply engaged with their children at the cellular level. Breaking that bond wouldn't be easy. Exactly how far would Terry be expected to go, if Sarah *didn't* come around?

"You trust him, Dad?"

Jacob Conlin pursed his lips and considered his response. "We're in a position to offer Eric Wheeler something of value. He needs a strong North American legal presence—preferably one headed up by his daughter . . . we solve that problem for him. I think . . . yeah, we can trust him, far as it goes. Like it or not, he's selected us, so the question becomes, do you want to act against him?" When Terry seemed to ponder the idea, Jacob continued, "That's a rhetorical question, son. No, you do not want to act against Eric Wheeler."

"Why? GCM doesn't have the same clout in North America as it does globally—that's the deal they made with the US, right? Preferential access to privatized US government military assets, as long as they stay out of the jurisdiction. I mean, Wheeler's not even supposed to be in continental airspace without reporting, right?"

"That was the deal, yes," Jacob said.

"So? It's not like he can just order a drone strike on us or nuke us or something, he'd . . ."

"Don't be an idiot. You think Eric Wheeler or GCM can't take action here or in the US? How do you think he rigged the fuckin' Four in the first place?"

Terry shrugged, sullen.

"Yeah, that's right. If he can fix a Program Spawning, he can sure as hell take care of people who double-cross him. And he sure as hell would. Like it or not, we're in bed with the guy. Take it like a man, and think of the upside. There are worse deals to be made, Terry."

Terry wouldn't have believed it of his father if he hadn't just heard the man suck Wheeler's cock and like it. But Jacob Conlin was right—there didn't seem to be a lot of operational wiggle-room on this. And he was also right about the upside. Terry had done some projections of his own when Eric had laid out the broad scope of his plans, and the net effect would make Terry one of the wealthiest and most powerful men on the planet. He was stuck as VP at Tyler/Brock without Wheeler's influence. Overall, the deal was a no brainer.

There was one other tangent on Terry's mind, and though he wanted to discuss it, he couldn't bring himself to ask the necessary questions. What he didn't ask was: "How far back does this go, Dad? When did we first get involved with this guy?" He knew his father and Wheeler had a long association, but did the relationship go back twenty years? Did Eric Wheeler have any input into selecting Terry's own genetic modifications, with an eye towards the current end-game? It struck Terry as paranoid to even wonder about that, but . . . it wasn't all that far-fetched. The man had rigged a Spawning Four selection: how much harder would it have been to go that one extra step, to insure he got what he wanted?

Terry watched the monitor as young Warren finally got the other hook in and rolled his opponent over. A groin strike with the heel of the foot; a thumb strike against the victim's eye and Warren had the rear-naked-choke sunk in.

Off camera, Terry could hear the polite applause of Warren's instructors and classmates as the victim tapped on the boy's throat-choking forearm.

By terrain I mean distances, whether the ground is traversed with ease or difficulty, whether it is open or constricted, and the chances of life or death.

—Sun Tzu, The Art of War

SHE'D STOPPED SHAKING eventually. She sat in her change room composing herself, refusing to leave until she'd regained her poise.

It felt good to shed the hospital clothing and wear her own things again. Though Sarah still felt a sense of dread, could still vividly recall the sights and sounds of her hallucinations, she was beginning to experience jolts of euphoria. It was the Quickening taking hold, pushing aside the emotions of her mind, and replacing them with the more visceral, tangible emotions of the body.

Fully dressed, she looked at herself in the mirror. She had showered, and her hair was kinked and heavy, having been towel dried. She looked . . . not younger necessarily, but vibrant, as she might have following a particularly vigorous workout. Or more specifically perhaps, following a particularly exhilarating bout of sex. *I'm glowing*, she realized at last, and chuckled at the cliché. Of course she was.

This time Gabrielle had been waiting just outside the change room, anxiously, so it seemed to Sarah. The nurse gave a reassuring smile now that Sarah seemed to have found her footing. *Aren't we relieved*, Sarah thought. Was every reaction to the Quickening so . . . gruesome? So vivid? Sarah didn't know, but she presumed that nurse Gabrielle had seen her fair share of badly rattled Program women following the treatment.

"How do you feel?" Gabrielle said, sliding her right arm in under Sarah's left and walking with her as friends did on the streets of Istanbul, or Mumbai. Sarah didn't mind. In fact, she found herself oddly grateful for the contact. For the first time, Sarah became aware of the fact that Gabrielle was older than she had appeared at first. She had that flawless Asian complexion, and she'd received some top-notch work besides. But the eyes were older, conveying more compassion than one might have expected from the high-browed, aristocratic face.

"I'm . . . conflicted, I guess," Sarah admitted, grinning sheepishly. "Is it always so . . ."

"Yes! It is always unique of course—no two women react the same way. But it is always meaningful."

"'Meaningful'," Sarah chuckled. "That's a good way of putting it!"

They walked back the way Sarah had come initially, exiting the changing room area into a short corridor that led to the main waiting room. Sarah was laughing by the time they arrived at the admittance desk—almost giggling. Whatever emotion she was experiencing seemed to slingshot just beyond her usual range. It was disconcerting, but not altogether unpleasant. At least it was not unpleasant until they arrived at the desk.

Sarah's laughter reduced to a smile, and then to silence as she stared at the figure sitting in the waiting room. The long, glossy black hair; the dark-chocolate, long-lashed eyes; the straight, slash-of-black brows; the exotic angles of the oval face.

Polly Walker, here for her Quickening.

Blonde and brunette locked eyes, neither moving. Sarah felt her heart rate pound to attack cadence in her chest—could hear the blood rushing in her ears.

"No," the desk nurse, Alicia, hissed. "Take her out the back way!"

Gabrielle pulled on Sarah's arm with some difficulty. Sarah couldn't look away from Polly, felt instead the urge to close with her.

"This way, Sarah," Gabrielle cooed. It would not have been the first time this had happened. With reluctance, Sarah turned as guided, back through the swinging doors. She glanced over her shoulder to see Polly still staring at her. It gave Sarah goose pimples to turn her back on the woman.

And then they were in the changing area, and walking down a different corridor, taking turns Sarah hadn't taken before. She was lost in thought, not paying attention as Gabrielle guided her through the hospital in a roundabout way to the parking lot. Gabrielle walked Sarah to her car and smiled. "You're in cabin four," Gabrielle reminded Sarah unnecessarily. That information had been in the orientation package online.

Sarah looked into Gabrielle's eyes and nodded. "Thank you," she said, her voice distracted. Then, before Gabrielle could turn away: "I mean it. Thank you, Gabrielle, for . . . you know. Being there."

The nurse smiled in a way that suggested she'd heard the sentiment before. The look of concern and genuine empathy on Gabrielle's face was disconcerting: it was a look that had rarely, if ever, been directed Sarah's way. Sarah was warmed almost to the point of tears at the expression. She was also repulsed, and vaguely resentful of the implications. She had no concept of how to reconcile her conflicted emotions in that moment. She didn't try, got into her car instead, didn't give Gabrielle another look.

It was another mile or so from the gatehouse checkpoint to the Spawning Ground proper—an area of several square miles that stretched from the western shore of the lake and on up into the hills beyond. The access road was unpaved—a gravel-topped course just wide enough for two cars to pass, and the trees on either side were wilder than ever. Sarah slowed her speed and smelled dust in the air, checking sign directions whenever the road branched off, as the area hadn't been formatted for GPS. Eventually, she came to a wooden sign with the numeral "4" embossed in raised metal upon it. Turning right, she drove slowly to a small, graveled lot and came to a stop.

Birdsong rushed into the open canopy of the convertible, and Sarah sat for a moment, feeling herself bathed in forest-sounds. The sky above was a bright, clear eggshell blue, the sunlight hot upon her brow. She wondered if her senses had been enhanced by the quickening procedure: her resolution on details seemed finer, more acute than ever. Then again, it was quieter out here in the woods, there were fewer distractions, fewer demands upon her attention.

Sarah got out of the car, opened the trunk, and withdrew her gym bag and laptop. Slinging the bag over her shoulder, she walked alongside the southern wall of a single story "cabin" that was more like a decent summer home—all varnished pine logs and deliberately rustic charm. The cabin faced onto a grassy lawn which sloped at a gradual decline to the tree line. Beyond this, Sarah caught traces of blue lake water shining in the sun. Circular paving stones in the grass tracked towards wide, wooden steps leading up to a covered porch; a swinging chair for two sat across a small table from polished chairs made from the trunks of large-diameter trees. The chairs had a smooth, flowing aspect to them, rather than displaying any formal structure. Chairs that looked as if they had been poured into place, rather than carved.

First things first, thought Sarah. The porch was inviting her to sit down and put her feet up, but she might only have as little as two and a half hours before Polly arrived. She needed to prepare herself.

Entering the cabin, Sarah made note of the general layout: a cozy living room arranged around a fireplace; a kitchen and small dining room immediately beyond the living room; sliding doors leading to a large bedroom and a modern bathroom. There were no electronics or communication hubs visible, save for a mounted tablet on the kitchen table. Heavy wooden rafters lined the ceiling, and the fresh scent of wood-polish hung lightly in the air.

The furnishings were sparse, adequate for two, and of high quality. Lacquered chairs in the living room reflected the molten motif of those on the deck, giving the room a high-tech, yet organic feel. A low-slung couch faced the fireplace, and Navajo rugs covered much of the hardwood floor, intentionally balancing the modern highlights with a more traditional foundation.

The kitchen was small, but fully functional, sporting a deep-basin sink and granite counter tops, and lined with a long bank of cupboards. Just off the kitchen was a fully stocked pantry, including a decent wine selection and a separate temperature control from the rest of the house. It was more than merely useful, Sarah realized. She wouldn't mind owning a lake property such as this.

As she passed through the kitchen en route to the bedroom, a voice spoke, startling Sarah and causing her to gasp inadvertently. It was the docked tablet on the table, activated by Sarah's proximity and biometrics. Beside the tablet lay a work booklet with a baby's skull silhouette in cerulean blue, set against a plain white cover.

"Welcome home, Sarah Wheeler!" enthused a chipper young woman with big Dallas Cowboy Cheerleader curls and bright white teeth. "Welcome back to the site of your birth, and beginning of your future. Please take a moment to familiarize yourself with our preferences package. Here you may select from over a thousand primary, secondary, tertiary, and optional traits with which to optimize your child. Please remember that both parents, if then living, must sign and date the preference booklet prior to processing. If you have any questions or concerns, please do not hesitate to contact tech support by touching the screen HERE." At the word "here", the female face dissolved to a TECH SUPPORT box which pulsed for a few moments before the monitor returned to dormant mode.

Sarah swallowed, staring at the booklet. *First things first.* Refocusing on the job at hand, she proceeded to the bedroom to change.

The bedroom was plain, but clean and honest in design. The bedframe, the drawers, tables, and chairs were all of varnished pine; the bed itself was king-sized and firm. Sarah threw her bag on the bed and got out of her jeans and sweatshirt, exchanging them for navy leggings to the ankle and a form-fitting, baby blue compression shirt. She drew her long blonde hair into a smooth, low ponytail, and swapped her low-heeled pumps for white neoprene slippers akin to mountain climbing or scuba footwear. Retrieving her phone, she left the bedroom, and headed out onto the front porch.

On her phone, she activated a commercially available military recon app developed by her father's company, Global Conflict Management Systems Inc. It would allow her to construct highly detailed topographical maps from her phone's photo-imagery, thereby giving her tactical command of the terrain.

Starting from the front porch, Sarah scanned the lawn into her phone, noting the six-degree angle of decline down to the tree line. The ground was relatively even, though lumpy—Sarah walked the area carefully, making sure the footing was consistent.

There was a partially obscured footpath leading through dense underbrush down to the lake. Sarah took the path, making note of low-lying boughs, and in particular taking care to photograph a large, yellow pine root which thrust across the path at its narrowest point.

Emerging onto a sandy beach, Sarah straightened and looked out upon the water. Cattails rose in a cluster near the bank to the south, where the beach merged once again with foliage. To the north, the beach widened into a ribbon of sand appropriate for tourists, though this side of the lake remained fairly pristine. Out towards the middle of the lake, Sarah noted the buoys in the water denoting the beginning of private StandardGen property. Ski boats, jet skis, and the like would be common in high-summer, but would never penetrate past that line of warning. On the far shore and well to the south, Sarah could see parts of the hotel and water park rising from the lakeshore. Cars glittered in the sun as they passed into and out of view behind the trees.

Sarah headed north along the beach, noting the footing, and scanning with her phone as she went. The sand might be a bit of an equalizer in terms of foot-speed, and would favour the kind of grappling approach Sarah preferred. The rudiments of a plan began to take shape, informed by the possibilities of the ground around her.

A few hundred yards on, a wooden pier pushed out into the lake. Sarah walked along the slatted surface, looking into the glassy-green water on either side. Along the pillar-supports of the pier, a thick green weed obscured the sandy bottom of the lake. Boats might be moored along here at some point during the year, though none were present now. Sarah stood for a moment at the end of the pier and took a deep breath, listening to the gentle lapping of the waves on the pillars beneath her. This would be a very restful place, Sarah decided. Afterwards.

Retracing her steps back to the beach, Sarah took a different footpath and headed west towards the hills. She crossed the access road and made note of a number of cleared areas amidst the trees, each separated from any surrounding clearing like individual camp grounds, though no camping apparatus like fire pits or wood-bins could be detected. There were, Sarah discovered, lights mounted in the surrounding trees. The cleared areas would be illuminated at night, she realized, and would likely not be used for camping at all.

She continued on up the hill, sometimes on delineated paths, other times not. Her camera took in the information from all sides and synthesized it into a coherent wire-image. Poplars and pines seemed to dominate the landscape, with juniper bushes creating frequent obstacles on the ground. The hills were tricky terrain, Sarah realized—potentially dangerous, but therefore potentially useful as a result.

Twenty minutes from the pier, Sarah stopped and frowned at an anomaly. A tightly grouped copse of cottonwoods amongst the pines looped and writhed up from the ground, creating a massive cluster of twisting trunks that would have supported a world-class tree house. The boughs were thick with fluffy white pollen seeds; the roots tumbled over and under each other in ropey chaos. Sarah took a picture, highlighting the site, and triangulating its position with the cabin.

She checked the time on her phone: 3:04 P.M. It was time to make her way back. Working quickly, but methodically, she covered the route back to Cabin 4, completing a fairly comprehensive map of her immediate vicinity. She arrived at the cabin at 3:45, and expected Polly any time after 4:00. She was in high spirits, and judged her attitude to be extremely positive. Arriving first at the cabin had given her an irrational sense of ownership. *This is my house*, she felt. *Polly's the visitor. She's the other woman.*

Sarah took a moment on the porch to upload her topo-map—not to the phone-cloud, but to her private server at home. It was a risk: there was a chance her father might be alerted to a data transfer, but it was unlikely. She was counting on him being more focused upon her voice communications into and out of the Spawning Grounds themselves. In any event, it wasn't all that strange. It would look to any outside observer like Sarah simply backing up her important phone-files to a secure location.

At 4:00 P.M. precisely, Sarah pumped out fifty straight-leg push-ups on the living room floor, then went outside to limber up with a variety of yoga and tai chi routines. These were as much to centre herself and calm her mind as they were to keep her body loose. Once warmed up, she worked out a variety of kicks and did some shadow-boxing, keeping her heart rate in her most efficient range.

By 5:00 P.M. she was hungry, which was to be expected. "You'll eat between two and three times as much as you normally would over the next couple of days," Gabrielle had warned. "The Spawning is very energy-intensive." Sarah fixed herself a light snack of toast and sardines, washing it down with plenty of filtered water. Staying hydrated would be important: one never knew how long these things would last.

At 6:00 P.M. she had a pee, brushed her teeth, then re-hydrated. Where the hell was Polly? Sarah paced the living room, then went outside to do another tai chi set, having completely cooled off from her earlier exertions.

By 7:00 P.M., dusk was settling in. There would be decent light for a couple more hours yet, but Sarah hadn't anticipated having to work at night. Lighting would be variable throughout the area she had scanned—from decent in the front yard, to partial along the shoreline, to pitch black out in the backwoods.

And then it hit her, as she was pacing the porch, swinging her arms to and fro, as she was starting in on her second cup of green tea, as she was fretting about the time, she realized: *she's making me wait*. Polly could have arrived hours ago, but she'd held off on her final approach—was probably just up the road or even . . . watching the place? Sarah peered off into the tree line from the porch and decided to move inside. There was just the front door to worry about, and it bothered her that her anxiety might have been apparent over the last few hours. If the game had truly begun, Sarah was already behind on points.

She made a fire and forced herself to be mindful of the stochastic pop and crack of the wood. She sat in one of the weirdly molded chairs with her legs tucked up beneath her, and faced the front door. She sipped at tea, and found herself admiring Polly's patience. *I couldn't have waited this long*, Sarah admitted to herself. Once the Quickening was in, she'd have headed straight for the cabin. She'd have wanted to get this over with.

She *wanted* to get this over with.

It was an indication of the differences between them.

Just before 9:00 P.M. Sarah heard car wheels on gravel,

coming to a stop in the lot beside the house. She stood, suddenly alarmed, and walked into the kitchen, resting her hip on the counter. She crossed her arms, then uncrossed them, uncertain what to do with her hands, and suddenly self-conscious about them.

Footsteps sounded out on the wooden steps. The screen door opened, and Polly stepped inside.

She had changed out of the clothes she'd worn at the clinic. Now she wore crimson, cotton spandex shorts to mid-thigh and a black zipper-front track jacket over a black sports bra. She'd drawn her long black hair into a high ponytail, and the slanting lines of her dramatic brows gave her face a decidedly Asian caste. Her ebony eyes immediately locked onto Sarah's arctic blues, and the women stood frozen in fascination with one another. Both became aware of seconds passing; neither knew how to break the spell.

The women subjected one another to an almost pornographic scrutiny, concentrating intently on the minute details of each other's person. Without losing eye contact, Polly removed her sport-sandals—Sarah noting the lithe economy of the woman's movements. Polly's quads were dense with fast-twitch muscle and deeply cut above the knee. She was a couple inches shorter, but configured along Sarah's lines with a broad-shouldered back tapering into strong, squared-off hips. There was something compact and ballistic about the woman—a torpedo-like efficiency to her physiognomy, and even as Sarah was registering that information, she realized that Polly was making the same critical assessments in return. Their bodies were aware of one another like twin tuning forks vibrating in resonance. Their cells, their DNA howled for the extinction of the other. It was knowledge encoded into their bodies at birth, and meeting now conveyed the sense of a strange, occult reunion.

The whole idea of the Executive Program had been to reduce individuals to pure, uncontaminated, rational market participants by constructing a true zero-sum game, for the highest stakes imaginable. All they were, all they had been, everything they had done and experienced as human beings fed into their performance tonight. And on the night, the market would decide which organism was best. It was a matter of giving oneself over to the market completely—to lose oneself in the mechanism of competition, and trust the verdict.

It was why, Sarah reflected, that "passion" was so highly prized by her instructors. Reason was the great betrayer, tricking participants into thinking their way to victory rather than simply acting, and letting the market determine victory. "One can't outsmart the market" was the constant refrain. The best you could do was to act—simply do what you do—and have confidence it would be enough. Holding back even the smallest part of yourself for the sake of reason could be the difference between winning and losing, life or death.

Except Sarah didn't buy it. Not completely anyway.

She had read Sun Tzu, and puzzled over his suggestion that rational strategy would trump tactical action. Nothing in the real world seemed to support that notion. Her instructors had constantly tried to get her to react instinctively to situations, to just "be herself", but her best, most authentic self was a thoughtful Sarah, a planning Sarah. A deceptive Sarah, in the Sun Tzu sense of the word. Try as she had throughout her life, she simply could not develop the faith in market mechanics that most experts insisted was the key to victory in any sphere, not just the Spawning Event. And now, she was about to experience the consequences of her skepticism, one way or the other.

"I don't know about you," Sarah said, keeping her voice low, even, and unprovocative, "but I could use a drink."

Polly nodded, staying relaxed in her posture, but alert in her eyes. Sarah pushed up off the counter and turned her back on Polly in a calculated show of confidence as she went into the pantry. "Red or white?" Sarah called from the wine rack.

"Whatever," Polly said, electing to remain inscrutable.

Sarah returned to the kitchen to find Polly moving in around the other side of the dining room table, keeping it between them. As she moved to pull out a wooden chair, the docked tablet came to life as it had earlier, for Sarah's benefit. The same cheery woman's face appeared, with the same upbeat message, with one awful amendment:

"Welcome home, Polly Walker!" the voice said, picking up on Polly's bio-presence. "Welcome back to the site of your birth, and beginning of your future . . ."

Sarah stood in paralyzed silence as the computer

acknowledged Polly and treated her as the assumptive victor. Polly seemed equally shaken, her own mood feeding off Sarah's. With a force of will, Sarah turned to the counter, opened a bottle of Cabernet Franc and poured two glasses. She turned to find Polly seated on the far side of the table, those dark eyes fixed upon Sarah like laser gunsights.

Sarah transported bottle and glasses both to the table and sat down herself. Her skin crawled to be so close to Polly: Sarah battled the urge to shudder. It was not hate Sarah felt, or if it was, it was a kind of hatred Sarah had never before imagined. After all, Polly was a complete stranger, and though her exotic looks implied a kind of brand-rivalry in a broad commercial sense, the women were not professional rivals or opposed in any other way than at the genetic level. Hatred seemed an insufficient term to describe their relationship.

Sarah was drawn to Polly—physically drawn to her—in a way that seemed antithetical to hatred. The overwhelming urge was to close and kill, not to shun or avoid. It was more a lethal sort of fascination; a primordial, biological reaction akin to antibodies attacking foreign agents in the blood stream. Sarah felt her dark twin writhing inside of her, begging to be given command. *Soon*, Sarah thought to herself. *Soon.*

But not yet.

The first glasses of wine were de facto shots, the second more properly experienced.

"I've seen you on shows," Sarah said, pitching herself as a fan. "That transparency show? You're good."

"Thanks," Polly said, non-committal. Her dark brown eyes seemed almost black in the low light, the pupils huge. *My own eyes are adapted to reflect light*, Sarah thought. *Hers take light in.*

"What've you got," Sarah continued, "like, ten million followers?"

"More like twenty-five."

"Wow. So, you're what . . . you're basically advertising?"

Polly smiled. It was the most overtly aggressive gesture either woman had made to that point. It said she had made her reads, that she was comfortable with where she stood. "Sarah," Polly said, her voice conveying authority, and a slight sense of irritation. "We should probably get down to business."

Sarah returned the smile, but it was forced, lacking in authenticity. The last thing she felt like doing then was smiling. She drained her glass and didn't taste the wine going down. She recalled the words of a boxing trainer years ago: "Fifty percent of fights are won at the weigh-in," he'd said. She recognized this moment as their weigh-in.

"I had this dog when I was little," Sarah began, trying to construct Polly as an interested party. A new acquaintance: Sarah sharing in order to kindle something deeper. "Golden retriever. You ever have pets?" Polly's flat gaze was silent, but seemed to say *you're stalling*. Sarah ignored the non-response. "I remember this one time . . . we were out at the cottage, me, my mom and dad, Ben—that's my dog . . . and this butterfly had gotten into the house. Gorgeous—big yellow wings and black markings . . . I still remember it very vividly. Anyway, Mom was going to kill it, but I was all 'No! No! Don't kill it! Put it outside! Put it outside!' So there we are—trying to shoo this butterfly outside . . . and we've just about got it—it's on the floor, ready to be swept up . . . and my stupid dog comes padding along, scoops the butterfly up in his mouth, and eats it! I just burst into tears, and Mom's trying not to laugh, you know? Because I'm taking it so hard. It was really . . . it was heartbreaking."

Polly's stare had become something of a bludgeon: it was all Sarah could do not to look away. "Why are you telling me this?" Polly asked at last.

Sarah hesitated, searching Polly's face for any sign of give whatsoever. "I don't know," Sarah said. "I guess I just . . . I wanted you to have something to remember me by, if . . . you know. So when you look back, you could think of me as that girl with the dog and the butterfly, and not just some lawyer you had to kill."

Polly nodded. "It's a pretty good story," she said, dark eyes glistening. "Or it would be, if it were true."

Sarah swallowed involuntarily. She was not used to being read so accurately. *Now*, she told her inner twin, and felt her blood boil with the release. Sarah rose and stalked purposefully to the front door.

Polly stood, and followed Sarah out into the night, with the moon rising near-full behind the trees. Porchlight spilled out onto the lawn: Sarah had removed her shoes and was rotating out her arms, loosening up her rotator cuffs. Polly rolled her head side to side and removed her jacket, the early evening air cool against her bare midriff. Tossing the jacket onto a deck chair, she trotted down the steps, made as if to lunge at Sarah, then stepped off to her right, hands open and raised to shoulder height.

Sarah turned with her foe, angling her left shoulder towards Polly. Only it wasn't Sarah, at least not the Sarah who had arrived at the cabin just a few short hours ago—not that Sarah alone. That Sarah had receded into the background, and the other Sarah who had been lurking in the limbic system all these years, *that* Sarah, finally came out to play.

Empty your mind, be formless. Shapeless, like water. If you put water into a cup, it becomes the cup. You put water into a bottle and it becomes the bottle. You put it in a teapot, it becomes the teapot. Now, water can flow or it can crash. Be water, my friend.

— Bruce Lee

BIRD SONG ROSE from the woods.

Insects chattered in the gathering dusk, in celebration of a waxing moon.

Light spilled from the porch of the cabin, casting long shadows of the women as they circled on cool grass.

It had begun, and their bodies rejoiced with the beginning.

Polly circled and feinted, gauging Sarah's reactions. *She's quick*, Sarah realized. Understanding that, Sarah set herself to deliver the left jab (*jab to control speed*), but she had to be mindful: a broken hand at this stage of the game could be fatal.

Polly changed levels and feinted for Sarah's waist from a wrestler's crouch, then rose and kicked her left foot at Sarah's body instead. Foot grazed chest as Sarah was nearly caught trying to defend the shoot, and she backpedaled to buy herself a little breathing room. Polly continued to roam to her right, patient, calm in her aspect. *This is who you are*, Sarah realized—about Polly, and about herself. *Truly, this is who you are.*

Sarah understood that she couldn't hang back indefinitely. She was the larger of the two women, the stronger: it would be to her advantage to impose will. Jabbing to approach, she shot in on Polly's waist, forcing her back with a powerful leg drive that carried the combatants several feet down the lawn.

Polly sprawled, encircling Sarah's head and left arm with her own arms and bearing both women to the grass. Sarah's grip had slipped to the point that she had her hands around Polly's left leg, pulling it forward behind the knee. Polly planted on that knee while dropping the right leg well back, leaning her weight forward onto Sarah's back.

Wrapping her left arm under Sarah, Polly began to pound her right fist at the kidneys and ribs of her foe. Thudding blows slammed to a halt in Sarah's solid core, or thump-skidded across her back. It was a bad position made worse when Polly began jackhammering the point of her elbow down into Sarah's spine. The single-leg had to be abandoned. Releasing Polly's leg, Sarah pulled out, catching a grazing elbow across her left temple en route. The women separated and stood, breathing hard. Polly had gotten the best of the exchange.

Sarah stepped to her right as Polly shook out her arms and circled. Suddenly Polly stepped into a right roundhouse kick—saw she was too far away—rotated with her own momentum and whipped around into a spinning heel kick via the left leg. Sarah withdrew as Polly's foot whistled through the space vacated by Sarah's mouth. *I'd have lost teeth there,* Sarah recognized: Polly's torque was incredible.

As moments passed, Sarah was becoming unsettled by her observations. Polly took risks—throwing closed fists to the head; executing spinning kicks on uneven ground—all things Sarah had been advised against. Either Polly was reckless, which didn't feel right, or she was just that confident. Either way presented unique dangers for Sarah.

Sarah closed behind her jab and tried to clinch, but time and again, Polly's arms would writhe clear of the grasp, and Sarah would pay the price of tightly clipped elbows and fists about the head, or well-placed knees up into the body. When she was forced to disengage, Sarah received hard kicks upon either side of her ribcage as Polly easily transitioned to offence after defending the grapple. *"You'll know in seconds who's better at what,"* Javier, her Brazilian jiu-jitsu coach, had always said. Sarah was finding out that Polly was the better woman on her feet, and if Sarah knew that, so did Polly.

Again and again, Sarah changed levels, trying for single or

double leg takedowns; trying to close and clinch. Polly wouldn't have it—either anticipating and sidestepping, sprawling, or simply shoving her way into the clear. Most Spawning Contests were finished in the first ninety seconds, but as Sarah's lunging shots grew more and more desperate, she realized the fight was moving into statistically unlikely territory. Polly was deliberately playing a long attrition game. Everyone knew it could take several minutes to systematically beat someone to death on their feet.

A gnawing worry began to claw at the pit of Sarah's stomach as she came to see the outlines of Polly's intentions. *Do I have the stamina to go ten minutes? Fifteen?* In terms of attrition, Polly had already gotten into Sarah's reserves; Sarah had barely scuffed at the surface of her foe. Polly saw the haunted look in Sarah's eyes; Sarah knew instantly that Polly had seen it by the increasingly aggressive and confident posture of the brunette's stance. One woman was slowly emerging as the predator, and it wasn't Sarah Wheeler.

After rejecting Sarah's sixth takedown attempt, Polly went over to offence full time. She pressed the pace; she dictated terms. She never rushed or over-pursued, however: she was patient and cold-blooded in her execution.

Polly began by kicking at Sarah's lead plant-leg, the left. Lead left jabs set up vicious roundhouse kicks to Sarah's left thigh—the shin of Polly's right leg sinking in deep with meaty, clapping contact. Disengaging and circling after connecting, Polly never gave Sarah a chance to fall-in and lock-up—the brunette was content to pick away at the blonde one vicious blow at a time.

Not that it was always pure pressure up the middle. Polly was as adept fighting backwards as she was coming forward—retreating in good order; issuing check-jabs; pivoting left around crisply turned check-hooks; rejecting Sarah on the inside with brutal elbow strikes to either cheekbone. Sarah had always been a good defender, and she parried a good deal of Polly's work, but countering was proving difficult. It wasn't Polly's reflexes—which were superb—that made Sarah ineffective, it was the brunette's *anticipation.* Whatever Sarah wanted to do, it was as though Polly saw the intention a split second before the action, providing answers before Sarah could ask the questions.

Sarah lost track of time, but the sky had grown dark, and cold, indifferent stars were beginning to pin-prick the sky. Polly's jab had cut Sarah inside her mouth, and lumped up her left eye. A deep and throbbing bruise was spreading upon Sarah's left thigh, out of sight beneath the navy blue leggings. Sarah laboured to draw breath as her ribs and stomach bore the brunt of Polly's well-timed kicks and knees. The phrase, *I'm losing* formed in Sarah's mind before she could shut it down, and the second the thought was out there, Sarah could swear that her own eyes had betrayed her dread to Polly.

A push-kick in the stomach aborted Sarah's weak overhand right, sending her stumbling backwards. It was now or never, Sarah realized. She was losing the energy she'd need to finish. She had to take the initiative *now*.

Sarah swept a three-quarters right hand over the top and lunged forward, swinging her left around as she stepped onto her right foot. Polly anticipated, backpedaling smoothly . . . as Sarah bulled forward with another decapitating right hand, Polly spun clockwise on the spot, simultaneously slipping the shot while walking Sarah into a devastating right-heel kick deep into the liver.

Sarah sobbed aloud as her knees gave way. The thudding impact actually caused Polly to lose balance—spilling her towards the cabin as Sarah staggered away from it. It was the first time either combatant had really given voice to her pain, and Sarah knew it was a turning point. She stumbled to her hands and knees—her right arm wrapped around her body, eyes shutting tight. *Get up*, she exhorted herself. *Get up or she'll finish you!*

Plan A wasn't working. Sarah had tried Polly on the lawn, and it was a losing effort. The brunette was too slick, too fast, too good. Both of them could see the outcome on the grass, it was inescapable, inevitable. That being the case, Sarah activated plan B . . .

POLLY WAS ASTONISHED: it was the first time Sarah had done anything that had truly surprised her. The blonde was turning and staggering off into the tree line. *She was running away!* Polly was momentarily amazed into indecision. Their bodies were wired to collide, to compete, to arrive at a decisive result.

Polly knew the strength of will it would take to override that wiring and she was impressed. Perhaps there was more to Sarah than met the eye after all. The moment of indecision passed in a heartbeat, and Polly quickly moved to give chase.

Sarah had been an easy read. Everything about her—from her nervy warm-ups to her lame attempt at manipulation over wine screamed jiu-jitsu stylist. The blonde was a sneak, relying on cleverness and deception. She was used to winning off her back using all the subtle distractions and false ploys of the submission grappler, so Polly's approach had been a foregone conclusion. It hadn't mattered to Polly whether they stood, or went to the ground, but it mattered to Sarah. That was all Polly had needed to know.

It was almost pitch black in the underbrush, and Polly ducked instinctively as juniper branches scratched her scalp and thighs. She ignored the pain in her left hand—the middle knuckle having been dislocated early in the conflict. It had been worth the injury to cut Sarah, and to control the distance between the fighters. As the blonde wore down, the jab would become less necessary. The pain was acceptable to Polly, and besides, she would have all the time in the world to heal once the fight was over.

Sarah crashed on ahead in the darkness, whining: Polly was almost certain she'd felt ribs give way beneath that last kick, and if true, this fight was almost over. Another . . .

Polly sprawled face-first in the dirt, tripped by a prominent root that bulged across the path. She reacted on instinct, rolling to her right as Sarah's foot stamped into the ground. Rising to her knees, Polly formed an X with her arms and blocked another kick she couldn't see. She could hear the blonde wheezing a curse, then turning to run. Clearly, this little pratfall had been orchestrated to some extent by Sarah: she'd known the root was there. Clever girl. Polly rose and gave chase, happy to let Sarah spend the energy running.

Out on the beach there was more ambient light—from the stars, the near-full moon, the street lights across the lake reflecting off the water. Polly slowed to a walk, bare feet swishing on sand. Sarah stumbled up ahead, right hand clutching at her ribs as she alternated between a reeling jog and a limping walk.

Polly heard the water lapping gently on the sandy shore in odd juxtaposition to Sarah's gasping, ragged breathing. She had the blonde's body breaking down. It was time to work on her psyche as well.

"Sarah?" Polly called out. "Sarah, is that rib broken?" No answer. Polly noted the soft footing of the sand and anticipated that at some point, the blonde would turn and attempt to grapple on the more favourable ground. It was a good idea, but Polly suspected Sarah had waited too long.

"Baby, if it's broken, you're through. It's over. I'll just work it until it punctures a lung, and you'll bleed out inside. Sarah, you'll suffer. You don't have to—it doesn't have to be like that. Just lie down and let me finish you."

Sarah looked back with an anguished expression and forced herself onwards. Polly pursed her lips. She was capable of situational cruelty of course—had built her reputation on it—but she wasn't cruel by nature. She took no particular pleasure in extending Sarah's pain—it was Sarah herself who had dictated Polly's attritional tactics. Though her words were meant to dispirit her foe, her intention was honest. If she could end Sarah's life without torturing her, she would. But for that, she'd need the woman's cooperation.

Sarah had made it to a long wooden pier and was heading out upon the lake. She was hurt and confused, Polly realized: the pier was a mistake. In one sense, it gave Polly less room to maneuver, less room to absorb and deflect Sarah's takedowns, but that didn't matter anymore. It was tactically decisive. Polly walked at a measured pace and stepped onto the pier, shaking out her arms as she made her final approach.

"What do you say?" Polly asked from thirty feet away. Sarah stooped in her stance, her right arm crossing her midsection. Moonlight pooled on the woman's cheeks, in the tracks of tears. Twenty years of training, of grinding out fifteen years of education in the space of three, of grinding out law school, of billing the hours it took to make junior partner, of living a high-octane professional life at full speed . . . it was all coming to an end on a ramshackle pier in the hinterlands of Alberta. The experiment that had been Sarah Wheeler was effectively over. Both women knew it.

Sarah hovered in her stance. *Fine*, thought Polly. She

guessed if the situation had been reversed, she'd probably have gone out the same way.

Polly approached and could see Sarah loading weight on her back foot. *She'll lunge for me*, Polly anticipated. That was fine. Polly felt strong enough now to simply stack Sarah up and finish her in the clinch.

Sarah cooperated as expected, lunging with arms outstretched. Polly waited in the pocket, walking Sarah onto a short right uppercut inside, while threading her left arm under Sarah's right. Sarah's right arm looped over Polly's left shoulder while the left roped around Polly's back. Polly dug her left hand into Sarah's ribs, working the impact site of that crushing heel kick. If a rib was broken, or even cracked, Polly would add to the damage. It was all going according to plan, until Sarah pulled Polly off to her right, and drove both women off the pier and into the lake.

Terrain was so important in warfare, so underrated. It had cost the French at Agincourt; Napoleon at Waterloo; beaten the Germans on the approaches to Moscow; made the reputations of the Spartans at Thermopylae.

It was illegal in Spawning Contests to use weapons of any kind. No low lying tree boughs could be pulled off and used as clubs. No bashing in of skulls with handy loose-lying stones. The civil penalties were prohibitive in such cases, and in any event, the wiring of the combatants tended to mitigate against such extra-corporeal contact.

Water, Sarah had realized, was a borderline case in legal terms. It could be construed technically as a weapon, but unlike say, a fistful of rock wielded by one combatant, water affected both contestants equally. Intent would be impossible to prove. "We clinched and fell into the lake, your honor." How could it be proved otherwise?

There was no training for this. The women sank as they thrashed and writhed, entangled in one another's limbs. Under water, it was good to be the stronger person, all else being equal. Under water, it really was just a matter of bodies struggling for survival. It was a matter of hunger, and will.

One woman's head broke the surface of the moonlit lake, her gasp drowning out the background noise of the forest. It was

Sarah Wheeler, and she was clutching at a wooden pillar, tilting her face towards the uncaring stars, sputtering as water splashed across her eyes and open mouth. Down below, her legs held Polly secure—the left looping over the girl's left shoulder; the right up under Polly's right arm; the right knee folding over the left foot to lock the woman in place.

Sarah sputtered and choked as Polly thrashed her last in the dark.

POLLY'S MIND BEGAN to wander as her lungs filled with lake water. She was so terribly disappointed. She had been looking forward to meeting her Other at last, and to raising a child together. It had all seemed so exciting and new a few hours ago. A new beginning. A new narrative. And now, it was over. Sarah had ended Polly.

WITH FADING STRENGTH, Sarah clutched at a wooden slat and pulled herself up, kicking at deadweight Polly in the process. The blonde slid along the pier like a boated bass, sobbing and choking as she rolled onto her back. She shuddered as the enormity of the moment overtook her. Sun Tzu would have said "all war is deception", or "every battle is won or lost before it is fought." She had thought her way to victory after all, despite all she'd ever been told. She had unleashed her dark twin in all her furious glory, but she'd retained control throughout. Fury alone would not have won against this opponent.

Sarah hugged her battered body and rolled onto her side so that she could vomit up lake water without choking herself. Beneath the waves, the weeds had claimed the body of Polly so completely, it was almost as though she'd never been there at all.

We had to re-draw "the feminine" within the context of the competitive matrix. The notion of the female existing outside the market, standing as a transcendent source of holistic meaning and collective, cooperative symbology was counter-productive and irrational.

— Katy Chow, "Silicon Valley Leopard Moms"

SARAH LAY AWAKE as the bedroom slowly grew brighter with the dawn's rising light. The open window allowed birdsong into the room. Sarah listened to the varying patterns and voices as she drowsed, feeling the crisp morning air upon her face.

She groaned like an old woman when she finally sat up to swing her legs over the side of the bed. She sat cringing for a moment before rising gingerly to her feet, hobbling slowly to the bathroom, her bare feet making muted clapping noises on the cold floor.

She looked at herself standing in her underwear in the bathroom mirror and felt a rush of conflicting emotions. An ugly mouse had hardened into bulging relief beneath her left eye; her lower lip was cracked—both the result of Polly's educated left hand. From the line of the breasts to her thighs, her body was a patchwork of bruised meat in thunderstorm shades of purple and yellow. If not for the Quickening, Sarah doubted she'd have been able to stand today. She could feel her accelerated metabolism humming, conducting emergency repairs, bolstering her for the trials yet to come.

She smoothed long blonde hair back behind her ears and allowed herself a moment of pride, if not exultation. All that was left of Polly were the marks she'd made upon Sarah. For a moment, Sarah was deeply moved, and honoured to have faced—and defeated—a competitor of such exquisite ability and effectiveness. Polly had been engineered for Sarah, and vice versa as part of a random selection process that also incorporated sophisticated "market-making" algorithms. The two women had grown up living separate lives, but had always been connected on a cellular level. They had always yearned, in a visceral, non-rational way, for reunion and completion.

It was one of the things that disgusted her about her father's plan. Though Sarah's test had been completely legitimate, Terry's would not be. It distorted and—in Sarah's opinion—cheapened the process. Her father had assured her that Terry's genetic potential was unmatched, but that wasn't for him to say. The market determined that: that's what competition was for. Not that it would matter of course. Sarah had no intention of following through on her father's design.

She got out of her things—wincing—and drew a hot bath, activating the jets for a soothing pulse-massage. Slipping into the water, she laid her head back and closed her eyes. "Music," she murmured aloud, but nothing happened. The house wasn't fully wired or intelligent: she had forgotten that. It wasn't meant to entertain or distract the occupants in any way. The people who stayed here would have to deal with themselves and each other in a way they might never have experienced before.

Polly could have won. Eric Wheeler could have intervened on Sarah's behalf, but oh no, *her* test would have to be a stern one. She hated him for his callous rigor in that regard. She respected him for it as well. In the event, she realized she would not have had it any other way. Despite her pain, she had never felt more alive or vital. The experience had deepened her, hardened her, made her more confident. Part of this was chemical she knew— part of it encoded response—but she couldn't help but think that a lesser challenge would have had a lesser impact. She was a better woman now than she had ever been before.

After her bath, Sarah donned a pair of loose fitting cotton pants that had come with the house, along with a cozy white bathrobe that fell to the knee. Ravenous, she made herself a three-egg omelet heavy with cheese, mushrooms, spinach, and onions, eating the results directly from the pan. There was regular maid service at the cabins, but not prior to the actual

Spawning. Sarah put the pan and fork into the sink, resolving to wash it later.

She made herself a large mug of green tea and put her neoprene shoes on. Tea in hand, she stooped to collect Polly's sandals, stepped outside and dropped them atop the jacket Polly had left behind as well. The cool air was invigorating, so after a moment lingering on the porch, Sarah stepped down onto the lawn for a leisurely limp-about.

She recalled the battle in flashes, remembering with chagrin how she'd been outclassed in the stand-up. It had been worth the attempt—seeing if a quick victory could be achieved. When it hadn't been possible, she'd resorted to strategy, and the turn to the beach had saved her life.

Emerging from the footpath onto sand, Sarah recalled how difficult it had been to disengage. One of the hardest things she'd ever had to do—a testament to the willpower she'd received from her father. But it hadn't been all willpower. Once combat had been initiated, her body had been wired to close and attack, so running should have been theoretically impossible, but she hadn't been running per se. She had tricked her body with the knowledge that she was still fighting, in fact, fighting in earnest when she'd broken off contact. Part of feigning a broken rib was to lure Polly forward, but also, to keep Sarah's own body from taking over completely. As long as she knew she was faking injury, Sarah had the ability to make a tactical withdrawal, because her body was able to register her aggressive intent.

Loons sounded in the distance, somewhere out of sight. Golden light played upon gentle morning waves as the lake seemed to slumber, and sunlight illuminated the treetops. Sarah sipped at her tea as she walked the beach, forcing herself to breathe deeply despite the tender ribcage, in the knowledge that she wouldn't always be breathing air this clean and fresh.

She had thought about a fighting retreat to the pier—attempting to re-initiate grappling routines on the sand, but had rejected the notion once she'd gotten out there. One, she no longer believed she could win a straight-up contest with Polly. Two, Polly had believed the broken-rib ruse and was convinced of victory: she'd pursue Sarah anywhere, with confidence verging on arrogance. "When capable, feign incapacity," Sun

Tzu had said—mere words, until you actually needed to win a conflict. It was surprising to Sarah that the *The Art of War* had been so thoroughly discredited by the current generation of reviewers. She'd never been more convinced of the book's wisdom.

Gaining the pier, Sarah walked its length, casually peering over the side in search of Polly, seeing only weeds. Perhaps the groundskeepers had retrieved the body, though Sarah thought this was unlikely. Reaching the end of the wooden walkway, Sarah looked out across the lake and changed her focus from the immediate past, to the near future.

She'd mate with Terry when he came through, and kill him in his sleep. It would be difficult; it would pit her against her own coding, but after what she'd been through, she felt up to the challenge. After that, though she recognized she had an opportunity, she had deliberately kept the parameters of her plans flexible. It was a time of great turbulence and transition . . . the ground was not solid—it shifted and rewarded only the most agile of those who would stand upon it.

"Anger his general, and confuse him," Sun Tzu had said. As always, the book only provided general headlines and broad outlines of action. It was, in essence, little more than a frame of mind. Angering her father would be a dangerous strategy, but worth the risk if she could get him to lose control. She had no intention of giving up her child, and she knew her father would never negotiate terms. That left only the timing and circumstances of their inevitable collision yet to be determined.

First things first, Sarah thought.

Terry.

Just win, baby.

—Al Davis

BIG PICTURE STUFF, Terry.

No shit.

Terry sat behind the wheel of his dad's Mercedes, staring through the windshield into the middle distance. Becoming aware of the guard standing beside the car, Terry realized he'd been addressed. "What?" Terry asked.

"I said, 'Good hunting', Mr. Conlin."

"Right," Terry nodded, managing a perfunctory smile. He realized how pre-occupied he was, but it couldn't be helped.

The gate barring entrance to the Spawning Grounds slowly opened and Terry put the car into drive. It was around 9:00 P.M.—getting dark. He drove slowly so as not to miss any of the illuminated signposts along the way.

He hadn't stopped thinking of the plane ride with Eric Wheeler since it had happened. It'd been like getting a sales pitch from Caesar, or Napoleon, or Steve Jobs—the grand sweep of the ideas; the clarity and certainty behind them. And the simplicity. Though there were moving parts a-plenty, Eric's discourse had revolved around the basic economic principle of comparative advantage—a concept with which Terry was reasonably familiar.

"Free trade's good," Eric had said, smiling his thin-lipped little mamba's smile. There was a grotesque aspect of playfulness about the man—that one blue eye somehow conveying mirth and menace at a stroke. "You do what you're best at; I do what I'm best at; we trade; we both make more money than if we'd decided to do everything ourselves. It's win-win." Of course Terry had heard the arguments before—at parties; on the net—but he didn't really need to be sold. He knew enough about comparative advantage to know that it was the engine of his own line of work, and that was where his curiosity ended.

"There is a problem with it, however," Eric had continued. "Goods and capital move friction-free throughout the globe—have done for decades—but labour . . . labour's trickier. Labour involves politics. You've got cultural differences that interrupt the natural flow of people towards jobs. You've got language barriers. Unions. Physical distance to overcome. But the biggest problem with labour, is that labour is people, and people identify themselves with a country. They buy into the illusion of 'connection'. They think they belong, as if by magic, in the country of their birth. It's the shape of people's minds, Terry, that is the greatest brake on progress. Free trade among nation-states has produced great wealth, but every time an efficiency is gained—every time an industry that would be better done elsewhere is outsourced—pockets of unemployment get trapped within national borders. Especially in the developed world. And those pockets, Terry—those angry, impoverished pockets—are the source of all the world's big issues these days."

Terry had sipped his drink, smiled, nodded his head in what he felt to be the right places, but as the scope of the discussion took shape, his attention wandered from Eric's words to the man himself. You couldn't think of Wheeler as an "economist"—the term wasn't broad enough. But he wasn't just a mercenary either, or a soldier. He was a policy-maker, Terry realized. A shot-caller. Maybe, Terry had begun to realize, Eric Wheeler was *the* shot-caller.

For the last forty years, Eric Wheeler had been working hard on getting the deals in place between nation-states and companies that would finally allow the full rationalization of labour. It hadn't *looked* like that was what he had been doing. As a hands-on director of Global Conflict Management Systems Inc., he had looked like an international mercenary and intelligence advisor deploying privatized military assets throughout the world in the name of global peace and security. The reality was a bit more complex.

"We're killing off the old analog world," Eric had explained. "The world of mass: mass populations, mass production, mass marketing—none of that makes sense anymore, but we're still top-heavy with those old societal structures. The 'old world' isn't geographical these days, it's a state of mind; it's a set of institutions and philosophies. GCM breaks down those rigid structures wherever they're proving to be most inconvenient, paving the way for a more flexible, open-source future."

"So when you put down a rebel uprising in Nigeria . . ." Terry had said.

"It's almost always labour, culture or environmentally oriented. We aren't necessarily at war with those people: we'd prefer to negotiate settlements where possible. We are at war with the analog mindset that believes policy can be instituted in a top-down, authoritative fashion based on say, human rights, race, custom, or patriotism, rather than by market-verdict. Only the market can convey legitimacy. Anyone who would take arms against that idea . . ."

"Gets to deal with you."

"Now you're gettin' it."

"And China's on board with the labour agreement?"

"They are finally on board. Got themselves into a bit of a demographic bind as you know—with all the rising costs and difficulties associated with a shrinking native labour force. Infusion of labour actually helps them out now—re-introduces competition to drive down wages. Concentrating labour in China, Africa, and South America brings down costs world-wide, attracting capital to those jurisdictions while reducing civil unrest and environmental stress in the developed world. All of that breaks down the old 'mass' society that's been holding us back. 'Markets' replace 'society': we go forward with a market of motivated individual consumers, and the old analog state—relieved of the need to support a mass population of 'citizens'—can finally be dismantled."

"What about defence?"

"What about it? Where do you think the threats are coming from? Promoting global security is one of the broad mandates for GCM: the highly interconnected free markets we want to promote are all mutually dependent. A network doesn't make war on itself: the rationale for war is simply removed. There's no need for a state to finance standing armies: private forces like mine can do whatever needs to be done. And once there's no need for a standing army, there's no need for a state, period."

"And you think people will just . . . board these new ships you're talking about and 'flow' to jobs in China?"

"Why not? That's where the jobs are. We're just getting rid of all the roadblocks. People in Canada used to think they were entitled to healthcare, but they got over it. Citizenship is the same thing: an outmoded analog construct. People will have the citizenship they can afford. If they can afford to live in North America, so be it. If not, they'll move to Africa, and we'll help them. The only reason anyone wants to be called 'Canadian' is pure sentimentality. National identity is like a religion. A labour unit should want to be called whatever it needs to be called, in order to survive."

"Well, when you put it like that," Terry had joked. But Eric Wheeler wasn't laughing.

It all unfolded logically from there.

Eric had shown Terry schematics for a new class of VLCS (Very Large Container Ships) being built in Korea that could carry over sixteen thousand TEUs (Twenty-foot Equivalent Units) and thirty thousand labour units across the Pacific. These "Atlas" class ships would need expanded port facilities, inter-ocean canals would need upgrades, exported labour-units would need temporary housing and support, and all of this activity would need to be financed.

That's where Terry came in.

Bringing GCM into the Tyler/Brock fold was the whale of all whales. Terry would go straight to the corner office for such a coup, and his legacy would be assured. The infrastructure-build alone would be astounding: logistics support for a permanent migratory labour force. But over and above that, the synthetic financial products that would be created to float this new productive revolution boggled the mind.

Low-interest loans could be made to people who wanted to relocate and start their lives over with opportunities overseas. Employers overseas would secure the loans, taking the costs out of initial wages paid on a staggered schedule. Any loan issue—any known cash-flow—could be stacked and securitized in much the same way mortgages had been, meaning an entirely new category of debt would emerge. Managing the risk, insuring it . . . the possibilities for financial innovation were endless. Terry had spent much of the night going over figures in his head, and couldn't sleep when he realized the kind of money he was about to make.

Then there was the domestic picture. The "smartening" of North American cities had stalled because of political resistance, cyber-terrorism, and generational conflict, but once Eric's "pockets of discontent" were processed, the redesign of North American cities around digital infrastructure and private networks could move ahead. The money involved in that upgrade would be staggering. So would the growth implied by the network density of wired urban centres.

GCM wasn't the only game in town, of course; Eric hadn't been the only one to realize where momentum was heading. But he had political clout few others could match. The groundbreaking work he'd done in Big Data econometrics in his twenties had paved the way to more efficient monetary policies and models that avoided the depression/inflation whipsaw of previous policy makers, putting his name right beside Keynes and Hayek in the pantheon. It had also made governments beholden to him, even as they began to hate and mistrust him.

He'd gotten even closer to governments at GCM, blurring the line between public and private operations until really only Eric Wheeler himself could tell the difference. He'd paved the way for corporations to own tactical nuclear assets, and was given a free hand outside of North America, as long as his operations broadly promoted American interests. Insofar as he slowly began to define what American interests might be, his compliance with the "authorities" had always been exemplary.

That was the league in which Terry was now playing. He'd always had it in mind to make insane amounts of money, but to actually take a hand at the rudder of history? To shape global events? The enormity of what he and Eric would accomplish over the next few years—along with Sarah at CWL managing the contracts and international agreements along the way—stunned him.

No one had ever talked to Terry Conlin the way Eric had—not even Terry's father. No one had ever thought Terry might be interested in grand machinations or geo-politics. Since his twelfth birthday, Terry had focused on mathematics, sales, and whoring—generally not in that order. The idea that there might be something huge about who and what Terry Conlin was had never occurred to him. But when Eric Wheeler spoke, Terry felt a sense of destiny for the first time in his life.

The truth was, the scale of Eric's vision electrified Terry more than his impending Spawning Contest, which, according to Eric, was a foregone conclusion. *Better cut that shit out*, Terry chided himself, refocusing his attention on the present. *Win first, count the money later.*

As he'd been driving, Terry had noticed a number of illuminated areas off-road, well into the trees. He finally pulled over to satisfy his curiosity, leaving the Mercedes at a bit of a tilt on the right-hand shoulder. He turned the engine off and got out, dressed in jeans, hiking boots, and a tan flannel shirt. The night was cool, but pleasant. All around him the sounds of insects and birds filled the air with a nocturnal symphony.

A slender footpath led the way through low-lying bushes to what turned out to be a rectangular clearing some fifty feet by thirty feet, surrounded on all sides by tall pines. Banks of floodlights had been mounted high in the trees, casting day-like incandescence on the scene and attracting a haze of moths and other insects out of the darkness.

It's an arena, Terry realized. A coliseum built for two. He strode casually through the area, toeing his boots at pine needles as his mind began to wander again.

There was still the nagging issue of Eric's historical involvement with the Conlin family, and the question of his potential input into Terry's own genetic heritage. During the plane ride, the notion had occurred to Terry, but indistinctly so—it was nothing he felt comfortable articulating. Later, when visiting his folks, his ideas had become more cogent, but he still couldn't bring himself to explore them out loud.

Had Eric Wheeler optimized Terry for this very Spawning Contest? It made a kind of quirky sense, in as much as Terry had often reflected upon how unlike either of his parents he was as a man. He'd inherited his father's size and muscle-composition, but where his dad was affable, and could affect a kind of gruff charm when necessary, nobody would accuse Terry of being the typical Albertan good ol' boy. He was as social as his old man—Jacob Conlin loved a drink as much as the next guy—but Terry's benders and casual violence seemed out of character with the Conlin line. He was a mean drunk; he was a mean sober. He didn't view it as a negative, and neither did his father, but the difference had always struck him.

Could Wheeler have been involved? Certainly: it was technically possible that he'd had conceptual input into Terry's optimization. Would he have had the foresight? After the plane ride, Terry didn't doubt it. The man had certainly controlled every aspect of his own daughter's development from the sounds of it: why leave anything else to chance?

Finally though, did it make any difference? This was what had stopped Terry from asking his father any questions. Terry didn't feel love from or for others very often, but he'd never questioned the affection of his own dad. The idea that Jacob Conlin might have been following orders didn't sit well with Terry, though he was hard pressed to say why. He was who he was, that was all there was to it. And given the situation that had evolved for him, would he want to be anyone else? So what if he'd been . . . directed to some extent: it was a phenomenal direction, wasn't it? Would he give back any of these opportunities if he had the chance? The answer was "hell no". If it was still bothering him after the Spawning, he could bloody well ask Eric as a formal son-in-law, and the father of Eric's precious grandchild.

That thought lifted Terry's spirits. He'd found that when he was troubled over the last couple of days, the feelings tended to drag him farther down than usual. With the sudden up-tick in mood, he found himself more upbeat than he would usually get, though he wasn't complaining. As he headed back to his car, Terry was almost humming—a sure sign that his adrenals were running hot.

He liked this new world according to Eric Wheeler. It made sense to him on a basic, visceral level. He liked the idea of doing something important with his life, even noble. Aside from the measurable benefits to himself, Terry could see that the "big picture" was a rosy one indeed. Staying in North America would be dependent upon a man's productivity rather than birthright, and that seemed just. Of course, if you wanted to compete on that basis, you better be in the Executive Program, or off to Asia you go, sah-hah. Less advantaged people could always take the pharma-route or get hot-wired for productivity's sake, but that was a one-way ticket to early burnout and health issues that made such measures counter-productive in the long run. That and all the fucking terrorist-hacks had made jacked solutions distinctly unpopular with anyone who could afford other alternatives. If you wanted to be *better,* you needed to be made that way from the get-go.

Terry had seen the numbers. Participation in the Program was growing exponentially. It wasn't just a case of haves and have-nots now . . . it was really Neanderthals and *Homo sapiens* all over again. The Program was open to all—just sack-up and pay for it. If you wanted to be well-positioned in life, it was your responsibility to get yourself in the game. That was fair, Terry reflected. It was the fairest deal anybody could ever expect.

The best part of it all was that nobody would ever be coerced to leave. As long as the market was the source of legitimacy, then market-forces would never be questioned. If you couldn't eat in New York, but you could in the Congo, you'd take the next available ship to the buffet line. As Eric pointed out, you didn't need government coercion to reinforce the market, you only needed it to interfere with the market. "We're not doing people any favours by making it so difficult for them to find opportunity," Eric had said. Blue eye dancing. Mirth. Menace.

Terry saw no downside to the mass export of redundant, often malcontented labour units who had been generated and sustained by decades of misguided inflation. The old analog society of mass had more people—and the wrong *kind* of people—than the new lean digital economy required. That was nobody's fault—certainly not Eric's and not Terry's either. The only real crime would be in maintaining the old order one day longer than necessary. The sooner things were rationalized, the better for everyone. Win-fucking-win!

As Terry neared the trunk of the Mercedes, he heard a car approaching from the way he had come, its headlights sweeping the tree line as it made the gentle left-hand turn. Terry's heart leapt into his throat as the BMW slowed, and the occupant, though shaded, was obviously getting a good look at him. He stared at the opaque glass, drawing himself up to his full height, squaring his shoulders to full spread. *Take a good long look,*

Terry thought to himself, stoking his ferocity.

I'm going to beat you to death with my cock.

"WELL, THIS IS unusually farsighted for you guys, isn't it?" Gannady Pike, Warren's best friend and quasi-legal adviser, had said with just the trace of a Slavic accent, when Warren had wanted to do up a will before leaving Victoria. It was standard practice for Program candidates not to have a will, consciousness of mortality being considered the wrong mind-set going into Spawn.

"Call me defeatist," Warren had joked. "I've got decent assets; I've got a private holding company and offshore accounts . . . I'm not leaving that mess for my folks to unravel, if . . ."

Gannady had nodded, smiling. He was an odd duck, Gannady Pike was. Not a lawyer per se, but he did things like wills and simple contracts which held up in court, and he knew all the ins and outs of setting up personal corporations—both how to do it, and what to avoid. Beyond admin wizardry, he was a writer who did steady trade in custom porn and fake social-media profiles—the latter so cunningly constructed that they included pictures, relationships, witty updates, upbeat conversations, and full timelines that went back as far as twenty years. Gannady knew the algorithms employers used to evaluate sosh-media footprints and could ensure that if scanned, his profiles would lead to a second interview. In his forties now, Pike had never held a "real" job so far as Warren knew, and didn't seem to want one.

Pike's office was a shabby rental, with a window that overlooked a parking lot, and a reception desk shared by a dozen other "professionals". It had been raining during Warren's visit; every now and again the wind would send squalls of rain-pellets against the glass in rat-a-tat bursts. The business with the will had been quickly concluded, with a well-organized Warren leaving all his assets to his parents. Pike had been able to E-register the forms online, and he printed off a hardcopy for Warren's records. After that, Gannady had pulled a bottle of whisky and two shot glasses from the depths of his desk, pouring himself and Warren a deal-sealing slug.

"No going away party?" Gannady asked as he reached across the desk to clink glasses with Warren. Warren had shrugged.

"Not really my style."

"You sure you're up for this?" Gannady quizzed, narrowing his eyes. "Most Program kids I know are more . . . rah-rah, you know?"

"You think I should get my swagger on?"

"Not necessarily. Long as you're confident, I guess it doesn't matter, right?"

Warren had sipped his drink, raising his eyebrows in lieu of another shrug.

"You *are* confident, yeah?"

"I am," Warren had nodded. "I'm worried and scared, but I'm confident."

Gannady shook his head, chuckling. "You're a weird cat, my friend."

"Why, because I tell the truth?"

"Exactly."

The drive to Sylvan had had—if not a therapeutic effect, then a numbing one at least. Warren had rented a BMW from the Calgary airport and the car practically drove itself with non-networked driver-assist, allowing Warren's mind to wander. Now that he had made the gates of the Spawning Ground, however, Warren's heart rate picked up and his anxiety returned. He drove slowly into the wooded gloom, painfully aware that he might never return.

Your whole life as a Program candidate boiled down to this moment, Warren reflected. Everyone's lives turned on a few decisive moments, of course, but in the Program, "decisive" took on a different weight entirely. You pushed yourself hard to get positioned going in, because coming out—if you came out— you'd have a family and a whole new set of responsibilities. But that wasn't the only reason you pushed, racing through those first twenty years to the fateful day of reckoning. Everyone wanted to have been tested in some way beforehand. Everyone wanted to know that they had the requisite steel inside. Every day was a public referendum on your mettle, when you grew up in the Program.

It was getting dark, and the winding access road was gravel, so Warren took it slow. Illuminated signs indicated off-roads to various cabins: number 4 was the one Warren wanted. Cabin number 4. It seemed so innocuous, all things considered.

Taking a gentle left hand turn, Warren saw a man standing just to the rear of a car parked on the right-hand shoulder of the road. Warren slowed to a crawl as he passed and looked up into the face of the man he recognized as his Spawning Counterpart.

Terry Conlin. In the flesh.

The man was a giant, and his bullet-shaped bald head turned on a corded neck to follow Warren's progress. The face was set in brutal stone, with just the hint of a leer on cruel lips. The eyes were dead—like fish eyes—and for just a heartbeat, Warren wished that his own eyes were as lifeless.

The BMW drove on for another thirty yards or so before Warren pulled over to the left and parked. His pulse pounded at his temples and he felt systolic pressure behind his eyes with each hammering beat of his heart. Once out of the car, there would be no going back. It wasn't how he had pictured the moment, just running into Conlin on a gravel road. He supposed that such haphazard confrontations happened all the time.

Warren swallowed, and his throat was dry. He turned off the ignition and lingered a moment longer, then pounded the heels of his hands against the steering wheel as rage began to take over.

"Just let your body do the training," Gannady had said on the second shot of Jameson's. "You're a fucking black belt in everything this side of thumb-wrestling—your body knows what to do." It was the same advice everyone always gave. Just get out of the way of your body, and let nature take its course.

Warren got out of the car and whirled about just in case. Conlin wasn't attacking, wasn't, in fact, even in sight. The back of Warren's neck bristled in the anticipation of ambush, but when he focused past the Mercedes he could see Terry's outline silhouetted against an illumination coming from the woods.

Good enough, Warren thought. He moved briskly to pursue.

A footpath led to a clearing in the trees that looked like a good place to either park an RV, or beat a human being to death with your bare hands. Terry had moved to the far side of the dirt lot and was removing his shoes. Floodlights poured hard, white light onto the area, casting Conlin into muscular relief.

"Nice fuckin' night, hey?" Conlin grinned as he removed his shirt, revealing a deep, broad chest and rounded shoulder heads. The man had been engineered for raw intimidation.

Warren removed his sandals and dropped his Rolex into the left one. He'd worn khaki board shorts and a tight gray t-shirt that wouldn't be all that easy to grab, but he removed it anyway, throwing it onto his footwear. He was a long, lean 6'1" himself, built like a swimmer, and he knew he had the endurance he'd need, but the power? Terry Conlin had the decisive advantage in that regard. Warren's mind instinctively began processing opening scenarios, eliminating the ones that led inevitably to Terry being able to employ his strength and mass.

"I feel like we should bow or something," Terry smirked.

It was the last thing Warren could remember, before his world turned crimson.

11:00 P.M. Calgary

KELLY LEE WAS used to hard work, but this was ridiculous.

She'd returned to Sarah's condo for the evening, since it was closer to the office than her own place, and she had the keys. She checked for packages with the concierge (there weren't any) and thought about an evening swim, but the truth was, she was exhausted. Sarah Wheeler took on the workload of three traditional lawyers and made it look easy. It wasn't. Covering for her was a nightmare.

Kelly poured herself a glass of Syrah—Sarah's favourite—and collapsed into the padded chair in the living room. She tuned the net to New York late night news and let the carnage breeze past her. Normally, she'd have picked up the day's events from her own monitor, but not today. Today, she'd been run off her feet, working the way Sarah did with a Bluetooth jack running hot and cold conversations in her ear while her hands hammered the keyboard on some other project and her tactical eye-lens gave her a fighter pilot's situational awareness of the various teams working parts of her projects. The lens worked on a firewalled corporate intra-net to mitigate hacks, so it was relatively safe to use, but that hadn't prevented Kelly from developing one savage bitch of a headache.

Aside from the volume of work, there was the intensity. Sarah's networks were conditioned to function on a razor's edge of fear-performance: they expected her seething rage to keep everyone on tempo. Kelly could summon the requisite anger, but sustaining it was another matter. It was a high-octane work environment that drew on reserves Kelly just didn't have.

Many Program kids weren't any more intelligent than a good Normal—certainly Sarah didn't seem to be. She could be humourless when stressed, which was ninety percent of the time, and she wasn't necessarily any quicker on the uptake than Kelly was. Despite her education, her taste was anything but high-brow as evidenced by her undying devotion to a string of vapid boy-bands, and any threatened trip to an art gallery would result in dramatic eye-rolls and lame excuses. But Sarah could grind hours out of a day that normal people just couldn't. She could sustain peak performance for hours on end, process high-density data streams without drugs, and when most people would be sleeping, she was prepping her morning priority list and getting her cardio in so she could hit the ground running. She would get extra mileage out of each and every day, and when you added up those extras over the course of a month or a year, it was a decisive advantage.

Sarah burned through legal aides at about the rate of 2.5 bodies per annum. On hot projects with hard deadlines, if Sarah worked late, her aides worked late, obliging them, if not mandating them, to take amphetamines to keep up. Still, there was no shortage of volunteers: Sarah's assistants made better money than junior associates, though they earned every penny.

In a world where accomplishment and drive was sexy, Sarah was overpowering. Kelly would have been attracted to her physicality anyway—to the sheer *meatiness* of her—but with the added cache of her work-rep, Sarah Wheeler was irresistible. It had been hard to watch her over the last few weeks as the Surge took hold. Kelly knew the toll the increased emotional load was taking, and wished for the ordeal to be over. It was inconceivable to her that Sarah wouldn't come through. Of all the people on earth, except maybe Sarah's father, Sarah would be the last person Kelly would want to face in a Spawning Contest.

For all her admiration of Sarah, Kelly Lee was an over-achiever herself, despite her lack of a Program pedigree. A Hong Kong city lawyer with mastery of six Asian languages and flawless London-accented English, she was a niche-player in an eco-system increasingly dominated by Program grads. Brought in by CWL as part of their global ramp-up, she'd made the jump to head office three years ago, based in no small part upon the recommendation of Eric Wheeler. Unbeknownst to CWL, Kelly had been a Global Conflict Management operative for years, and still took a regular paycheque from the Old Man himself.

Which reminded her: her day wasn't over yet.

Picking herself up out of the comfy chair, she took her wine into Sarah's office and booted up the computer. She knew the passwords and accessed all recent updates. She brought up the terrain-scan Sarah had sent to herself and studied it, paying close attention to areas Sarah had marked in the hills surrounding the cabin.

In the midst of her analysis, her phone rang. *Speak of the devil*, Kelly thought. Removing herself from the office, she retrieved her phone from the kitchen island and answered the call.

"Hey," Kelly said. The face on the view screen was somehow more severe than ever. The single blazing blue eye seemed even more incandescent in high-def. Kelly felt a familiar plummeting sensation in her stomach at the sight of Eric Wheeler.

"Well?" Eric said.

"Nothing yet." Kelly knew Eric monitored Sarah's calls when he could, but the Director was a busy man. Kelly was his eyes and ears at the firm, and he checked in with her at unpredictable intervals.

"Perhaps you should call her."

"I will. If I haven't heard from her soon, I'll call."

"Tomorrow, perhaps."

"Sure."

"Get some sleep, kid. You look bagged."

Kelly smiled in spite of herself. Eric could do that to people, catch them unawares with words and actions that seemed like kindness. "You know it," Kelly smiled. "Covering for your daughter is no easy task."

"All right," Eric said with a nod. He hung up.

Kelly considered the phone for a moment, then set it down and returned to the office. She transferred the terrain map to her own computer and would do a complete diagnostic in the morning, although when exactly, she hadn't the faintest notion.

Kelly took a quick hot shower, brushed her teeth, and applied moisturizer to her face as protection against the dry Calgary air. She went to Sarah's bedroom and dressed in one of the many nightshirts they shared as a matter of convenience. She got under the covers and assumed she'd drop right off, but that didn't happen. Her mind was racing, and it conjured Sarah in a familiar thought-loop that was as irritating as it was unstoppable.

Kelly wasn't exactly certain when it had happened, but somewhere along the way, she'd fallen in love with her assignment. At first, she'd told herself that it made the job easier, and that was true, as far as it went. Her job had been to keep an eye on Sarah and she was executing that mission to perfection. But.

She thought of the vacation to St. Croix. Sarah's idea. Totally out of the blue; they'd only been casual hook-ups to that point. Sarah had laid it out for Kelly in typical sledgehammer style: "I'm Program, and I don't want any messy entanglements. I know you probably work for my dad, and I don't really give a shit. I guess he's got good taste: I'm enjoying being with you. Like, I don't really want to see anyone else right now—that kind of enjoying."

"So what are you saying?" Kelly had asked.

"I'm saying I'd love it if we could just cut through the bullshit. Make your reports, do what you need to do, but let's make some real time for one another. I don't have any right to ask you for a commitment, obviously. But if you're up for a poignant romance with a doomed ending, I'm in."

Kelly had been in—not all-in, not right away—but she'd been intrigued, and that was the fast track to love, for her. They both worked hard and work took precedence, but what they lacked in time, they made up for with intensity. Sarah made sure of that. When she focused her attention on you, it was like sunlight being concentrated through a magnifying glass. It was thrilling for Kelly, but she was more than aware of the potential scalding effect of such light.

Kelly Lee was in danger now. Beholden to Eric Wheeler and in love with Sarah Wheeler, she would have to pick a side soon, and for keeps. Sarah meant to defy her father, and she needed Kelly's help to pull it off. *You're using me*, Kelly thought to herself, thinking the words at Sarah. It probably wasn't as simple as that—Kelly couldn't believe the feelings were all one way—but she wasn't naïve enough to believe it wasn't partially true.

It was a horrible feeling to know that you were so attached to someone that they could do anything to you and you'd forgive them. Kelly feared she had allowed Sarah that kind of power, and she feared that Sarah knew it. But Eric Wheeler killed human beings for a living. There was more to it than that, but in essence, that's what he did, that's who he was. And the thought of opposing him terrified Kelly.

Sleep, when it finally came, was a furtive, skittish thing barely worthy of the name.

All consumer-driven, supply-side art trends eventually and inevitably towards some form of pornography. All consumers care about is what you can do for them. In the end, if they're not getting off, it ain't worth paying for.

—Chthonic Sun, internet personality

SARAH FOUND POLLY'S last public address on YouTube:

"Hey everybody, good morning. Well, wow . . . it's here, you know? It's time. I don't really know what to say—which is weird, right? I feel . . . I'm excited. I'm really excited; not scared yet, maybe I will be but right now, I'm just anxious to get going."

The voice, the presentation . . . it was all so young and upbeat. It was a good performance, just the right tone for her audience. The real Polly had been a damn sight more frightening and formidable in person.

Sarah closed the laptop and set it down beside her on the porch swing built for two. The overhead light of the covered deck attracted flying insects, but no mosquito dared venture too close. *One of the side-effects of the Quickening*, Sarah realized. Bugs wouldn't want any part of her blood now.

Sarah was dressed in the loose-fitting drawstring pants that had come with the cabin, and one of her own t-shirts. The evening air was cool upon her forearms. Robins sang throughout the woods while frogs provided a throaty bass line, and insects improvised a syncopated melody between. The nocturnal farrago was oddly soothing, and compelling. Sarah let herself linger in the moment, which she realized was unusual behaviour for her even as it was happening.

Polly was everywhere on the internet, once you knew what to look for. It would be a difficult presence to live with, Sarah realized—that constant reminder. More than a ghost, less than the actual girl, or perhaps simply a different format of the girl: Polly's digital, immortal self. *There will be grief*, Sarah mused. She hadn't considered that there might be a public mourning for Polly; couldn't imagine how surreal such an experience might be. It was an odd feeling to know that she, Sarah Wheeler, had been a presumed underdog in terms of the expectations of the wider world. She'd never been an underdog at anything in her entire life.

Sarah took a deep breath and stretched out both legs before her. She was feeling better—her enhanced metabolism working feverishly to repair her damaged cells. She'd slept the day away—a first, as far as she could recall: another effect of the Quickening, shutting her down in order to better heal her. Her thigh still throbbed—that wouldn't be going away any time soon—but it no longer hurt to breathe. The bruising on her torso had actually receded in some places, though it was still tender to the touch. *I'll live*, she thought with some satisfaction, tempered by the knowledge that the acceleration of metabolic function during the Spawning could take as much as five to ten years off a person's life. It was worth it to feel as good as she felt just then.

She was about to check in on work when she heard a sound from the beach in the distance: splashing, someone running through the surf. She heard someone crashing through the underbrush along the footpath; could imagine a blundering, reeling gait. In a moment, a man came into view, stumbling clear of the tree line, emerging from darkness into the edge of the porch-light's range. He didn't see her at first, but when he did, he halted, reeling on the spot as though drunk. Or hurt. As he staggered closer, Sarah thought he was wearing latex gloves on both hands, but upon resolution, she could tell it was blood-staining to the elbow. His nose bled—possibly broken: she could hear his laboured breathing as he stopped at the first of three large, circular stepping stones laid into the grass leading up to the porch steps.

Sarah stood: alarmed; thrilled. Blood hammered in her ears; her mouth went dry.

The man came to the bottom step, looking up at her. His dark brown eyes swam as though he were on something, but Sarah supposed it could be pure adrenaline. His hair was wet, matted. He had a lean, sinuous, swimmer's physique: broad shoulders tapered to an athletic waist. His chest rose and fell with exaggerated breathing.

"Are you. . . ?" the man asked. His voice was raw—as though he'd hurt his throat somehow. And then she saw the abrasions upon his neck.

"Yes," she whispered.

The man growled, his eyes baleful, glaring up at her through his lashes.

"Do you . . ." she faltered, ". . . do you want to get cleaned up first?"

The man wiped his nose on his forearm. A vein in his forehead pulsed. His jaw clenched.

He came to her slowly, eyes staring into hers. His hands took her biceps, gripping her hard enough to hurt. He kissed her— teeth clicked on teeth—and she tasted the coppery tang of blood on his tongue. He forced her back against the screen door, forward progress momentarily stymied. "Wait," she panted, reaching behind her to fumble with the door handle. She opened the door without looking, her mouth still engaged, and she backed into the cabin with the stranger upon her.

She felt as she had when she hit the water with Polly. Her body took over, but this time even more completely than when she had been engaged in mortal competition for air. Sarah was a passenger inside her own flesh once again.

The man took her to the hardwood floor of the cabin, and in the first mating-throes she hardly noticed the pain against her vertebrae, shoulder blades, elbows, skull. He tore at her clothes, kneeling between her knees to reef at her sweat pants even as she kicked at the restraints herself. Clawing his back, she felt his muscles writhing like bunched piano wires. She gasped when he thrust into her, his body slamming down upon her deeply bruised left thigh. Heedless of the pain, she wrapped her legs around his back, holding him in closed guard, pushing at his face, making him fight his way forward.

The man came that first time in a spasmodic seizure—more like an epileptic fit than a sexual act, and in the immediate aftermath, he seemed stunned by the ejaculation. Sarah briefly came back to herself, though foggily, and she took the opportunity to pull the man to his feet and lead him to the bedroom. They were both panting from the sheer savagery of their exertions. If the man even felt his injuries, he gave no sign of it.

They shed any last remnants of tattered clothing as the man hardened into rapid re-arousal. They stared at one another throughout these moments, trembling with the horrible, alien need to be at each other.

He revived quickly, and lunged upon her with renewed vigor. The Spawning was upon him, activated and released by the killing, and Sarah knew the man would never perform like this again in his entire life. She didn't dwell on that. She couldn't dwell on that. Cogent thoughts of any kind came to her as in a dream, and seemed to fade away like smoke in the wind.

She was as hungry as he, and whenever he hesitated to catch his breath, she was on him, pushing him to his back, pulling his hair, baring his throat. Her vitality fueled his, and he would reverse positions with muscular effort, but she would lift her knees to his chest and make him fight through the obstacles. Her laughter seemed wild and strange to her own ears. It was the sound her body made, when it was fully engaged in realizing its own destiny.

He drove her into the walls and floors as her body clenched at his like a closed fist. She baited him and provoked him like a matador sticking swords into a bull's haunch. He gored her in return.

All through the night, again and again and again, the man's body rallied and pulsed with seemingly endless vitality. The smell in the room was the same pungent musk that it would be normally . . . with an extra tinge of something else—something almost chemical—that Sarah couldn't quite identify. And the blood of course. That was in the air, too.

The blood on the sheets and pillowcases was the visceral evidence of their virginity in Spawning. That much of the blood belonged to a slain third party was an indication of how much virginity had changed in the twenty-first century.

The moon rose full above the lake; insect and bird song continued on into the night. Inside Cabin number 4, two bodies tore at one another in mindless consummation, slaves to the DNA that drove them.

"WARREN MILNER," SARAH muttered. She was dressed in a floor-length cotton shift, her hair damp, freshly showered. She sat in a large, comfortable chair across from the bed, her legs up over the arm as she went through the man's wallet. Morning sunlight strobed through the pines outside, dappling the cabin light-and-dark.

"Focke-Wulf North America," she murmured, "senior engineer." She hadn't seen herself with an engineer, but whatever. She liked the idea of their children having her verbal skill, coupled with his mathematical precision.

He was well-established—almost as accomplished in his own field as she was in hers, by the looks of things. Not that she was keeping score.

Platinum card. Laurentian club key-card member. The Banker's Club gym. He had good cards, did Warren Milner.

"Find what you're looking for?" Warren mumbled from the bed. He sat up and grimaced, immediately favouring bruised ribs. Gingerly, he touched at his swollen nose, deciding it wasn't broken after all.

She smiled, continued her investigation. "You live in Victoria," she stated. "That's fine. Wilhelm Loughren has offices there. I can get a transfer."

"Where do you live?" he asked, his voice husky.

"Calgary."

"We've got offices there too. Let's not rush to judgment on it. I can move, need be."

She nodded. Looking up, she asked: "Coffee or tea?"

"Coffee. Please. Black."

She rose to put the water on.

WARREN WINCED TO see the smears of dried blood upon the bed.

He got up with a groan, making his halting way to the bathroom. He ran a shower hot enough to nearly scald, scrubbing at his rust-coloured hands with the plastic nail-brush provided. Revived, he dressed in the ubiquitous cotton draw-string pants he'd found in the closet, and stared at himself in the mirror.

His memory was fragmented at best. He recalled Terry's leering grin, remembered biting the man's ear off. Terry crawling. The hideous, whimpering noises Terry had made.

Warren brushed his teeth hard enough to make the gums bleed. Eventually, he smelled the odor of strong coffee.

Warren wandered into the kitchen as Sarah puttered. She poured him a cup of coffee and handed it to him as he approached.

"Thanks, um . . ." Warren frowned.

"Sarah," Sarah smiled.

Warren nodded sheepishly as he sipped. The Executive Program made your Spawning Counterpart transparent, but you never knew who your One was beforehand. It was really the first time he'd gotten a good close look at her while being lucid enough to appreciate it, and he actually felt a slight sense of vertigo when she'd smiled. Partially, he knew this was a result of the serotonin-wash triggered by the Spawning. Still. She was so painfully beautiful to him in that moment that he didn't feel competent to speak.

Sarah had brought one of the white terrycloth housecoats from the closet and draped it over one of the kitchen chairs. Warren obtained it, put it on, and joined Sarah out on the porch, the better to enjoy the morning.

Loons called in the distance as Warren sat to Sarah's right on the swinging chair. Steam rose pleasantly from the coffee as they drank, warming their faces in the cool morning air.

Warren fought himself for control: his heart was pounding just because Sarah sat so close-by. It made him self-conscious, gave him the irrational fear that she might be able to hear the tell-tale thumping noise drumming out from his chest.

"So," Sarah began, blowing on her coffee. If she was nervous, she didn't look it. If anything, she looked slightly amused by it all. "You're an engineer."

"Is that bad?" Warren asked.

"No, no. Just unexpected. Never really saw myself with an engineer."

Warren nodded, thrashing about in his mind for something to say. His gaze fell upon her black laptop with the crimson CWL sigil upon it. "CWL," he managed. "Good firm. Partner?"

"Junior."

"Nice. What's with the antique?"

"What, the laptop? It's military—all the partners have one. Can't be hacked, or so they tell us. You could back over that thing with a truck and it would still download cat videos for you."

Warren chuckled. They didn't say another word for close to five minutes.

It was the longest time Warren could ever remember sitting in silence with someone to whom he thought he should be speaking. On the one hand, it was agony, and yet . . . he felt oddly relaxed. The morning was a tourism brochure, the girl was an advertisement for Outdoor Life Online, and he felt as though he'd known her forever. His *body* felt that way, he realized at last. He was far more comfortable with her than he should have been, all things considered.

Only their minds were strangers.

"This is very odd," Sarah said at last, turning her head to look at him. Soft blonde hair flowed behind her shoulders, shining lustrous in the morning light. "This . . . knowing and not knowing at the same time."

"I know!" Warren grinned, relieved not to be alone in his perceptions. "You read about it, but . . ."

Both nodded, and returned to their coffee.

"You think it worked?" Warren offered after a moment.

"I don't see why not. I took the Quickening at the lab, and it definitely activated. And you did your part." Sarah smiled, made eye contact. Warren grinned back and looked out over the lawn, suddenly self-conscious.

Sarah reached to take Warren's left hand in her right, giving it a reassuring squeeze. "Are you okay?"

"Yeah. You know. You are handling this really, really well."

"I'm handling it well because you're here. We're here together, and we'll handle whatever we need to, right?"

"Right."

Beautiful and poised, Warren reflected. *I am one lucky bastard.*

"Boy or girl?" Sarah asked, her eyes dancing at the thought.

"Don't think they let you choose that anymore."

"But if you could?"

"Oh man . . . both! Twins!"

"Ouch! Thanks a lot!" Sarah was playing it for comedy, but she remembered the twin monsters she'd envisioned during the Quickening uptake. There were good reasons why all Spawning births were single children. She repressed the memory and kept her smile in place.

"Sarah," Warren said after a moment, gathering his thoughts. "I can tell you're special. Even if you weren't my One, I'd be drawn to you. I would."

Sarah smiled a different smile, as if accepting the compliment while gently chastising it. It was the smile one gave when wondering about another's naiveté without necessarily wanting to crush it. The fact that Warren was wistful about overriding his DNA imperative struck her as quaint. "How would you know?" she said quietly, and Warren could only shrug. How *could* he know? They were vessels for their DNA, and their DNA demanded species propagation. A profound, emotional bond between parents maximized the chances for offspring survival, and success. There was no way to separate his emotions from his deeper, cellular motivations.

He reached to brush a thumb gently across the swelling under Sarah's left eye. She flinched at the touch, partly because it was sensitive, partly because the mark wasn't hers. Warren nodded in understanding, and finished his coffee.

A phone rang from inside the cabin. Warren looked at Sarah, and she said: "That's mine. I should . . ."

"No, of course," Warren said.

Sarah rose from the swinging chair, taking their coffee cups with her en route to the kitchen.

Dropping the cups off in the sink, she took her phone off the counter and checked the caller id. Smiling, she answered: "Hey!"

"Thank Christ," Kelly Lee smiled, visibly relieved on the view screen. "I thought you were going to call me?"

Sarah headed into the bedroom, taking a seat in the large chair. On reflex she draped long legs over the arm. "You're right," Sarah grinned, "sorry for making it all about me, Kel. The big question is: how are *you* holding up?"

"Ha. Is it over?"

"Yes," Sarah said, lowering her voice. "I mean—he's still here and everything. But yes, last night we . . . we met."

"O.M. fucking G. How was it? Are you okay?"

"I'm fine, Kel. Sore."

"How many times?"

"Jesus, Kelly! Like I was making a chart!"

"What—like I wouldn't be curious?"

"It was . . . I don't know. A lot. It's a lot, Kel. And it's not like a normal . . . it's just . . . it's not normal."

"Is *he* okay?"

"He's pretty banged up. But he's okay—nothing broken. There's fucking blood all over the place though. I'm going to have to wash the sheets."

"How do you feel? What's he like? Is he good looking, or . . ."

"No—he's got swag. A little spooked, I suppose."

"Spooked?"

"I'm trying to get him to relax, but—you know—it's weird. Talking to him. I feel like I've known him forever, but then, we're talking and . . ."

"And what?"

"And, I mean . . . we don't know each other, you know? As people? We just know each other physically."

"Well, that's the deal, right? You guys're matched pairs—he's coded for you, you're coded for him."

"It's pretty intense. But it's good, being with him. He's sweet."

"I'm sorry . . . did you say 'sweet'? It sounded on this end like you just said 'sweet'. That's not really your type, is it?"

"Shut up, I can be sweet. And he really is, I think—for an engineer."

"An engineer," Kelly repeated, blinking.

Kelly hid it well, but Sarah saw the slight double-take. *Are you listening, Dad?* Sarah thought. *Bet you're double-clutching too.*

UN-HACKABLE, HEY, Warren thought as he reached for Sarah's laptop. *We'll see about that.*

The desktop was orderly—just a few folders—some encrypted for work, others public for music and other entertainment. He did a quick diagnostic code on the encryption and she was right, at least as far as a quick penetration was concerned. Anything important was locked up tighter than a drone's target-acquisition matrix.

A quick peek at her reading list revealed a number of titles, mostly non-fiction. Classics like *The Prince* and *The Art of War*. Econometric titles like *Japanese Deflation of the late 20th Century* and *China's New Asset Bubble*. *Meltdown: The EU and the Collapse of the Sovereign Bond Market*. *Guns as Ideology*. *Social Media Wave Theory: An Introduction*. And so on: Sarah didn't read for entertainment.

Her music was much more lighthearted, at least in Warren's humble opinion. Mostly synth-pop bands where each new song was algorithmically generated, based upon previous selections and preferences. Producers took that information, aggregated it, and slotted in appropriate performers for various markets, to make the videos, conduct local-media publicity, and do the "live" shows. It was all consumer-driven, with fans essentially voting on group-member composition such that it changed from show to show, based upon popular preference. Glancing through the titles, it was almost as if Sarah bore a grudge against actual human singer-songwriters, so studiously did she avoid them. *Well, we'll work on that,* Warren grinned.

He activated a public internet channel, then accessed his Executive Program page. Way too early for an official text message—instead, he simply updated relationship status from "Candidate" to "Victor". An automatic message would go out to his friends, followers, and family, which would ease their minds until he could have a proper chat.

As he logged out and closed the laptop, he found himself thinking of Ellen. He pursed his lips and tried to get a handle on his emotions. He felt guilty because as much as he had loved Ellen, he remembered the relationship now as a shallow, transitory, hollow thing. He had never thought of her that way—even when she had periodically hit the brakes to manage his ardor—she had always seemed like the most solid, the most real thing in his life. But his perceptions had been altered by the Spawning. When he looked at Sarah, his stomach plunged and his mouth went dry—he could actually feel the physiological impact of her presence. But more than raw sexual intensity, he felt a familiarity in his bones that all the years with Ellen hadn't produced. With some regret he realized that those years *couldn't* produce the same depth of feeling as the Spawning. It wasn't just a difference between two relationships: it was a difference in kind between the two relationships.

Warren heard the screen door open, and right on cue, his heart leapt. He looked up at Sarah—into those washed-out Husky-dog blue eyes and noticed her glancing immediately towards her laptop. *Sharp cookie,* Warren thought. *She doesn't miss much.*

"Sorry about that," Sarah said.

"Everything okay?"

"Yeah—just a friend checking up on me."

"Mm. What'd you say?"

"That I lucked out."

Warren chuckled, feeling her gaze upon him. Her stare almost seemed to have palpable weight to it. He looked out over the lawn rather than meet those eyes and said: "Hey—I've got some clothes and things in my car. Feel like a walk?"

"I'll get changed," Sarah smiled.

KELLY ROSE, CLOSED her office door, sat back down, and thought hard about her next few moves. *An engineer,* Sarah had said. Was it possible that Terry Conlin had failed to come through?

Eric had probably been monitoring the call as soon as it was made, but if he hadn't been, and Kelly didn't alert him? That would be a mistake.

On the other hand, Kelly had a natural, understandable aversion to giving Eric Wheeler bad news. It was better to do so over the phone than in person, of course, but either way, the results could be . . . volatile.

In the end there was no real choice at all. Kelly realized she'd only been hesitating to buy herself some composure. She found her phone in her purse and hit Eric's mission-dedicated number.

He didn't respond immediately. Kelly let the phone ring twice, four times . . . she was just beginning to wonder if she should call back when the familiar glaring features of Eric Wheeler filled the view screen. She couldn't tell from the background where he might be, but he seemed bathed in an odd, blue-tinged light.

"Ah," Eric said. "Ms. Lee."

"Hey. Were you monitoring any of my last conversation?"

"I'm actually in the middle of a sensitive negotiation at the moment. Afraid I missed it."

"I just got off the line with your daughter." Kelly was watching for any hint of an internal reaction in the man's eye, or face. She found none.

"I trust she's doing well."

"She's fine. I don't think Terry Conlin came through though."

"You don't think Terry came through, or you know beyond a shadow of a doubt that he didn't?"

"Sarah mentioned that her One was an 'engineer'."

"Mm. Well, nobody's going to mistake Terry Conlin for an engineer. The other fellow just won't do, I'm afraid."

"What do you want me to do?"

"Confirm status. I need to know ASAP if Terry Conlin is in fact dead. If he is, Sarah knows what to do, but just to be sure, use your influence on her—make *certain* she takes care of the situation as per plan B. I want full and docile cooperation from Mr. Warren Milner vis-à-vis my grandchild. Failing that: plan C, Kelly."

"The bonding's already taken place. You know that, right?"

"Look, I've got to go. You haven't fucked anything up yet: call me when you do. I have confidence in you, Kelly."

"Yes, sir."

Eric disengaged, leaving Kelly staring at the blank view screen of her phone for several moments.

ON THE ONE hand Eric was elated: his daughter had come through! But it wasn't the time or place to revel in her triumph. He put the phone back into the breast pocket of his suit jacket, took a single deep breath through his nose, then turned back to the command bay of the "Republic".

The "Republic" was a helicopter carrier of Russian design—formerly the "Zhukov"—purchased at a tremendous discount during one of the frequent insolvencies endured by the Russian state. Retrofitted for drones and cruise missiles, the "Republic" represented one of several capital ships owned by GCM, and was currently deployed just beyond the limit of US territorial waters off the coast of southern California. Any closer and the vessel would have been submitted to American operational oversight, given that a private drone-strike was in play.

The bay itself was circular in design, bordered on one side by a glass observation gallery in which the shadowed outline of Eric's clients could be seen. Computer monitors oversaw a variety of functions, and Eric moved to stand behind the young man who had taken command of the drone's final approach. Miguel Reyes was the lad's name, a thirteen-year-old Chilean boy who Eric had rescued from a Brazilian slave market three years previously. The kid was as good as it got, possessing reflexes and instincts which allowed him to compete in online wargame exercises with Program kids his own age.

Crosshairs passed over low, green-canopied hills deep in the Mexican interior. Terraced farmland was visible, as were the outlying buildings of a town, from which a few main roads extended. GCM also provided the ground-level intelligence to identify and verify kills: this particular operation was the culmination of a six month investigation that had incorporated informants, military assets, and diplomatic pay-offs. A bit of a loss leader in business terms, but Eric knew the job would lead to bigger paydays to come.

Clients enjoyed the fact that at GCM, the directors and chief executives were hands-on. They didn't just do the deals and delegate; someone like Eric Wheeler—a world-class economist and visionary—would actually oversee the operation all the way through. Unlike executives of other security firms, Eric Wheeler had actually gone in-country on a gun-ship; had actually put muzzles to temples; had actually pulled triggers and coerced cooperation out of captives. Then he would go on CNN in person and deliver the spin, if necessary. You just didn't get that kind of full-spectrum service from every outfit.

The drone had completed its ground-to-air sweep, detecting no installed defence-signatures. Miguel's eyes never left the screen: Eric couldn't even be sure if the boy had blinked. Across the room, Ana Torres engaged the jamming drone from a much higher altitude, essentially blocking all communications to and from the town-site.

Eric fought to keep his attention on-mission, but he couldn't help thinking about the Spawning Event. If Conlin had truly failed, it wasn't a deal breaker. His participation served a multi-layered purpose that couldn't entirely be replaced, but the financial details themselves could be re-routed. It was the kind of set-back for which Eric was always prepared. It would be up to Sarah to manage the situation.

Warren Milner was a curious sort, Eric reflected. His biometrics hadn't tracked as neatly as Terry's had done, leading to a so-called long-tailed statistical chart. The margin of superiority for Terry had been so great that Eric had felt comfortable with the margin for error inherent in Milner's metrics. Still, Spawning Events were always dicey affairs. One never knew with absolute certainty what might happen, on any given day.

Which is why he felt so proud of—and vindicated by—Sarah's performance. Winning on the day meant everything he had done to her—*for* her—had been the right move. He had never really doubted it, but the mathematician in him had known that she was in very tough with the Walker girl. Still, he had built Sarah for certainty. Certainty was an odd, anti-market objective, and aiming for it had ironically required market methods, but in the end, she had proven herself to be special. She hadn't exceeded his expectations, but his expectations had been astronomically high to begin with. Meeting them was exceptional.

If only he had shown the same wisdom with Samantha.

The three-story apartment building housing the union organizer and rabid nationalist Leon Ortega, had slowly slid underneath the drone's crosshairs. Readings displayed wind, humidity, and other modifying conditions as Miguel took the drone down to attack altitude. Pedestrians strolled dusty sidewalks in the broiling Mexican sun; the odd car wove slowly in and around small children playing soccer in the street.

Miguel smiled as he engaged the firing system. In moments, three fer-de-lance missiles punctured the ceiling of the building, blowing out windows on all four sides. Incendiaries followed, penetrating deep into the building before unleashing their particular brand of hell.

Eric put a firm hand on Miguel's shoulder and said, "Good lad," in the tones that had once motivated Alexander's men to follow him into an unknown desert, or Napoleon's rear guard to hold fast against murderous Russian Cossacks. Miguel turned and grinned up at Eric not as a child-assassin, but merely as a thirteen-year-old boy for whom such praise was priceless.

Eric turned to the gallery, smiled, and held his arms out wide in an expansive gesture. In truth, he felt no particular emotion at the clinical execution of a routine mission, but these were hard-drinkin', back-slappin' Gulf o' Mexico oil-men and geologists in attendance. They had their expectations.

Behind the glass, Eric could hear the muted applause and hoots of glee from satisfied customers. He turned his attention to Ana and said in English, "Get me on-site confirmation and let's wrap this up." Then he returned his broad grin to the gallery and gave those boys their money's worth of teeth.

The Executive Program makes people the way Wall Street creates financial products. One must assume that the consequences will be similar.

— Pope Boniface XIV

WARREN CONTINUED HIS story: ". . . so my dad owns a bunch of waste disposal contracts and landfills and stuff, and his big idea was always to have me work at some of the sites, you know? Show me how lucky I am; teach me responsibility, that kind of thing. Anyway, this one time—I'm probably thirteen or something—I'm in this garage with a crew—and these are rough old boys, you know? I mean, good guys, but they're not exactly members of the country club or anything. So we're on a break, and there's all these mousetraps lying around, right? And these guys are taking turns setting off the traps with their fingers— just seeing if they can trigger the things without getting caught—until finally, this one guys goes: 'I bet I can do it with my cock!'"

Sarah laughed so hard, so in spite of herself, that she snorted. The break in her reserve was an encouraging sight to Warren: her laughter was louder and goofier than he had expected.

They stood on the pier overlooking a lake turned molten gold in spots by the rising sun. In the distance the tap-tap-tapping of a woodpecker could be heard. Water lapped against wood, and across the lake, a jet boat headed out from the hotel's marina. Warren was dressed in a white bathrobe over cotton pants and no shoes. Sarah wore a white t-shirt over form-fitting light blue jeans and tan hiking boots with the laces undone.

"You're kidding," Sarah grinned, eyes dancing.

"Nope: not kidding. That's who these guys were. So sure enough . . . trap's on the table; money's on the table—and they were using actual paper currency, right? Like in the movies. So the trap's there at the edge of the table; guy whips out his rat, and he's taking a few sort of practice dangles, right? Then he goes for it—swings his cock up and around . . . and the trap snaps shut as he's spinning 180. Trap's empty—it's there on the table, sprung over upside-down—and the guy—wish I could remember his name, Gerry, Harry, something like that—the guy stumbles to a seat on this swivel chair, slowly rotating around, right? We think he's actually done it, but when we see his cock in his hands, the helmet is all black and swelling like a bastard. Poor guy's just staring at this thing in shock, right? MEDIC!—you know? So that's it—we're off to the hospital—the whole deal—it was insane. Took his money of course, but damn, I still somehow doubt that's the lesson my dad was hoping I'd learn there."

"Oh my God," Sarah laughed, shaking her head. "That did *not* happen."

"That happened. That's a scar I bear. Not as bad as the guy with the mousetrap penis scar, but still."

"So disgusting!"

"So, what about your dad?" Warren asked when they'd regained their composure. "What's he like?"

Sarah's smile became smaller, and her eyes grew distant. She gave Warren that stare of hers for a moment before looking out over the water."

"He's . . . he's not like your typical dad," she managed, pursing her lips in thought.

"Come on—everybody's dad is unique. Give me something."

"Well . . . he's a great man. I mean like, in the way you would say 'Alexander the Great', you know? Great in a formal sense, not 'great' in the sense that you'd want to go drinking with him."

"Do tell!"

"I don't know, Warren . . ."

"Are you serious? Babe, the shit you don't want to talk about is exactly the shit I need to hear."

Sarah nodded, then said: "You ever heard of the Wheeler-Fukuyama-Hicks transformations?"

"I'm guessing your dad's the 'Wheeler' in the title?"

"It's part of a new econometrics model that uses Social Media Wave Theory to predict and prevent big market collapses and depressions. My dad was chief economist on that. Oh, and Social Media Wave Theory? My dad invented that. It's like math that couldn't have existed before the internet."

"Math geek. Man after my own heart."

Sarah laughed again, but it wasn't the big, full-bodied laugh she'd unleashed moments ago. Warren sensed the ruefulness of the new laugh, the bitterness. *Best travel lightly here*, he thought.

"Wait though," Warren said as his brain engaged. "Social Media Wave Dynamics . . . that's like forty years ago. How old's your dad?" The way Program generations worked out, Warren had expected Sarah's father to be roughly as old as his own—early forties.

"Old," Sarah replied, lifting her eyebrows for emphasis. "He's the only human being to have ever survived a second Spawning Surge. Artificially induced. After his first kid died on her Spawning Run . . . he insisted on trying again."

"Jesus Christ, Sarah," Warren breathed, thinking it through. Having just been through one Surge, Warren could not imagine going through it again. If Sarah's story was accurate, Eric Wheeler had apparently gone into Surge in his *forties*, and survived against prime competition. It seemed inconceivable.

"Cost him his left eye," Sarah concluded, "but he got what he wanted. He got me."

"Are you serious? I didn't even think a second run was possible."

"It's not supposed to be. But his first family didn't work out, and my dad doesn't accept negative outcomes, so . . ."

"Damn."

"Gets better. He's a director of Global Conflict Management Systems."

"Holy shit!"

"Anyway, I never saw him much growing up. He's a Wikipedia entry to me. Haven't seen him in years, actually."

"Wow. I'm so sorry to hear that, Sarah. Maybe that'll all change now."

Sarah crossed her arms, frowning across the water.

"Something I said?" Warren offered, probing as gently as he could.

"No," Sarah said, shaking her head. "No, you have the right to know. My dad's probably not going to be a big part of our life is all. It's not like you and your parents."

"Well, that's fine. How about the rest of your family? Any brothers and sisters?"

Sarah turned her head to look at Warren in confusion. "What do you mean?"

"Well, you know . . . siblings."

"You have . . ."

"Sure—one brother, one sister."

"And that's safe for them?"

"Oh yeah, it's fine. Mom and Dad had them outside of the Program. There's no clinical rivalry or anything between us."

"That's . . . wow."

"What, you never wanted a little sister growing up?"

"God no!"

"Would you ever consider, you know . . . having children outside of the Program? After this one?"

Sarah blinked and frowned, unable to conceal her inner conflict. "I don't know, Warren," she said at last. "Honestly, I've never even thought about it before."

Awkward, Warren thought as they both gazed across the lake, momentarily at an impasse. Obviously, everything would be negotiable, but Warren was getting the sense that his One was a complex, prickly individual even by Program standards. He had always liked the thought of a bigger family—had pictured Christmas dinners with his folks, his siblings, and their children alongside his own. Sarah obviously came from a much different place when it came to family. He needed to ease up, he realized. They would have time to understand these things about one another.

Lost in thought, Warren never saw Sarah's t-shirt flying towards his head. It wrapped itself around his face, and when he removed it, he could see her shimmying free of her jeans.

"I'm going in," she grinned, tanned body solid and strong in her athletic under-garb.

"Looks cold," Warren smiled.

"Looks can be deceiving." With a wink, she dove off the end

of the pier, cutting the surface with expert form. Warren could see her body glistening beneath the waves as she dolphin-kicked once, twice, then emerged several yards out into the lake.

Pushing hair out of her eyes, Sarah yelled: "You should come in!"

"Not much of a swimmer!" Warren laughed.

"I'd catch you," Sarah said, treading water effortlessly.

"No doubt."

"Hey—what's your favourite food?" Sarah asked, voice dripping with irony. It was the perfect trite question, asked in the least trite circumstances imaginable.

Warren puzzled for a moment, then answered: "Curry!" He hesitated as she submerged again, then rolled over into a supple backstroke towards him. "Favourite colour?" he asked.

"Pink," Sarah said as she sculled back into upright treading position again. Warren couldn't tell if she was serious: her voice carried the same ironic attitude towards the interrogation. "Dogs or cats?" she shot back.

"Parrots," Warren said without hesitation.

"Oh, we are not getting a parrot, mister!"

"No, but they're cool. They're the Cadillac of pets."

"The what?"

"Forget it."

Sarah submerged again and did a pass near the pier, then broke surface and began plowing water in earnest. Warren smiled in simple appreciation of the woman's strong shoulders and sleek form propelling her torpedo-like through the resistance. He felt his body responding at the sight of her in motion. She was absolutely breathtaking to him.

When she returned at last to the pier, she extended her arms, and Warren pulled her from the lake. He took his own bathrobe off and put it around her shoulders, rubbing her arms as they stared at each other. The sun was warm on their skin, bright in their eyes. She leaned forward as he was drying her and kissed him impulsively, the two momentarily frozen in time. Then she cringed involuntarily as his hands found her ribs.

"Sorry," Warren said, though he was grinning.

"You should see the other girl," Sarah smiled.

"I'll bet. Who was she?"

Sarah's smile faltered. Just like that, the stare was back,

beaming into the farthest reaches of Warren's soul like a searchlight sweeping about for escaped prisoners.

"What does it matter?" Sarah said.

"C'mon," Warren poked playfully at her ribs: she caught his right hand in her left.

"Don't tease me about her." Sarah dropped her eyes. Warren pulled her in for a hug, rubbing her back to dry her.

"Okay," he said. "Sorry. Off-limits."

"Not off-limits," Sarah murmured in close. "Just too soon. I want my hooks in you good and deep before we talk about her."

Warren laughed. "Your hooks get in any deeper they're gonna be poking out the other side."

Sarah chuckled at the image. "Good," she said.

Therefore I say: Know the enemy and know yourself; in a hundred battles, you will never be in peril.

— Sun Tzu, The Art of War

STROLLING NORTH ALONG the sandy beach, just off the waterline, Sarah realized that Warren had taken her hand some time ago. She wondered if he even knew, wondered if he'd even had the intention to hold hands. It was unnerving to be so unaware, but that's how their bodies were together: instantly comfortable; instantly compatible. Never one for public displays of affection in the past, Sarah found herself delighted by Warren's touch. Delighted, and bewildered.

They chatted as they went, trying to get their minds caught up with their bodies. They were very different people, Sarah realized, they saw the world in two very distinct ways. It didn't repulse her—if anything the differences were more intriguing than anything else, but they were a source of anxiety all the same. Warren had entered into the Spawning a deeply committed family man. Sarah did not think those values could be negotiated away. That would be a problem.

They turned inland eventually, taking one of the many grassy footpaths through the trees to arrive at one of the trunk roads. Warren placed his steps carefully in the dirt-filled ruts, avoiding gravel with his bare feet, while Sarah strode on ahead. She caught him appreciating the muscular jut of her backside and smiled. She felt the same way—as though she could simply look at Warren all day, and never get tired of the sight.

"So," Sarah said, as squirrels chittered in nearby boughs, "what's the girlfriend situation like, Warren?"

"Well . . . I've got one. Had one, I guess."

"Mm. I'm not opposed to, you know, some kind of open, transition-period thing . . ."

"Not necessary. She knows I'm in the Program—knows the whole deal. She was pretty amazing about it, actually. I would like some time to say a proper goodbye though, when we get back. Things felt so rushed when I left. She deserves better."

"I'll bet she does."

"Jealous?"

"God," Sarah realized, looking up and frowning in amazement, "I am! I've never been jealous before in my life, Warren, I swear. This is so weird."

"Well, if you promise not to kill her, you should meet her. She'd be a good friend to us. Our first friend as a couple, maybe."

"My God, you *do* like her. No promises on the no-killing thing!"

"Well, what about you? Don't tell me you don't have anything going on."

Sarah flashed on her tropical vacation with Kelly—a time that had seemed to be the most couple-like experience that Sarah could remember. There had been candlelit dinners and tropical nights; lying together in a hammock beneath the stars; tanning by the ocean, and lovemaking whenever the mood had arisen. Other than that, a host of one-night and office-related trysts with various faces and names swept past in disjointed procession. *Shirt buttons clicking along a boardroom table.*

"Nothing serious," Sarah said. "No strings."

"Smart," Warren nodded. "Mom always told me that was the way to go."

"Sounds like a wise . . ." Sarah had lost track of Warren, so she stopped and turned around. He had stopped walking; was staring at her with a perplexed expression.

"I'd take a bullet for you," Warren said as though trying to explain it to himself. "You know that, right?"

Sarah gave a demure smile, lowering her eyes, then looking back up at Warren. "I know," she said.

Shaking his head in wonder, Warren started walking again. His gait was slow, as was hers: both had their fair share of nagging aches and stiffness to consider. Soon, they walked side by side, coming to a T intersection with the main access road. They turned left and started heading south.

"What's the worst thing you ever did to get ahead at work?" Warren asked.

"A 'head' or ahead?" Sarah quipped. "Because it's not like I ever had to cheat to get a head."

"Shut up: ahead, as in 'advancing'."

Sarah considered for a moment. There had been some positioning battles at CWL when she'd first articled; a few confrontations to be forced, and when power was insufficient for confrontation, she'd used finesse as necessary. She wasn't sure these were conversations she wanted to have, however, so her answer was: "Nothing."

"Nothing," Warren scoffed. "At a law firm. At Conlin, Wilhelm, and Loughren no less. You're telling me you stabbed no knives into any backs?"

"You're talking about deception, dirty tricks," Sarah qualified, "my answer is 'nothing'. I passed the bar at fourteen, articled for a year, then pounded out twenty hour days, seven days a week, and said 'beat that' until I made junior partner. My 'dirty trick' was being better."

Warren grinned, nodding his head in acknowledgement. "That's good. Competitive."

"That's who we are, right? Smarter, stronger, faster. My firm's not even hiring new associates who aren't Program now. Normals can't keep up."

Warren's face was non-committal, but he offered up a "yeah," as though he would take her word as evidence.

"It's good though, right?" Sarah continued. "'Productivity Begins in the Cradle'—all that stuff."

"You believe that?"

"Sure. It's working isn't it? Adding another computer to the office isn't going to make you any more productive . . . people had to change sooner or later."

Warren shrugged. "That's true."

"You know what my dad says?"

"What?"

"'If you're not in the Program, you're deadwood.'"

"I'm getting that your dad's a real sweetheart."

"You have no idea. But he's not wrong."

Warren pursed his lips, rolled out the kinks in his neck. Sarah could tell he was uncomfortable with the conclusions she was drawing, but they were inescapable. Anyone who elected not to undergo some form of personal enhancement was obsolete. And obsolete these days was a death sentence.

After a moment of contemplation, Sarah changed tack again, asking, "You like yourself, Warren?"

That got his attention and respect: a real question. "Most days, yeah. You?"

"Not particularly. But I wouldn't trade lives with anyone else in the world, you know? I wouldn't want to actually be anyone else. Weird, right?"

Warren shook his head, impressed. "You are really honest," he said.

"Yeah," Sarah lied. "I really am."

They rounded a gently sweeping left hand curve in the road and two cars came into view up ahead.

One, a Mercedes sedan, lay off to the right in the foreground. The other, a BMW, was parked on the left hand shoulder in the distance.

Warren had grown quiet, agitated. He stared at the Mercedes as he passed. Sarah followed slowly, her instincts telling her not to intrude. She glanced around but could see no evidence of an altercation in the immediate vicinity.

Eventually, Warren got to the BMW, opened the driver's side door and popped the trunk. He removed his bathrobe and put on a clean white t-shirt. Sarah stood nearby, admiring the sinewy lines of Warren's torso as he dressed.

With a solid, German-engineered "chunk", Warren closed the trunk, hoisted his gym bag, and said, "Hey. I think there's something I have to do."

Sarah searched his face, detecting the nervy apprehension lying just beneath the attempted calm façade. "Want me to come-with?" she ventured.

"Yeah—would you? I think I'd like that."

"Sure."

Warren led the way. He retraced his steps back to the Mercedes, then headed off-road along a footpath leading to a grouping of pines. Sarah followed in his wake, and could make out a clearing amidst the trees ahead.

They heard the buzzing noise before they saw anything. Then they entered the clearing.

Flies covered a corpse lying on its back; magpies took flight at the approach of living humans. Terry's face had been battered beyond recognition, the caved-in crater of his dented sinus cavity encrusted with blood and flies. His mouth was open in rictus, most of the teeth shattered or missing. The birds had taken his eyes and lips. His throat had been torn away; his left ear was missing.

Ashen-faced, Warren staggered away. His shoes and Rolex lay where he had left them. He made it halfway towards his possessions, then doubled over, retching into the dirt.

Sarah drifted closer to Terry, staring in fascination at what might have been. He was a huge figure, thicker and taller than Warren, but Sarah noted the broken left ankle that had undoubtedly hobbled him. *Smart*, she reflected. Warren had made size a non-factor early on. She appreciated the sense of scheme that lay beneath the evident savagery. *Just like an engineer,* she thought.

A whining noise snapped Sarah out of her trance, bringing her attention back to Warren. He had wandered off a ways, then taken a seat in the dirt with his knees up, elbows on his knees, hands in his hair. He couldn't look directly at the corpse, but he couldn't avoid it either. His eyes made furtive, sidelong glances at the body.

Sarah frowned in confusion as Warren closed his eyes. Was he *crying*?

She hardly knew what to do. She approached slowly, cautiously, as one might a large sleeping dog that hasn't been chained up. She knelt onto her heels, placing a tentative hand on Warren's back. The physical ease and familiarity wasn't there now: Sarah had never consoled another human being in her entire life. She rubbed her hand on the man's back as though applying suntan lotion.

She urged herself to say something. "This isn't your fault," she managed.

"Um," Warren muttered, voice thick with emotion. "Yeah, it is. This was one hundred percent me, actually."

"It's coded in, babe. Your DNA killed this guy. You had no choice. None of us did. Survival of the fittest gets me."

Warren swallowed, blinking away tears. Sarah's skin crawled at the sight of them.

"Did you use a weapon?" Sarah asked.

"No, of course not."

"Then you're good here. It's not murder. You're covered under the Program: it's a fitness killing, nothing more."

"Fuck, Sarah. It's not about this being legal."

"Well what, then? Baby, you won. I don't . . ."

Warren emitted a hideous half laugh/half sob, his body shaking.

Sarah resolved to strike him if he started crying again. Instead, Warren said: "I should bury him."

It was too much. Sarah stood up from her crouch, wiping pine needles from her seat, tightly pressed lips betraying her anger.

"You're pissed," Warren said, looking up at Sarah.

"No," Sarah said rigidly. "No."

"I should . . ." Warren began, but Sarah cut him off.

"Yes. Warren, yes, I am pissed."

"Sarah . . ."

"What the fuck? What do you mean you 'should bury him'? Warren? Leave him for the groundskeepers, that's what they're here for!"

"Sarah, listen . . ."

"What the fuck were your parents thinking?"

"What are you talking about?"

"Compassion? Empathy? How the hell could they select that for you? Knowing what you'd have to do one day? How could they be in the Program and not give you everything you'd need to compete?"

"They didn't select it. I mean, they didn't select it *out*; they just left it in."

"Left it in? What, like, they just . . ."

"I'm . . . aside from coding-in the Spawning, there wasn't a whole lot of tinkering in my make-up. My folks didn't check off a lot of boxes. *They* were highly engineered—they figured that would be good enough. They just let nature take its course with me."

Sarah was astonished. "So . . . what are you saying? You're a Normal?"

"Not exactly. Close, I guess. Sure."

"Jesus Christ!"

"Sarah, we're still a matched pair. That's in me, there's no changing that. You're my One. I feel that in my fucking bones. But other than Spawning Response, I guess I'm pretty much random."

"Random! Fuck!"

"Sarah, what's the big . . ."

"The whole point of this is 'species perfection'," Sarah snarled, cheeks hot with growing rage. "They put natural selection back into the process to give us back our teeth; stop people from obsessing over cosmetic details. It's supposed to be engineered solutions, put to the ultimate test. Warren, you killed a man with your bare hands, and now you're crying about taking out the fucking garbage? I don't want that for my kid!"

"I killed a man with my bare hands, Sarah, for you."

Sarah's mouth opened and closed, momentarily out of ammunition. She turned and paced back and forth, seething. "Do what you have to do here."

Warren stood, stepping towards her. "Sarah . . . don't leave like this." He reached for her arms but she brushed his hands away and stepped back.

"Do what you have to do," she repeated, eyes blazing. "Pull yourself together, then come and find me at the cabin. We'll . . . talk."

Warren reached for her one more time, but Sarah wouldn't have it. She turned and left the clearing.

Jesus. Fucking. Christ.

Getting back to the road, Sarah focused with one deep breath, shutting out the noise—those goddamned birds—so she could process.

You want to know who I am? Really?

I'm somebody who lies about her favourite colour—picking the most harmless sounding on reflex. Just in case.

I believe in the Program. I believe in the motto "Better in the Cradle". Otherwise life is just a numbers game.

You Bastard. I believe my body loves yours, my cells love yours. I fucking yearn for you.

And you are broken.

She shook her head.

She retraced her steps back to the lake, her fury cutting the travel time in half. She wanted to hear water breaking on sand. Wanted to see a deeper, darker green than the woods. She wanted to be away from this place, this situation. She crossed her arms against her body as she walked, scowling.

Arriving at the pier, Sarah's shoes thumped against the wooden planks: she found the sound vaguely comforting. Across the lake, she could see the opposing tree line, and the traffic just beyond. To the south, she saw the public water park; heard an outboard motor running in the distance.

"But you won," she muttered aloud to herself. Whatever crippling compassion Warren had been burdened with, it hadn't hurt him on game night. In fact, as she thought clearly about it—the dead man had been a formidable physical presence: his folks had selected strength, maybe sacrificed a little agility to get him strong. Jacob Conlin had been a big man; had probably wanted to cast Terry in his own image. Whatever the case, the experiment had come to a full stop last night.

Sarah loved the lean lines of Warren, the wiry muscles; they had proven themselves in battle, and afterwards. He'd been busted up as they say, but the bigger man hadn't really been all that competitive. Reconstructing the battle in her mind, Sarah could see that Warren had taken his opponent apart—first crippling him with the heel-hook, then systematically going about the kill when the big man was grounded. In the clinch, Warren had had the stones to bite the man's ear off: that was impressive. And overall, the engineering sensibility shone through loud and clear. The precision; the sense of design.

He just couldn't be a dud.

The thought of killing Warren made her physically ill. How easy in theory it had been to plan such an outcome for Terry. It was common for a victor to be so badly wounded that he or she died after the energy-expensive Spawning—so the rationale was already in place. It was a plausible scenario. She had judged her chances of getting away with it as reasonably good, if not guaranteed.

But she had underestimated the neuro-chemical bond. Even knowing that Terry was her father's pawn might not have given Sarah the strength, she realized now. And Warren was a complete innocent. *I'd take a bullet for you,* he'd said.

She was drawn to him. She was made that way. Killing Warren would cost her in ways she couldn't anticipate. All her life, even as a little girl, she had dreamed about her Match, and what it would be like to be with him. To know that you were destined to be with someone—truly destined . . . there were pop songs about the new market-driven unions; books about the new, richer, deeper, scientifically verifiable love. Romance wasn't just a hollow, chivalric ideal anymore: it had sinews; it was flesh and blood. It was real. She wanted to participate in that. And she had: you couldn't just shrug off an experience like the Spawning, no matter how strong you were inside. Warren had made an impact. It warmed her to think of him, even now, when she so desperately needed to hate him.

How the hell had her father done it? Knowing what she knew now about the Spawning Bond, she hated Eric Wheeler more intensely than ever before, but also, she felt a kind of pity she'd never had for him. How it must have hurt him, to commit so totally to the shaping of his daughter that he would separate himself from two wives. Perhaps the bond was stronger in women because of the Quickening; perhaps there were other factors involved. Sarah just didn't know.

A breeze picked up: she raised her face into it, closed her eyes. Water lapped against the supporting posts, lulling her. Looking down, she took in the beautiful blue-green of the lake; could see the underwater vines winding along the poles, growing along the sandy bottom. It was treacherous down there, she remembered.

Squinting, she could see a pale object in the weeds, recognizing it at last as a hand, attached to an arm, attached to a body that lay entangled and hidden from sight. *There you are,* Sarah thought. She'd almost forgotten about her own test, passed with flying colours just the night before Warren's arrival. Polly Walker—good martial artist, bad swimmer. Polly: Sarah thought of Warren's beloved parrots. *Polly want a cracker.*

Sarah stroked her tummy with her right hand, staring down in thought. Warren was a keeper, she realized. And whatever weakness he passed on, would just have to be nurtured out of the child. Whatever was missing, Sarah would teach. It would be all right. She hoped for a tall, sinuous girl, with blonde hair, and dark, lake-green eyes.

She really should have mentioned Dead Polly's whereabouts to the lab techs. They did regular clean-up patrols of course, but this was unfair—they probably hadn't anticipated a drowning. Looking at that pale hand slowly waving from the weeds, Sarah thought of scavenger hunts she'd had as a kid—searching her parent's estate for clues, being so delighted when she'd found the treasures. Polly was like that now: a hidden treasure; a thing to be found. A mystery to be solved.

And suddenly, Sarah *knew*. She felt a sense of flight, a towering sensation, a perspective shift. Though she had come to view her capacity for workload as her primary "gift", this, whatever it was, this *state* was surely part of her unique package. She had experienced it half a dozen times during her career—always during moments of duress, and high-stakes potential payoffs. When this gift kicked in, she felt she could see all the pieces of the machine working and moving together—a level of perception she knew others didn't share.

The world had forgotten about the "rational" interpretation of game theory, focusing instead upon the "evolutionary" aspect. Whenever an adjustment process tended to eliminate less fit choices and competitors, the end result was always a Nash Equilibrium. It was why CEOs didn't have to be geniuses to be effective: the *market* was the genius. The idea of anticipating game outcomes, of strategically trying to *shape* game outcomes, had fallen out of favour. It was why game theory was as relevant to the animal kingdom as it was to the capital markets, because what was important was the adjustment system, not the actors themselves. Sarah had known all this since she was six years old; had been drilled in the mathematics of game theory and probability all her life; had been the daughter of one of the most visionary mathematicians since Nash himself.

But in her heart, she knew it was a lie. Or if not a lie, then not the whole truth. She knew by virtue of her special gift that it was possible to skip ahead in the "game", to perceive all details without conscious control of them, to intuitively make the right moves at the right times, thereby inducing the right counters, which would ultimately result in an equilibrium. An equilibrium shaped and pre-determined by strategy. Sun Tzu's equilibrium.

If you had Sarah's gift, you didn't have to react to market-signals. You could cause them. You could shape the market itself. You could lead it where you wanted it to go.

Any plan needed to be flexible; any planner needed to be adaptable. She saw the game unfold before her like steps in an equation; like a chess match as witnessed via time-lapse photography. There were no guarantees, only preferences, and probabilities. Warren wasn't necessarily a problem; he could be a key component in her next series of moves. If Warren wanted her as much as she wanted him, then he would help her no matter the cost. And if Kelly didn't collapse under pressure, if her father reacted as Sarah was certain he would . . .

Sarah straightened her back, hardened her heart. The tests weren't over, she realized. They were really just beginning.

THERE WAS A multi-purpose tool in the BMW emergency-service kit that contained a collapsible spade-blade. Warren used it to dig a shallow grave for Terry.

The sun was rising, heating up the day, and as the breeze shifted, it brought the smell of violent death to Warren's nostrils. Sweat pooled in the withers of Warren's back as he hacked at the soft, loamy soil of the clearing. Hungry magpies kept watch from the trees, making odd, quorking vocalizations, waiting for the man to finish.

Warren couldn't remember much of it—not in sequence anyway. Terry had been smiling—leering—at the beginning, enjoying himself. He'd thrown Warren off like a man against a boy, laughing at the pathetic takedown attempts. He'd head-butted Warren at one point: that's when Warren thought his nose had been broken. But when Warren had rolled into that heel-hook, everything had changed.

Terry had whimpered—actually sobbing aloud—when his ankle had been popped out. The man had been a juggernaut when whole, but when any part of him had been broken? He had shattered. All Warren could remember was disengaging to circle like a wolf around a still-breathing doe, picking his spots to attack. It had taken a long time—longer than expected—to finish. Terry was a big man; there had been a lot of meat to process. He hadn't offered a lot of meaningful resistance off his back, but the sheer bulk of him had taken some effort to reduce. If he'd had the mental resilience to go with his physical vitality,

Terry certainly would have prevailed.

Warren flashed on his elbow strikes smashing Terry's teeth out of his mouth; the erection Warren had received at the sound of Terry's death rattle. That had been the trigger for mating, Warren realized: the death of the other. Victory had unleashed his full potential, engaging him as a reproductive vessel. Terry's death had been Warren's Quickening.

When the hole had been dug, Warren tried to breathe only through his mouth as he approached the corpse. He stooped to grab at Terry's calves, the left foot dangling obscenely by a few distressed tendons. Panting, Warren backpedaled, pulling hundreds of pounds of beef and bone through the dirt to its final resting place.

With the mission accomplished, Warren took a moment to catch his breath. He sat with his arms around his knees, forcing himself to look at what he had done. What his elbows had done to that face; what his hands had done to that throat. He felt as though he owed at least that much to the dead man: to look honestly and unflinchingly upon the consequences of the actions taken.

Warren didn't know any prayers. "I'm sorry," he muttered at last.

He had told Sarah a bit about his summers working for his dad at the landfills, but he'd kept the conversation light, playing it for comedy. He hadn't told her about everything that got processed at a landfill these days. People bringing dead relatives around in biodegradable body bags, throwing them into the disposal trenches with little or no fanfare. There would be some weeping and standing around, but very little in the way of real ceremony. Those frills cost money, as did burial plots and formal crematoriums. Families would leave after paying the nominal processing fee, and the bodies would be taken to the incinerator. "If they can't pay, do the job anyway," his dad had instructed. If the family had been organized enough to harvest organs in time, they'd usually pay the disposal-fee without question. But nobody liked to take a loss on a corpse.

"We all have to play the game," his father had always said, "but you don't have to like it." That was the thing for Warren. You'd have to be a fool not to be Program these days if you could afford it, but you didn't have to buy into the whole Program world-view. Warren had felt the atavistic hatred welling up inside him for Terry, because hatred triggered adrenaline and performance. You felt hate, because it was a mechanism the body used, to do what it had to do. Now, Warren allowed himself to feel sorrow, guilt, even shame. For Terry, and for himself.

Warren rose, breathing through his mouth once again, and started shoveling dirt onto Terry's rigid frame. *Christ, I wish I could remember*, Warren thought. He felt as though it were his responsibility to act as witness. Without the formal record, Terry had simply come to an abrupt end. He may as well have died in a traffic accident en route.

Sarah's a true believer, Warren realized. Probably not a real choice on her part, if the sketch she'd drawn of her father was at all accurate. But all the hallmarks of the Program acolyte were there. The market-normative sensibility. The lack of belief in intrinsic value. The consumer ethos that might makes right. All of it. He hadn't talked to her about her own test just yet, and though she had seemed somewhat traumatized by it, Warren had little doubt that her reaction to it would be entirely different than his own. She would evaluate the test using the metrics of winning and losing. The death of a human being was an externality, not a material consideration. The market had spoken through Sarah, and for Sarah, that would be the only logical consideration.

What are we going to do? Warren wondered. He couldn't blame Sarah for these emerging difficulties—*he* was the outlier. Most people thought the way she did, Program or no—it was the default sensibility. The hard truth was, she had a right to be angry with him, not the other way around.

There was one other thing that bothered him beyond the philosophical chasm between himself and his One. He had not failed to notice that "Conlin" was the family name of both his Spawning Counterpart *and* the firm for which Sarah worked. True, the Executive Program in Canada was a small world, but *that* small? Then again, if it wasn't a coincidence, what was it? Warren couldn't imagine any significance to the connection, but . . . something about Sarah's demeanor had made him cautious. Maybe even slightly suspicious. When they got together again, they would talk about a great many things, and Warren decided that the "Conlin Question" would be one of the items on the agenda.

Warren heard car doors shut and squinted through the trees. He could just make out the approach of men wearing white coveralls, carrying body bags of the exact same manufacture as used in the landfills owned by his father. *Small world, indeed,* Warren thought.

All warfare is based on deception.

— Sun Tzu

AN ELECTRIC GOLF cart sat parked outside the cabin as Sarah approached. Various tools, bags, and plastic containers were mounted thereon: the stock in trade of janitors everywhere. Sarah strode past the cart, eyes smouldering.

Inside, two maids dressed in rubber gloves, denim shirts, and jeans were hard at work. A large plastic tub containing the bloody sheets of the Spawning Bed sat upon the kitchen floor. One woman was applying air-freshener to the bedroom. The other was wiping down the kitchen counters and smiled as Sarah approached.

"Get out," Sarah seethed, in a voice her co-workers would have recognized. The smiling woman's eyes immediately betrayed her fear: she knew what Sarah was; what she was capable of, and what she'd be entitled to do if "provoked" during this sensitive time. The maids gathered up their things quickly, avoiding eye contact as Sarah stood rooted to one spot, standing still as the cleaning staff scurried to either side of her en route to the exit.

Alone again, Sarah released her breath in a hiss, forcing herself to relax. *Do I really want to do this?* she asked herself. There were alternative paths to be taken—paths of lesser resistance. As lucrative and comfortable as those paths might be, however, they weren't pain or cost-free.

Fuck it, Sarah thought. *Resist. You'll never be stronger or have more leverage. You'll never again have the pieces in place. If you don't fight for your life now, you don't deserve it in the first place.*

Resolved, she took a deep breath, grabbed her laptop off the counter and headed into the bedroom, taking a seat on the bed.

Another deep breath and she opened her laptop, engaged a video-conference screen, and enabled encryption.

"Call: Kelly Lee," Sarah said, noting the tremor in her voice. She steeled herself, killing that tremor in her throat through sheer exercise of will.

In moments, Kelly's smiling face came on-screen. Sarah could just make out the familiar details of Kelly's office in the background.

"Hey blondie," Kelly smiled. "*Ni hao ma?*"

"Can you go to encrypt, please?" Sarah said briskly. Kelly's aspect changed from friendly to cold-blooded in a heartbeat. She rose from her desk to close the office door, then resumed her seat to enable a secure feed.

"Okay," Kelly nodded.

"Program abortions," Sarah said. "What are my options?"

Kelly double-clutched, momentarily speechless. "Jesus," she breathed at last, "everything okay?"

And Sarah broke down.

She covered her mouth as her tears came in a sudden torrent. It wasn't just the stress of the last twenty-four hours, or of the weeks preceding. It wasn't merely the neuro-chemical overdrive, or the issues with Warren, or the fact that she had ended another woman's life. It was all of these things, and all of the events of her life that had led to this moment. She was crossing her own personal Rubicon with this phone call, and the emotions were overwhelming.

"It's okay," Kelly soothed, frowning with concern and confusion.

"I'm sorry," Sarah gasped.

"It's okay, Sarah. Relax. Breathe. Focus. Okay: what?"

Sarah gathered herself, breathing deeply through crying-congested nostrils. "I don't know if I can go through with this," she managed in clipped tones.

"Listen," Kelly said. "Either you go through with this, or it's going to go through you. Just state the case, Sarah."

"My One. He . . . he says he's 'random'. Says his parents just 'let nature take its course' with him."

"And?"

"And for whatever reason, they left his empathy on full fucking auto. And God knows what else. If they didn't touch him, then there's no record of the mods. He says they only coded for reproduction—nothing else—I mean . . . how is that even legal?"

"It shouldn't be, but not making a choice is a choice, right? Long as the parents are unanimous, it's legal."

"Christ. My father . . ."

"Shhhh . . . come on . . ."

"My father will not accept this."

"Let's not even go there yet. What's your One's name?"

"Warren. Warren Milner."

"You're certain he wants to go random on all traits? You need to talk him down from that."

"He's not like us. He doesn't . . . he has a lot of weird ideas about family, the Program, life. He's not exactly a true believer. Maybe that's a good thing—I don't know. I don't think . . . I don't think he's going to come around on this. Not the way Dad wants."

"Maybe he doesn't have to."

"What do you mean?"

"I mean a lot of people don't survive the Spawning. It's very energy expensive . . . internal injuries; head injuries . . . things that take a while to manifest. He could die in his sleep. It happens."

Sarah stared for a moment, registering the none-too-subtle innuendo. "I can't."

"Sarah . . ."

"No, Kelly—you don't understand. Even if I wanted to, the feelings I have for him . . . there's no way."

"Those feelings are encoded responses. You know that."

"They're still real."

"They can be overcome."

"No. They can't."

"It's your child's life on the line. Your father's grandchild . . ."

"Fuck my father, Kelly. It's my decision either way. I have to think about this."

"Sarah, listen to me . . ."

"No, Kelly. Warren won. He passed his test, random or no.

He's earned his say. I should focus on that."

"Look: you know your dad. You do not want to have this conversation with him, Sarah. You need to get Warren onside, or . . ."

"Send me the precedents and a précis on Program abortion, Kelly. Please. I need to know my exposure."

Kelly hesitated on screen, considering her options. Reluctantly, she said: "Okay, I'll pull it together. Just promise me you won't do anything until you've really, really worked this through."

"Thanks, Kel. I mean it. Thank you for everything."

"De nada."

Sarah managed a half-hearted smile, and ended the conference.

She wiped at her eyes, her composure snapping back upon the conclusion of the performance. Like all good manipulations, it had been grounded in fact. She *was* hanging by a thread emotionally. She was confused and distraught over the things that were happening to her. Calling forth the tears had been no problem. The real challenge had been holding them back all this time.

She engaged her home server and checked Kelly's notes on Eric's whereabouts, making a rough estimate on distance and travel time.

He'll be here tomorrow, Sarah calculated. That didn't give her a lot of time to deal with Warren, but it was what it was.

So much for the honeymoon.

KELLY COULDN'T MOVE for a few seconds, could hardly breathe. She got herself together in increments, not rushing. She wanted to be totally composed for her next conversation.

She took her phone from its charger and held it a moment, then punched the hot-mission number for Eric's personal line. His face filled the screen on the first ring, and before she could speak, he hissed: "Shut up. Assemble a team—one masking squad; one escort duty for me. Have it ready to go at the Springbank airport within twenty-four hours. I'll be there as soon as I can."

"You heard."

"I heard the word 'abortion' used twice, yes. The rest of it is a blur."

"She's not rational. I still think I can . . ."

"Kelly. Not to put too fine a point on this, but without that child, there's really no reason for me to continue on. Those are fairly high stakes, wouldn't you agree?"

"Yes sir. What about air-support? I can arrange drone re-assignment from Fort McMurray. We'll just need a little time to . . ."

"What part of twenty-four hours did you not understand? If I wanted this to look like a GCM tactical strike, I wouldn't have called you in the first place. I'll send further mission specs to your phone—just source the assets listed. I need to spank my daughter, Kelly: far as I know, drones can't do that yet. Are you understanding me?"

"Yes, sir."

"Outstanding. And get James for my personal detail. He's good at this kind of thing."

Eric ended the call abruptly, his one good eye blazing with such intensity that Kelly could almost feel heat emanating from her phone.

Sarah had made her choice, had put her life in Kelly's hands.

It's still not too late to betray her, Kelly realized. Just thinking the words made Kelly Lee's hands tremble.

Evolution implies a lack of intention.

— Eric Wheeler

IT WAS EARLY evening when Warren returned to Cabin 4 to find Sarah seated on the swinging porch-chair made for two, a small pot of green tea on the table before her. Robins sang in the trees, out of sight. A light breeze carried the scent of the lake into the cabin's front yard. *What a difference a day makes*, Warren thought as he recalled the first time he'd come upon Sarah sitting in that very same place, under markedly different circumstances.

Their bodies had sung to one another then, and they sang now, drawing Warren forward to the porch steps. From a distance they would have looked like an old married couple the way Warren ascended the stairs with a weary gait, sitting beside Sarah on the swinging chair as though they'd been enjoying late afternoons in the country together their whole lives. He took her right hand in his left and pressed his lips together in chagrin. They sat in silence for long moments, feeling their way forward.

"So," Sarah said at last. "Did you bury him?"

"Yep," Warren nodded. "Then the groundskeepers came, dug him up, and carted him off. You were right. Waste of time."

"What now?"

"I'm going to have a shower, get changed, then I thought I'd take you into town for dinner."

"Okay," Sarah said. "Sounds good."

They put the plan into action. Warren washed the grime of his fruitless labours away, dressing in jeans and a salmon-coloured shirt. Sarah wore blue jeans and a white t-shirt, and somehow managed to look put together. *Doesn't matter what you wear, does it?* Warren thought as he gazed upon her.

They took his car; listened to his music. Paul Simon's "Kodachrome" provided an oddly inappropriate backdrop to the scene as Warren turned onto the access road and headed for the Spawning Grounds' gated checkpoint. Leaves from the overhanging boughs reflected upon the black hood and tinted glass of the BMW, flowing across the surface of the car as though drifting down a river.

Sarah turned her head to look out the window. She wasn't speaking.

Warren stopped analyzing and simply sat next to her, letting his body sense hers. He felt her anger, but it had abated from the white hot fury it had been. It was anger fueled by frustration and resentment, which was understandable. Warren sensed that she was oddly hurt by what had happened, possibly mistaking his actions as an indictment of her own inaction. He sensed her confusion, and her profound unease at being confused in the first place. And there was something else, an anxiety, or else a rigidity of control that bespoke the suppression of anxiety. This last vibe Warren couldn't put his finger on, but by the end of the night, he hoped to have a handle on it.

They wouldn't be able to simply fight this out, Warren realized. There was too much subtext, too much subtlety. Too much at stake.

How many second nights go this way? Warren wondered. The wild, unrestrained ardor of the mating night leading to a mess of unresolved, unarticulated feelings the next day. *My fault*, he realized. He had cried taking out the garbage just like she'd said, and it wasn't the first time either.

"Kodachrome" bled into "Sounds of Silence" and "I am a Rock" as the car swept around the north shore of Sylvan Lake. "Homeward Bound" passed without comment, but when "Bridge Over Troubled Waters" played, Sarah finally looked over and said: "Seriously?"

Warren smiled. It was something.

By the time they'd made the Hotel Eden parking lot, "Here Comes the Sun" was playing, and Warren wondered whether Sarah would wait until the car stopped moving to get out.

They walked through the small marina of sailing vessels and

motorboats to the restaurant's outdoor access. The place was nautically themed, with a large bay window overlooking the lake and the water slide off to the left. It was early for dinner, and early in the season, so the restaurant was largely empty. A friendly young hostess guided Warren and Sarah to a table at the window and took their drink orders.

Warren watched Sarah take inventory of the fellow patrons. A family of four treating their youngest to a birthday dinner. An elderly couple sharing a plate of fish and chips. Two girlfriends occupying a booth across the room, their laughter and gossip audible nonetheless.

Warren shook his head, giving a rueful smile.

"What?" Sarah said.

"Your contempt is showing."

The server brought their drinks: scotch for Warren; Perrier for Sarah. Their eyes locked throughout the interruption.

"My contempt is being provoked," Sarah said.

"Doesn't take much."

"This how it's going to be, then?"

Warren hesitated, then went all in. "When you get right down to it, you're not a very nice person, are you?"

"No," Sarah said without hesitation. "I'm not."

"Christ, Sarah. Are you *trying* to push me away?"

"No!" The girls across the room briefly turned their heads to look: Sarah lowered her voice. "No. I want you to *know* me. We're too close to be strangers. I can't handle the disconnect, Warren. I can't."

"I know," Warren nodded. "You're right. I see that you're right, it's just . . ."

"It's just that you can't stand me."

There, for just the briefest of moments in those otherwise opaque, reflective eyes, Sarah betrayed her hurt. *She's letting me see her*, Warren thought. *Don't fuck this up.*

"You're pretty hard-core, Sarah," Warren said, offering the trace of a smile with the assessment. "I'm just going to need some time to get used to your ways."

"We'll have the time," Sarah said. "I'll show you who I am, but . . . you're not going to like all of it. Chances are, you're never going to want me to have Christmas dinner with your family. Your siblings. That might never change."

"You're honest as hell, I'll give you that."

"Sometimes I am. Sometimes I just say pink's my favourite colour because it sounds the most harmless. You said you would be drawn to me no matter what—even if you weren't my One. That's just not so, Warren."

Warren nodded. When you're right, you're right.

"I have cheated at work," Sarah continued, admitting wrongdoing without apologizing. "I've stabbed backs. And my dad . . . you just have no concept of the kinds of things he's done. We've done. I can't say that I've always acted independently of his interests."

"How can I judge you now?" Warren asked. "You saw my counterpart. What I did to him. My hands are definitely no cleaner than yours."

Sarah was about to answer when the waitress made a tentative approach. They took a moment to sort out their orders, then regrouped when the server left.

A sailboat with a striking, rainbow coloured sail drifted out of harbour as Sarah and Warren collected their thoughts. Finally, eyes staring at her plate, Sarah said: "I can't just leave things to random chance with my child."

"Our child," Warren corrected.

"Absolutely: our child. I can't. I wasn't raised that way. Wasn't built that way."

Warren reached across the table to take Sarah's left hand in his right. An effortless gesture with all the smooth execution of habit, as though he'd been taking her hand for years.

"You lack faith," Warren said, not unkindly.

"I've got faith. In myself. In the Program. We make choices, and we put those choices to the test. We don't just throw our hands up and hope for the best."

"But aren't you just throwing your hands up and saying 'this is the way it is—there's nothing we can do?' Yeah, we're in the game, but we don't have to play by the Program's rules. We can be more than that, Sarah."

She looked away again, suddenly demure. Warren frowned. *There it is again*, he thought. *What is it, Sarah. What are you hiding?*

He continued on as gently as he could. "I don't like you much yet. I don't know your mind yet. But I love you with everything

I've got—everything I am. You have to know that."

She looked up again, searching his eyes with her own. "Yes," she confirmed. "Yes, of course I do. I feel the same way."

"Okay then. That's our starting point. That's where we come back to, whenever we get lost. We can't feel this way, and not trust one another."

"I know."

"I know what I'm doing, Sarah. I won. Trust in that. Put your faith in that. I got tested, and I passed. Whatever we were before—separately—maybe we can be something new together now. Don't you feel like that? Don't you feel like this is a new beginning?"

Sarah's arctic blue eyes wavered, her mesmeric stare faltering, once again allowing Warren accidental access to the girl behind the gaze.

He sensed that background emotion she'd been concealing, seeing it more clearly than he had before. He recognized it, though the better resolution hardly translated into better comprehension on his part. It wasn't anxiety exactly, or nervousness alone. It was the heightened form of those emotions; the primal driver itself.

Fear.

THE SPRINGBANK AIRSTRIP lay to the west of Calgary and served as a heliport as well as a hub for small-plane agricultural and recreational users. It wasn't designed to take jets on its short runways, but Kelly knew the Immanov Command jet wouldn't have any problems. Commercial lines housed military engines and an overbuilt undercarriage: the plane was engineered to make use of airstrips a lot smaller and more primitive than Springbank. Landing here would circumvent a lot of paperwork that couldn't be avoided at Calgary international, and Eric hadn't left much margin for bullshit on his spec-sheet.

As the plane taxied towards the designated hangar, Kelly took stock of the assets she'd pulled together. Two black, four-wheel drive Mercedes SUVs: check. Eric had personally routed in two GCM shooters from Seattle: Kelly had collected them and briefed them on the mission particulars. Weapons and ammunition had come with the vehicles: Kelly had assigned guns appropriate to the various tasks, though everyone would have special Sig Sauer 9s coded to their own palm-print.

The most difficult procurement had been a bottle of forty-year-old McCallan's Special. Fortunately, Calgary was one of the world's most avid scotch-drinking communities, sporting a number of specialist shops that catered to rarified tastes. *Twenty thousand dollars for a bottle of scotch*, Kelly mused. *Must be nice.*

James had arrived via helicopter from his home in nearby Cochrane. In his fifties now, and retired, the man still carried himself like the US Special Forces operative he'd once been. Close-cropped salt and pepper hair framed a tanned, raw-boned face. Every now and again, the corner of his mouth would spasm—a telltale sign that he'd been a juicer during his active career. He would have had to have been, Kelly reflected, to work alongside Eric all those years.

The small task-force waited by the cars as the plane came to a halt and powered down. In moments, the door opened and the automatic gangway descended. Kelly repressed the urge to snarl as Eric's pet cobra Miguel exited first—leering grin set upon his thirteen-year-old face. Another of Eric's electronics command group appeared behind the boy—a dark-featured girl Kelly didn't recognize. Eric himself came last, dressed in a dark suit and long trench coat. The three approached at a brisk pace, Eric overtaking and passing the other two en route.

"Ms. Lee," Eric nodded, then extended his hand and said: "James. Thanks for coming on such short notice."

"Happy to oblige, Eric."

Kelly noted the ease with which the soldier interacted with the old man. She couldn't help but be envious. Then she noticed Miguel smirking up at her and pursed her lips in silent irritation.

"All right," Eric said, checking his phone, "it's 19:30. I've got a little personal business to conclude before we head out, and then I need three hours sleep. Travel time to Spawning Ground Sylvan, Kelly?"

"Two hours."

"Good. We'll leave at oh-three-thirty hours, and arrive for breakfast. Holding pattern here until I get back. James, how'd you like to drive me across town?"

"My pleasure, sir."

"Kelly, where's my scotch?"

Kelly pointed at the appropriate SUV.

"Let's go," Eric concluded.

Eric and James got into the Mercedes and pulled out of the hangar. Miguel took out his phone and immediately started playing a game that involved shooting other people who were also playing on their phones. The others all fell into practiced time-killing routines: they'd relax, while maintaining their alertness. It wasn't a terribly dangerous mission by strike-squad standards, but it was a mission being led in person by Eric Wheeler. Mistakes of concentration were to be avoided at all costs.

Kelly forced her face to look bored, while inside, she willed herself not to throw up from the tension.

You think that because no one intends the market, that market-forces aren't a form of coercion? You think that by spreading absolute power out amongst consumers, that it doesn't corrupt absolutely? Fuck. You. All.
— Caleb McWhirter, defendant's statement at trial, Murder in the first degree/terrorism charges

THEY ATE LIKE famished ranch hands after a hard day of mending fences and branding cattle. Soft whole wheat dinner rolls devoured before the salad course; full pear-and-gorgonzola dinner salads, with a cream-of-leek soup. Sarah had the salmon fillet, but it wasn't enough, helping herself to half of Warren's prime-rib, which led to side orders of pasta for both. For dessert, they shared a large plate of rich cheeses and fruits, and could have gone in for the frozen nougat as well, but were beginning to be a little self-conscious at the consumption. Though the Spawning Bond had been consummated, it was clear that their respective metabolisms were still revving on "high".

Warren felt Sarah gradually uncoil throughout the meal. She was still guarded, but she was relaxing, even offering up the odd half smile. They weren't going to solve their differences tonight, but they could establish good-faith negotiations for the future. Warren felt as though a series of strong starts had been made, and allowed himself to be encouraged by the progress.

Sarah had even brought up Polly for the first time, calling her the "Noir Vodka Girl". After describing some of Polly's ad campaigns and game-show appearances, Warren nodded: "Right. I've seen her. Gorgeous." That got a look from Sarah, but also the trace of a grin. They were finding a way to account for the dead counterparts in their lives. It would be an ongoing process.

Warren didn't bring up Terry's name just then. He wanted to, but he was enjoying the thaw. And he could still sense that Sarah was spooked by something, didn't want her to get any more distant. Now that Polly was on the table, there would be a natural segue available, and a better time to talk about Conlin.

As night descended on the Sylvan Lake hills, the marina lights came on, casting a warm yellow glow around the hotel. The restaurant lights dimmed, and candles were brought around to all the tables. Sarah sipped at her espresso and smiled as Warren stared at her with heartbreaking longing in his eyes.

"I just can't get used to the sight of you," he whispered, seeing her as though for the first time, yet again.

JACOB CONLIN WAS a bear of a man, but he seemed shrunken within his own skin. Standing at the great double-doors to his mansion beneath an impressive sandstone arch, his red-rimmed, haunted eyes seemed to be receding into his skull. His broad-shouldered back seemed bowed beneath the invisible weight of his grief.

"Eric," Jacob acknowledged. "Thanks for coming."

Eric held up twenty thousand dollars' worth of scotch and said: "Let's drink this piss."

Jacob led Eric through a gigantic maze of rooms and hallways. Completed just two years previously, the house was thousands of square feet of prime real estate, set in the finest fortified gate-community in Southern Alberta. It contained a full spa complex and indoor pool. It contained a grand staircase that would've been at home on the Titanic. Hardwood floors shone like polished metal; Italian crystal chandeliers cast a brilliant, brittle light. There was a ball room for entertaining; a games room for gaming; turrets and secondary staircases and alcoves full of architectural whimsy. It all seemed like too much house now, for this shrunken man. Ghostlike, he led Eric to the Victorian study, and closed the live oak doors behind them.

Eric proceeded to the bar, bringing up a pair of tumblers and pouring them each an inch of amber heaven. Jacob had gone to the window, staring down into the large man-made pond that was communal property. In the winter, it became a skating rink, and hot chocolate parties were held in the large, octagon-shaped gazebo on the far side. The gazebo was lit with tiny white lights up and down its eight supporting shafts and all across the roof. The pinpoints of light reflected in the still, dark water like stars as the sun began to drop behind the Rockies in the west.

Eric set Jacob's drink down before his padded leather chair behind his massive desk. Eric took the seat opposite, folding his trench coat over the back and crossing his legs as he sat. He sipped his drink and waited, feeling the smooth bite of the rare liquor grace his throat.

To Eric, Jacob Conlin was an asset first and foremost, but that didn't preclude him from being a friend. It was a kind of affection that Eric could switch on or off, run hot or cold, in a broad fast stream, or in a dripping trickle. It was the nature of all friendships these days, Eric reflected: a purchased friend was still a friend of a kind. And the two men now shared a bond that went beyond business. They'd both lost children to the Spawning, and it was as hard a fate as a genetically-engineered man could have.

After a while, Jacob took his seat. He reached for the glass and appreciated the heady aroma before downing the drink at a bolt. Eric smiled, leaning across to refill the man's tumbler, then took another sip of his own portion.

"How'd you do it?" Jacob shook his head. "How'd you get past it?"

Eric pursed his lips in thought. "I never did," he said at last. "I think of my Sam every day. Your own genes won't let you forget it. It's the first thing you think of when you wake up, each and every morning."

"Count on you to sugar-coat it for me." Jacob gave a wan smile.

"Sugar won't cover some things. This is one of them."

"I should've listened to you. With Terry."

"Don't. End of the day, it's up to them. They win or they lose on their own."

"No. Should have listened. You had the right of it, Eric. You told me how I should have optimized him, and I thought I knew better."

"The kid was a machine, Jake. He was all but a lock to come

through. You couldn't have hoped for better."

Jacob finished his drink, started his third. "How's Sarah?" he asked at last.

"She came through. Says she's okay—no permanent injuries. Clean win."

"Good for her. Goddamnit, good for you, too. I woulda hated to see you lose a second. That woulda been just too fuckin' much."

They shared a silence then, each man thinking of his own losses. Finally, Jacob asked: "What do you know about the . . . you know. The other kid."

"Not much," Eric said, blaming himself for the oversight. Warren hadn't modeled well because he hadn't been engineered properly. The diagnostics had assigned him attributes based on standard distribution, but in the event, obviously there had been some statistical divergence from the Bell curve and the real one. Not that it would matter. In a few hours, Eric himself would put an end to the experiment that was Warren Milner.

"It's funny," Jacob looked up with a puzzled expression. "I don't hate the son of a bitch as much as I thought I would."

"Wouldn't do you any good if you did," Eric said, speaking from experience. "Hate just adds to your load."

Jacob nodded, spilling a couple hundred dollars' worth of scotch into his tumbler. "You're the right guy for this, Eric. I'm fuckin' glad you came."

"Wish like hell we were celebrating," Eric said honestly. He would have come either way.

"Well," Jacob exhaled, opening a desk drawer and withdrawing a large manila envelope fastened by a red drawstring. "There's still something to celebrate I suppose." He slid the envelope across the table to Eric. "Sarah's partnership papers. Her name'll be on the masthead—end of the week."

"Thank you, Jacob."

"Worked out well. I'm gonna be stepping away for a while— take Liz to the Bahamas or something. Ship's in great fuckin' hands with Sarah."

That much was true. Deal-flow was going to be non-stop for the next several years, and the firm needed to execute. If Jacob couldn't perform, it was better that he not be there. As for Sarah . . . Eric was confident that after being reminded of her priorities, Sarah would be the ideal person on the legal front. She was rattled and hormonal right now, but she'd get back in line once things had been clarified for her.

Abortion, Eric thought, his blood simmering. The fuck could she be thinking? Terry Conlin had died in the making of that child, not to mention all else riding on the offspring. It was more than insulting and short-sighted, it was disrespectful. How could she expect to return to CWL if she aborted, with Jacob Conlin sitting there, wondering why his kid had been used up? Stupid, selfish, and if he knew his Sarah, spiteful as well.

Enjoy the night, Eric thought grimly. *Love him while you've got him, because those memories are going to have to last a lifetime.*

Eric poured them both another round. He drank to Terry, while mulling over the very best way to have him replaced in the command-chain.

THE DRIVE HOME was quiet, but more comfortable than the ride out had been. Instead of looking out the side-window, Sarah turned her head to gaze upon Warren as he drove. Warren felt her attention upon him like a physical weight, and reveled in it.

They made love back at the cabin without preamble: both had felt it coming. Warren built a fire in the hearth while Sarah brought out blankets from the bedroom. The low-slung couch facing the fireplace was perfect for the occasion—almost as though it had been designed to accommodate lovers by firelight.

And this time, it *was* lovemaking, not the angry, adrenaline fueled reproductive response of the Spawn. What it lacked in intensity, it made up for with tenderness. It hurt Sarah to bear the weight of Warren upon her bruised ribs, so he rolled in underneath her instead. Such consideration would have been impossible during the Spawn, and in fact, the pain would have acted as a spur to performance. It was a completely different act altogether, despite the superficial resemblance.

Sarah's mouth kissed at the scars she had left upon Warren's collarbone the night before, and pulled gently at his cock to bring him around. Arousal, though not as rapid or as volcanic as it had been under the Spawning, was just as constant. The touch of Sarah's body had a galvanic effect upon Warren, bringing him around again and again. And Warren's slow, rhythmic writhing played Sarah perfectly, effortlessly. There was no need to give instruction, no negotiations required. Their bodies knew instinctively just what to do.

Eventually, sated, they lay together bathed in the flickering glow of orange embers, Warren glorying in the weight of Sarah upon his body; Sarah lying with her left cheek on Warren's chest, staring at the fire as she listened to his heart. Warren stroked at Sarah's damp blonde hair, marveling at the softness of it.

"I hate that she hurt you," Warren murmured. Sarah felt him stirring beneath, aroused by the mere thought of extinguished Polly. Competition informed everything they did, everything they were. The dead counterparts would be with Sarah and Warren forever, the memory of the dual conquests a visceral signal of their own supremacy, manifesting in sexual behaviour. It was the new kink of the twenty-first Century: a fetish that could not have existed before the Program.

"No," Sarah whispered. "You would have liked her. She was very . . . direct." *And she was better than me*, Sarah didn't say. In many ways, she knew that Warren would have been better off with Polly. The realization hurt Sarah more than anything else Polly had done to her.

"Mine was an asshole," Warren grumbled. "You'd have hated him."

Sarah felt herself tighten involuntarily, knowing that it was too late to disguise her reaction. She took a deep breath and said: "Ask me."

"Excuse me?"

"You know you've been wanting to ask me about your counterpart. Ask me."

Warren swallowed. "My counterpart's name was Conlin. Terry Conlin. He was out of New York, but . . ."

"His father is senior partner at my firm. Jacob Conlin."

"Sarah . . . what's going on, exactly? I mean, *is* there something going on?"

Sarah propped her chin on Warren's chest so that she could look into his face. Such a handsome, friendly, but strong face. Wide, guile-less eyes. Sarah hoped that this wasn't the happiest either one of them would ever be again.

"We'd better get dressed, Warren. We need to talk."

IN TWENTY MINUTES they had each showered and dressed themselves. Warren had made a pot of strong coffee and was bringing himself up to full alertness when Sarah joined him at the kitchen table. She placed her closed laptop on the table top, and took a seat, gratefully accepting a cup of coffee.

"I'm not going to like this, am I?" Warren said, making it more statement than question.

"I don't see how you could."

"Did you know him?"

"Who? Terry? Not as such. I knew of him."

"Well, how . . . I mean, how could . . . was he actually deliberately *chosen* as my counterpart?"

"We all were. The whole four. Somehow my father got Terry coded in with you. Polly and I were a legit combination because he wanted me properly tested. You weren't supposed to survive your test."

"How the hell does that even happen? And why would your father be involved?"

"My dad makes things happen. That's what he does. You fucked up his models by winning."

"I'm guessing he hates when that happens."

"I was supposed to be with Terry. Terry would head up Global Con's new financial division for North America; I would be senior partner at CWL; Terry's dad would get a shitload of revenue from the projects I'd bring in from my dad's initiatives . . . you get the picture. We were all nodes on a high-level network my dad was building."

"Jesus Christ."

"There's more. My dad wants our child."

"You mean yours and Terry's child—the child you would have had."

"My child. His direct genetic legacy. He wants to make the optimizations, control the upbringing. That's the child he wants."

"Well, fuck him. My family doesn't have Global Con pockets, but we're not totally without resources. He wants to fight us, we'll see him in court. Plus, my wife's the new senior partner at a hot-shot law firm. I'll take those odds."

"You're not getting it," Sarah said, putting down her coffee and fixing Warren with her washed-out gaze. "My dad . . . he's got a vision for how things are supposed to go. He sees the shape of the world he wants, and he's making it so. It's not all just him, of course—he's in a race with other heavy-hitters and companies all over the world, but he's definitely special. He was the first to precisely quantify what the internet was doing to business—to countries and cultures. He got how boundaries of all kinds were breaking down, how things were freeing up. He didn't create the trends, but he saw them more clearly than most—created models to describe and predict them.

"Decades ago, he bought out the special forces from the US government and took them private. Leased nukes for corporate use. He worked for years to negotiate global labour contracts and revamp old free-trade pacts—taking all the 'friction' out of the system. No citizenship boundaries, no obstacles to prevent people from going wherever the market tells them the jobs are. Massive, transformative labour migration—basically the break-up and export of the American middle class. And once the middle class is gone—once North America's essentially a head-office jurisdiction—you can go ahead and dismantle the state. Get rid of taxes and all the public infrastructure supported by taxes; go to perfect privatization. At every step of the transformation, there's money to be made, and my dad's at the head of that curve.

"End of the day, you'll have a North America populated by the best, most productive Program graduates, living in an environmentally green, crime free, smart-wired paradise. No citizens, just networked consumers—rational market participants whose decisions will conform exactly to my dad's models. The internet replaces the state, and firms like Global Conflict Management provide for our collective defense. They're the new military of the free market, my dad's the director, and his algorithms will not just accurately predict trends, they'll shape them. Are you getting this, Warren? Are you starting to see who my father is now?"

Warren blinked in astonishment.

Sarah continued on. "Thing is, he can't do it all himself. He's done a lot, but he's sixty-some years old, living on amphetamines and six hours sleep a week . . . he's running out of gas. He needs me and CWL handling the corporate business. And he needs my child to see his plans through. And that child has to be a particular kind of person to pull it all off. Do you see? You see why this isn't going to court? My dad doesn't go to court. He's not going to let anything happen to our child, that he doesn't want to have happen. So we need to get ready."

"Ready?" Warren frowned. "What do you mean?"

"He's coming." Sarah paused for effect. "He's coming, and he doesn't need you."

Warren let her words hang in the air for a moment, then: "What about you," he said. "Do you need me?"

Sarah was caught short. She knew what he was asking. "If I were planning to do things his way, you'd be dead already," she said simply. "I'm choosing you."

Warren stared into Sarah's crystalline eyes—stared so long that eventually she had to ask: "What?"

"Trying to decide if you're choosing me, or if you just need an accomplice."

Sarah held his gaze with her own, pouring all her considerable willpower into the exchange. "I love you," she said, in a voice that would brook no argument. "I need you. And I'm sorry."

Just then, Sarah's laptop began to chime, ringing loudly until she opened the cover to disengage the warning signal. "They've just left Calgary now," Sarah said as she typed. In moments, the schematics of the terrain around cabin number 4 came up.

"If you're with me, then this is what we need to do," Sarah said.

Borders don't count for much, or stop much, good or bad, anymore.

— Bill Clinton

IN THE SILVER-grey gloom of early morning, Will Bennett sat in the guardhouse overlooking the access road to the Spawning Ground, watching porn on his personal tablet. The air was cool and dew-scented; the high-low call of starlings in the trees sang throughout the forest, each echoing the others. A low ground-fog receded off the road into the trees, lingering gas-like in the underbrush.

Nubile Asian women fornicated and beat one another to no apparent purpose on Will's screen. Will was not particularly aroused, though his appetite for the stuff was insatiable. He liked 'em little and brown and wriggling, and would gravitate to Malaysian porn channels in preference to most other alternatives during his down time. And the job was *mostly* down-time—hell, it was ALL down-time. Midnight 'til noon and he wasn't even halfway home.

The couple in Cabin 4 were settling in, and although he'd heard about the woman from the day-guy, he hadn't seen her with his own eyes. "Ice queen," Milt had called her, comparing her patrician blonde looks to some actress on a show Will had never seen. Milty'd been pretty impressed. Even when he labeled the woman a "stone bitch", it was with a kind of lustful reverence.

Will got that the Program chicks were hot—they were—but he could never quite get into them. Even the one he'd passed-through to the clinic a little while ago—a striking, bright-blue eyed brunette—Will just didn't see the attraction. If anything, he was always slightly repelled by these women. Their cold-eyed stares and shitty manners. Like he needed to be reminded they were out of his league.

Movement in Will's peripheral vision made him look up from a spanking to see a dark-featured girl standing in the road in front of the guardhouse. The sudden shock made Will flinch towards his sidearm, but he relaxed immediately. She was a slender thing—not Asian, but in the ballpark physically—the same black hair and exotic eyes. The girl smiled, and Will smiled back. This was . . .

THE BRAINS OF Will Bennett splattered against the bulletproof glass of the guardhouse as the 9mm slug punched a gaping hole in his forehead via the entry wound in the back of his skull. Bawling Asian girls tumbled to the floor as Will's lifeless hand spasmed and his bowels released. He slumped forward onto the desk, his long shift brought to an abrupt end.

Miguel grinned. Blue smoke curled up from the cruel barrel of the Luger parabellum—a gift from Eric for Miguel's eleventh birthday. It was a collector's item, an actual World War Two weapon whose provenance could be traced to Eastern-front Einsatzgruppen and the concentration camp at Riga. It was a gun that had delivered many a kill-shot in its long and distinguished career.

The parabellum was an expensive gift to give a child, but well worth it from Eric's point of view. Miguel killed exactly as directed, without compunction or hesitation. He killed all targets with equal enthusiasm: women, children, pets. There were no non-combatants for Miguel, nothing outside the game. No "externalities", as Eric would call them. And alone of Eric's subordinates, Miguel killed with great affection—even reverence—for his boss. The Luger was a symbol of their bond, and Miguel cherished it, taking care of it exactly as Eric had taught him.

Miguel waved to Ana through the pane of brains and glass, and she relayed the signal down the road. Pushing the corpse of Will Bennett out of sight, Miguel operated the gate-switches, opening the roads to both the StandardGen facility and the Spawning Ground proper. Mission accomplished, Miguel left the guardhouse, leaving Will face down in his own gore.

"This was supposed to be much less complicated," Eric mused as the command SUV moved forward into the Spawning Ground. It was James driving, Teller riding shotgun, Wallace amidships, and Eric and Kelly in the back seat. "Fucking fat-tails."

Eric popped an amphetamine from a small silver box, offering the pills to Kelly, who declined. He had dozed on the trip to Sylvan, aided by a drowse-inducer, but he was rousing quickly to full alertness, and, as Kelly could tell, he was still angry. The single blue eye began to blaze with the same smouldering intensity as it had earlier, shedding the glassiness of drugged sleep with the sheer force of Eric's will.

"Simple, clear instructions," Eric went on. "Should have known her passive-aggressive shit would get in the way. Are you all right, Kelly?"

Kelly almost came to attention in her seat, feeling her body tense. "I'm fine," she said.

"You look nervous," Eric smiled, eye staring.

"It's the first time I'm confronting Sarah as your . . . in my official capacity. As it were."

Eric nodded. "Guess so. Of course, way this is going, this is working out well for you two."

"I suppose so. Hadn't thought about it in those terms, actually."

"No reason not to continue on." Eric shrugged. "Keep an open mind. She may actually reach out to you, once this is over."

"Yes. Perhaps."

The car wound its way along the sinuous track of the access road, finally slowing, then turning left onto the trunk road towards Cabin 4. Approaching the small parking area, Eric noted Sarah's Porsche and Warren's BMW. "This is far enough," Eric said, reaching into his coat to withdraw his Sig Sauer 9. Eric engaged the internal sound-suppressors built into the gun as the other members of his strike team did the same. Kelly took out her phone and brought up the tactical map of the cabin.

"No back or side doors," Kelly said. "Entrance at the front, facing away from us. Bedroom on the right side as we approach."

"Shall we?" Eric said, smiling as he opened the door. Kelly's blood curdled at the sight of that smile, wondering what gesture the man would make if he were happy. Then she shuddered to think that perhaps he was.

MORRISEY WENT ROUND to the back of the clinic, using the service entrance and killing the bay attendant with a single shot between the eyes. Securing the area, Morrisey held up, his tactical glass covering his right eye as he waited for the signal to continue.

While Morrisey had been making his approach to the rear, the sliding doors of the clinic's main entrance whispered open and Ana walked through, carrying a silver Halliburton. A single patron sat near the door, far away from the reception desk. It was early yet, and though the clinic operated round the clock, full staffing wouldn't occur for a few more hours.

The client awaiting her Quickening treatment read news from a tablet, ignoring the Spanish girl with the suitcase as Ana took a seat nearby. The Spawning Candidate—a striking figure with midnight-black hair and startling blue eyes set in a high-cheekboned face—continued to ignore the girl as Ana set the suitcase upon a low, glass-topped table, opened it, and began to manipulate the contents. It was only when the news-feed on the candidate's tablet cut out, rendering the screen a glowing, static blue, that the woman reacted at all. Frowning, she hit her tablet against the side of her hand, muttering, "What the hell?"

The Spawning Candidate, a sports-agent with Temple-Hall Assoc., never heard Miguel's approach, and although she sensed his presence in her peripheral vision, he had already pulled the trigger by that time. Shot in her right ear, the woman's blood and brains—expensive, carefully selected blood and brains; the blood and brains of a champion, born to create champions—splashed onto the wall behind her as she slumped into an awkward, sprawling pose in her chair.

Miguel grinned at the upcoming challenge. With a good forty feet to cover, he raised his silenced weapon as the receptionist lifted her head and took a moment to process the scene. As her eyes widened with understanding, Miguel placed his shot, the 9mm slug catching the woman on the left side of the throat, throwing her into shock even as it spun her in her chair and sent her gagging to the floor. Miguel smiled: he was three for three so far.

As Miguel approached reception—stepping around the expanding pool of blood from the alive-and-dying receptionist—Clarke stayed in the parking lot, awaiting any unwanted guests. New arrivals or additional staff weren't anticipated for a few more hours, but there hadn't been time for a full tactical plan, so a safety-trigger seemed prudent. Ana's jamming equipment prevented any monitoring or communications electronics from functioning, save for the strike-team's own band-signatures, effectively sealing off the clinic from the outside world. With the parking lot covered, the team was free to process the remaining liquidations.

Miguel took the receptionist's seat, ignoring the wet, gurgling noises the woman was making on the floor, and turned his attention to the clinic's computer system. Moving from a general admissions screen to an employee management program, he quickly identified and located the few technicians, nurses, single doctor, and janitor on-station at the moment, and relayed their coordinates to Morrisey's heads-up-display.

Targets thus acquired, Morrisey left the service area, killing the janitor en route to the elevator with two shots centre-mass.

"Are you good?" Miguel inquired of Ana. "I'm off to see security."

"I'm good. Go."

Miguel rose from his seat, and without looking down, he shot the dying nurse in the back as he passed her by. It was cool, not looking down—Miguel was intensely aware of the killing being exactly like those he'd seen in American movies. The same casual, disdainful efficiency that always got a chortle of amusement from the audience.

The brass shell casing of the expended slug rang against the linoleum floor, and the sound also reminded Miguel of the movies he'd seen, games he'd played. It was the sound of authenticity.

While Miguel made his exit, Ana shook a can of neon green spray paint while casting a speculative look at the dead Spawning Candidate. Ana couldn't help but feel the irony: children of slaves killing the children of the Gods? Wasn't that what the Program People were? Surely they were no longer merely human in the truest sense of the term. They had left the ape behind, and were ascending to be something else, somewhere else.

Ana proceeded to spray green paint on the off-white wall, making sure she trailed the stream through the blood and across the dead woman's face. "DIE PROGRAM FREAKS!!!" Ana wrote in large, unsubtle letters. She worked methodically, taking no particular pleasure in the desecration. The vandalism was more for the media than it was for any security service that came. Global Con would work through back-channels to make sure only the most cursory of investigations took place. No one, for instance, would trace Miguel's shell casings, or think to order expensive forensics on-scene. As Ana understood it, Global Con could operate domestically as long as it didn't embarrass the government. The false-flag operation would be enough of a cover story to satisfy all interested parties.

A child of slaves. Ana stared at the corpse as she stepped back from the tagging, thrilled at the *wrongness* of the scene. *People like me and Miguel,* Ana thought, *we shouldn't even touch people like you.* Slavery in South America wasn't like the "voluntary" slavery used to get around the 13th Amendment in the US. In South America, you could be born into slavery; unwanted children could be sold into it; you could fall into it through debt. There was still some stigma attached to the practice—not enough to stop it of course—but enough to keep it a relatively uncommon, though growing, industry.

It was almost as though people had lost the language they needed to protest the act. Certainly this was the case for Ana, who understood all people—even Program People—to be commodities of one kind or another, some more valuable than others. After that, why be delicate about the notion of slavery? She had the same hardened sensibilities as the world around her, and although she had hated her time as a domestic asset, she had never truly questioned or protested it.

She was grateful to Eric for his purchase, for the purpose he had given her. For the power he had bestowed upon her. In that she was similar enough to Miguel, for both of them would execute any instruction from Eric without hesitation, out of sheer, profound gratitude alone. But whereas Miguel reveled in the killing, and longed to do it, Ana never rejoiced at the sight of blood. *It was you, or it was me,* she thought as she stared at the paint obscuring the dead woman's features. It was the way of the world.

Ana replaced the spray can in the Halliburton and headed to the reception desk. She hardened herself at the sight of the dead nurse and realized that Miguel had deliberately bled the woman a bit with that neck-shot before finishing her. It was repulsive, and yet . . . as hard as Ana's life had been before Eric, she knew it was nothing compared to the misery of Miguel's. A party in comparison; pig-tails and puppy dogs. People might hate the boy, Ana reflected, but they should never judge him. It takes a village to raise a psychopath.

She set herself to monitoring the surviving employee-blips, and ignored the coppery smell of blood rising from the otherwise pristine floor.

"You piece of shit," Dave Martini muttered under his breath, farting around with the motherboard that controlled his security cameras. The equipment was twenty years out of date and it was only a matter of time before the circuits fried. With every monitor showing a blue-screen, Dave had come to the conclusion that that time was now.

"Son of a bitch," Dave breathed as he gave up, sitting back in his chair and thinking things through. In a way, he was lucky. The reason the surveillance electronics were old was because Alberta had one of the lowest security-threat indexes in the entire western world. Fuckin' commies in New York might riot when you took their schools away, but people in Alberta just sucked it up and soldiered on. It was why StandardGen had established one of its premier facilities in this jurisdiction. Places in Europe had to be enclosed by walls and towers and razor wire and electric fencing. Here? Just being out in the fuckin' boonies was security enough.

Anywhere else in the whole world, and Dave Martini would have been a whole hell of a lot jumpier when his monitors went down.

In Africa, things had been different. Working perimeter defence on a Global Conflict Management contract for AgroDyne—one of the gigantic international farming outfits— Dave had had to be on his toes. Coons—correction, *poachers*—

tested the fence just about every other day—day and night—and they weren't always half-starved desperate types who were basically hoping to be plunked. Some of those boys came to fight, and African farm units experienced some of the highest attrition rates of all Global Con contracts. But the pay had reflected the danger, and with kill-bonuses, a man like Dave Martini had been able to make a damned good buck over there. Best of all, the company actually *did* maintain the wildlife preserves, which went a long way to silencing bleeding-heart criticism surrounding such contracts. People didn't like the thought of slaughtering Africans trying to get to their own water supplies, but gunning down ivory-poachers or tiger-nad merchants was a whole different ball o' wax. Still, it was a numbers game, and after a couple of profitable tours, it had been time for Dave Martini to ease up on the old stress-levels.

StandardGen Sylvan Lake had been perfect. Rotating between the clinic and the guardhouse, the shifts were longer than hell, but nothing ever happened. It was no exaggeration: in six months, Dave hadn't so much as kicked a reporter in the ass much less fought off any suicide bombers. The job even came with a little walk up apartment in town, which normally one of the three security men had to himself as the other two worked their shifts. With meals at the clinic cafeteria, the job was a damn good gig by North American standards. The best balance between pay and hazard Dave had ever seen.

Still. It was weird, all the monitors going down, all at once. And for the life of him, he couldn't find anything wrong in the circuit boards or breakers. It damn sure wasn't a short, and it didn't look to be a hardware problem. If Dave hadn't known better, he'd almost have suspected a localized EMP attack. But that . . .

"*Quién enes más macho?*" said a voice from the doorway. Dave looked up to see a little boy who matched the voice perfectly. The kid was grinning, like he'd just told the best joke in his whole repertoire, and he was waiting for the impact to register.

Dave Martini was not without instincts. When faced with danger in Africa, he'd actually been able to rely on his gut more than once. He'd seen child-soldiers before and although Miguel didn't look the part, he *vibed* the part once you really saw him.

Once you looked into those heartless eyes, you could see the bloodlust and excitement. The kid gave off the killer's reek in waves, once you knew what it was that was setting off the hackles on your neck, or the goose bumps on your arms.

BUT YOUNG AS he was, Miguel was an old hand too—vastly experienced at dominating the moment of hesitation his child-like features inevitably induced in his opponents. As Dave went for his gun, Miguel already had his leveled: two in the vest to stun; one in the face to finish.

"*Cuatro*," Miguel smiled as Dave tumbled out of his chair.

Eric was going to be pleased, Miguel decided. He advanced to Dave's work-station, stepping over the corpse and engaging system diagnostics. Everything was on time with no surprises. Eric appreciated either precise execution, or successful improvisation, and he was getting the former in spades.

As Miguel worked, he fished his tactical lens out of his breast pocket and fixed the flexi-arm over his ear so he could watch Morrisey's clean-up in real time.

No new signals in civilian bands were being processed in the clinic, but the monitors could still access video archives. Miguel brought up footage from the early morning and erased all traces of their approach. Next, he erased and disabled the perimeter cameras around the Spawning Grounds proper. Security was apparently not a real issue at this facility, but on the perimeter at least, electronics had been installed. For all the good they would do.

In his right eye, Miguel watched as Morrisey shot the doctor in his office (twice in the chest), killed two nurses in the spa area, cleaned the cafeteria, then advanced as per the employee management signal to process the remaining targets. Miguel reflected that if the surviving eggheads stayed calm, they could probably adapt that signal to send out some sort of coded instruction to the world beyond, but in the boy's experience, hunted people rarely thought of such things. It was why Kelly had elected to leave the management protocol unblocked in the tactical plan, and for that, Miguel had to give her some credit. The girl wasn't worth shit in a fire-fight, but she could game-plan with the best of them.

As Morrisey walked a hallway with a measured pace, Miguel

actuated Ana's mic and asked: "Everything all right?"

"*Sí*, Miggy—we're good."

"Nice. Morrisey's almost done."

"Let me know when we're clean, and I'll give Eric the heads up."

"*Bueno.*"

Miguel fixed his attention in the operational plane again as Morrisey approached a laboratory. Stepping through an open door, the shooter put two into a lab-coat wearing, bespectacled tech, then whirled to target a second tech, when a complication arose. Miguel's breath hissed through his teeth as a third figure from the far end of the room produced a sidearm and began shelling the top of the doorframe, causing Morrisey to drop and roll into the lab. Now it was a bit of a mess as the targets were actively seeking either to engage or flee.

Miguel reloaded his weapon and considered moving up in support. *Let's wait to see what develops*, he cautioned himself. It was Morrisey the former SEAL versus a bunch of lab rats, after all.

Panicked shouts and cries carried across the comm-link as Morrisey let the panicky lab-tech spray bullets. Rising from behind a bench, Morrisey shot the opposing shooter in the shoulder, sending the man sprawling out of sight. Morrisey fired off a suppression-burst to stand and take stock of the room while switching to his second sidearm.

Now it was a matter of tracking down signals on his heads up display.

A young woman who looked like a university student cowered under a lab bench and screamed as Morrisey came into view, then stopped screaming as bullets thumped her chest.

A middle-aged aged man hiding under a sink died without a sound, cowering in abject terror without even looking up at his assassin.

Another man made a mad crawling dash for the door, his palms clapping out loud against linoleum when nine-millimeter slugs caught him flush on the starboard side, punching out his lungs.

An insurance-bullet in the chest finished the panicky, gun-toting tech. He died with a sigh.

And as Morrissey approached a final table, he stooped,

paused, and reached in to retrieve a woman's security pass.

Holding the card up to read the name "Gabrielle Dhaliwal", Morrisey said "Shit," without any undue emotion.

"What's the matter?" Miguel asked.

"Looks like we've got a runner."

201

Take time to deliberate, but when the time for action has arrived, stop thinking and go in.

— Napoleon Bonaparte

THEY CREPT ALONG the left side of the cabin—the side opposite the bedroom—James leading the way, Eric in the 2-spot, the rest following in column.

Emerging into the yard at the back, James headed for the deck, but Eric wandered out onto the lawn. Kelly frowned as the man seemed to linger on the spot, looking out towards the lake and breathing deeply of the clean rural air. Loons cried in the distance; invisible robins sang in shadow-shrouded tree boughs.

Kelly approached Eric from behind, joining him on his left flank as the men fanned out around the porch.

"Memories." Eric smiled.

"I can imagine."

"You forget how . . . peaceful it is out here. You overlook that part at the time. But this is lovely."

Kelly had no idea what to say, so she stayed rooted to the spot, watching the tree line. Eventually, Eric turned and headed to the cabin.

James led the way through the unlocked front door, ready as ever to take a bullet for the Old Man. Eric followed, face rigid with tightly controlled, yet seething rage. As they entered the living room, seeing the ashes from the previous night's fire in the hearth, Eric took lead and called out, "Sarah honey. Daddy's home." His voice carried a mocking, jovial tone not reflected in his face.

Into the kitchen and Eric saw a quarter-full glass pot of coffee on the stove; dishes in the sink.

Eric moved towards the bedroom in anticipation while James covered the rear and cleared the bathroom. Staring at the empty, unmade bed, Eric's jaw worked silently, the muscles at his temples grinding into harsh relief. Nodding in acknowledgement, Eric exited the bedroom, headed back into the kitchen, put his pistol on the counter, and poured himself some cold coffee. Men milled in the living room, making the room look small with their bulk. James wandered into the kitchen/dining room area; Kelly scowled.

Putting his cup in the microwave for a thirty second burst on high, Eric said without turning around: "Well, they must be around here someplace. Cars're here. We saw no one leaving on our approach." The timer on the microwave rang: Eric removed his cup, blowing steam off the surface of the liquid as he turned around.

"Gentlemen, I'd like you to find my daughter. Bring her back to me safe and sound. Kill the man, using as many bullets as you possibly can. Kelly."

Kelly moved to face the former-SEALs. "I'm downloading topography and optimal search patterns to your phones. When you clear a grid, indicate it on the map so I can keep track." Kelly's thumbs moved quickly on her device, tasking each member of the team in turn. With that done, she sent a quick text to the masking squad at the clinic, expanding the time-envelope for their holding action.

The operatives departed with a tromping of shoes on wooden steps, dispersing quickly. After a moment, Eric wandered out onto the deck, staring off into the distance, sipping his coffee as Kelly moved to join him. Together they stood in silence for some time, listening to the forest, feeling the fresh morning breeze upon their faces.

"You know what would've been really handy right about now?" Eric eventually asked without looking over.

"Sir?" Kelly responded.

"Drone coverage. Little aerial recon would be just the thing."

"You had to act quickly," Kelly shrugged. "A plan today is always better than the perfect plan tomorrow, right?"

"Mm. Still. You were right to have considered it."

"Doesn't matter. We'll find them."

"Yeah. Lemme ask you something. When did you warn them,

Ms. Lee?"

"I'm sorry?"

"Not yet, you're not." Eric sipped at his coffee, then said: "Up to you how you play this, but acting dumb is going to turn this physical from the jump."

Kelly swallowed, heart slapping about in her chest. A thousand scenarios seemed to flash across her mind's eye, none of them good. Though Eric's exterior was calm, Kelly knew he was right on the edge of homicidal fury. The slightest provocation, and he would kill her where she stood. "When we left the city, I signaled so Sarah would know roughly how much time she had," Kelly said, keeping her voice even, her tone laconic. "You were dozing."

"Fuck, right from the car you did that? Ballsy." Eric took a moment to finish his coffee, contemplating the moment. Kelly felt her body slip into terror-paralysis. It was all she could do to keep breathing.

"Tac-lenses for the masking squad of course," Eric mused, now putting the pieces together, "but we wouldn't need them. Because we didn't anticipate any need to split up. Because that wasn't in your ops overview." Eric nodded in appreciation. "How long then, Kelly?"

"Sir?"

"Don't be coy, kid. I'm proud of you. How long have you been doubling for her?"

"Since . . . since you first approached me. She knew right away—somehow. And . . ."

"Fucking lesbians," Eric chuckled, shaking his head. "I guess I always sensed there was something really there between you two. Overestimated my charm, apparently. Think she loves you, or is she just playing you?"

Kelly flinched: it was a question she asked herself every day. "Bit of both, I suppose," Kelly said, giving Eric the answer she'd always given herself. "She's her father's daughter."

Eric nodded. "What was the plan then?"

"Get you back in the country. Get you out here with minimal coverage. Separate you from your men."

"Nice. Flexible. If Terry had won though . . . he'd never have gone along with it."

"If Terry had won, he'd have died in his sleep. Sarah knew he was your man. And with only Sarah out here, you would've moved with even fewer precautions. It actually would've been easier."

Eric smiled without any discernible happiness. "I was angry," he murmured, more to himself than Kelly. "Rash. That 'abortion' talk made me up-tempo. Nice. You come up with that?"

"Your daughter."

"That's my girl. Well, what do you figure, Kelly? Are you in love with my Sarah?"

Kelly pinched her lips together, her gaze going flat. She didn't owe Eric the answer to that question. If he was going to kill her, he was going to do it regardless of the answer.

Eric chuckled. "I'll take that as a yes," he said. "What I'm paying you, it's gotta be love, make you turn against me like this. You know . . . I may be leaping to conclusions here, but I think it's safe to say that at least some of your feelings are being reciprocated."

"Dare to dream, right?" Kelly said, feeling defiance creep back into her backbone.

"For sure. Dare to dream. But see, that's the flaw in the plan. There's always a flaw, right? You took away my security screen, but you left me leverage."

Eric smiled out into the yard, good eye dancing. He was enjoying himself, Kelly could tell.

For her part, Kelly had gone rigid and felt like vomiting. Eric was right.

She was the leverage.

Mira "Gabrielle" Dhaliwal was not one to panic.

She'd been a trauma nurse at a state hospital in Mumbai and had seen plenty of terror first hand. She had the professional sensibility to compartmentalize her feelings—to stow away that part of herself that had gone numb with shock, and to keep functioning with nerveless efficiency while the world fell apart around her.

She'd seen shrapnel and gunshot wounds—even in real time, as the clinic she'd worked at in Mumbai had once been the site of a gangland shootout. Then as now, she'd reacted quickly, decisively, the active part of her mind refusing to speed things up or slow them down. Then as now, her first move had been to get down, out of sight. After that, it was a matter of escaping the immediate kill-zone.

Her second move, decided upon as Schwarztman took fire, was to remove her name badge. It had occurred to her almost on the level of instinct, triggered by the glimpse she'd gotten of their assailant. It was no terrorist—not with that black battle dress uniform and tac-lens kit, and certainly not with that precise, economical work rate. She'd seen men like that one before—pirate-hunters; slum-gunners; private security . . . such men left little to chance. In a heartbeat, it had occurred to her that she could be tracked by her badge—that tracking her was, indeed, the *purpose* of the badge—so she'd torn it from her lab coat and left it under the desk.

A terrorist might have simply sprayed the room and moved on, but "Gabrielle"—Mira to herself and blood relations—knew this man would be more methodical. She'd had the will to wait, shutting out the screams of her friends and co-workers and focusing on the moment. Once Gil had made his crawling dash for the door and been stopped in his tracks, she knew the killer probably wouldn't linger in that direction. He'd mop up the room in sections like a pro, and when he did, Mira would escape on the very same line Gil had taken. Only Mira had been a good deal swifter, quieter.

Now, sitting in the semi-dark of a maintenance tunnel underneath the hospital, Gabrielle could hear her own wheezing breath echoing off pipe and concrete. She shut her mouth and fought back a moan of despair, telling herself: *keep it together, Mira. You are not out of this yet, and you cannot stay here.*

Then she thought of Khalil, her husband, and almost lost her composure. He would be so heartbroken if anything were to happen to her. They'd moved because his job with StandardGen paid them more than they could have dreamed possible in Mumbai. He'd gotten her on staff, and even though it meant long periods of separation—he in the branch office in Calgary; she on-site at the clinic—there had never been any doubt about seizing the opportunity.

I wanted it too, she thought at Khalil, as though he could feel the impulse. This, whatever this was, was not his fault.

She knew there were surveillance cameras in these tunnels,

but not so many as in the hallways above. She assumed the attackers—she refused to call them terrorists now—would have control of security, and she had stopped herself from running directly to the main exits. She was a rat; they were cats, and they knew where the obvious holes were.

She still had her cellphone, but was terrified to even turn it on. She had no idea what could be done in terms of locating her via her phone, but she feared the worst. She could not bring herself to destroy or abandon it, however: at some point, she'd use it to get help. Failing that, she might even turn it on and leave it somewhere, pulling the same ruse she had with the identity badge. The thought gave her a small boost of confidence—just knowing that she was coming up with such ideas, under this sort of duress.

Catching her breath, slowing her heartrate, Mira forced herself to think. She could get out through the loading bay— from there it was a short sprint to one of the open-use service cars . . . but then what? The small RCMP detachment in Red Deer would respond to a terrorist threat, but . . . Mira had her doubts about their efficacy in this case. She didn't want to give in to paranoia, but she knew this was no terrorist attack. That being the case, it was possible that the RCMP already knew of and possibly even condoned the action. What if she called, and they asked her where she was? *Stay right there, we'll come and get you.* It wasn't completely out of the question. She had seen men like the man in the lab before, knew for whom such men worked. Without more information, calling the RCMP could very well be the end of her.

Who else then?

She could call media in Edmonton. She didn't have footage to give them, but if she were convincing enough, they'd come out with cameras and start causing havoc. With the media on-site, *then* perhaps the authorities could be engaged. Except . . . surely there was reputation-risk at stake here for StandardGen. They'd want compliance oversight on any media relations. Going to the press on her own would cost Mira her job. And yet . . .

That man, that private-security man killing her friends . . . that was an additional complication. If he'd been a terrorist, then StandardGen Head Office would have been her first call. Now? Warning claxons were sounding in her head, alerting her to the fact that there was much more to all this than met the eye. StandardGen employed exactly the same type of security personnel as the man upstairs. She didn't know what that meant, but the similarity was too close for comfort.

Khalil. Khalil would know who to call, who to trust. And she could—and did—trust him with her life.

Up, Mira commanded herself. She rose from the cold, heavily painted-over concrete and peered down the cramped and gloomy hallway. Bare-bulb lights in wire cages provided sporadic illumination, but there was plenty of shadow. The omnipresent hum of machinery in the background would disguise her footsteps. It was now or never. Sitting in one place felt like a wish-of-death to Mira, and she simply wasn't the type.

Creeping resolutely down the hallway, Mira puzzled over the things that she knew, guessed at the things she didn't. She knew that StandardGen facilities were frequent targets in Europe, but here in Alberta, this particular Spawning Ground had never had a security incident. There hadn't even been a press inquiry, not even so much as a trespassing blogger attempting to catch a fitness kill on film. Sylvan Lake and environs had truly been an idyllic setting. So what were these people after?

It did not take Mira long to think of Sarah Wheeler. A lovely girl—one of the tense, haunted ones who brought out the maternal instinct in Mira. Unable to have children herself, the irony of working at StandardGen in Quickening support had never been lost on Mira. She felt strongly about the Spawning Candidates entrusted to her care. She liked to think she made a difference for them. She knew she had in Sarah's case.

The blonde girl with the mesmerizing eyes had been so different from her counterpart. Where Sarah had been tortured by her Quickening experience—writhing and moaning in hallucination—Polly had been comparatively serene. Polly had drifted off with a smile on her lips, completely at peace with the violence being done to her metabolism. It happened that way sometimes—some women took to the Quickening, and others didn't. It had been Mira's experience that the easier the Quickening, the more successful the combat. She had not heard the result of Sarah/Polly, but if she'd had to wager upon it, she would have put all her chips on the brunette.

The problem, the thing that caught Mira's attention, was that

Sarah Wheeler was the daughter of a director of Global Conflict Management, and it was quite possibly one of their men who was currently engaged in slaughtering the inhabitants of the clinic. She had no proof for such a wild allegation, but the elements of coincidence were there, and it made her mind strive for connection.

What could they possibly want?

What was being achieved?

The Executive Program had never caught on in India. Genetic manipulation was common of course—especially illegal sex-selection—but the entirety of the program, the fitness killing in particular, that had never gained traction on the subcontinent. Culture was a fragile thing, and the more you gave in to commodification, the more disposable your people became. In India and throughout Asia in particular, that idea was abhorrent. It was one innovation from the West that many eastern countries had trouble adopting and adapting. Mira had had her own private reservations, but these had been overridden by the money involved. Now she wished she had given the decision to leave Mumbai a little more thought.

She had no idea why assassins were killing her associates above, but she recognized *how* it was being done. Cold-bloodedly. Ruthlessly. Efficiently. It was *processing* more than murder per se. Strip out the horror and it had the feel of a logistics exercise. India had been reluctant to embrace the notion of "vat-grown" predators and competitors, because it was difficult to keep that kind of thing penned up on Spawning Grounds. The people StandardGen was making did not play well with others, and when they returned to their homes after their fitness tests, was it so hard to believe that they took a piece of the Spawning Ground with them? As their numbers grew, was it so hard to believe that the fences between the world and the Spawning Grounds might one day disappear? All the world a Spawning Ground and every man a killer?

Who could say what such people might do? Who could speculate upon their motivations? North America had been willing to wade into the risks with typical swaggering indifference. Perhaps this clinic assault was part of the price to be paid. It was all happening on a level that Mira Dhaliwal couldn't comprehend, but she knew she wanted to survive it.

Whatever game was being played, she had resolved not to be one of the pieces.

The only game she wanted any part of was the get-back-to-Khalil-alive game. Everything else would unfold from there.

So she crept from shadow to shadow; doorway to doorway, crouching in the darkened mouths of branching corridors, ears straining to detect the booted footfalls of pursuit. She wasn't overly familiar with the access tunnels, but the general layout wasn't confusing. The main hallway ran straight to the loading bay. The loading bay opened out onto the parking lot. Simple as that.

Eventually she came to the service elevator, and beside that, the switchback staircase leading up. She hesitated in the darkness, feeling the blood in her ears pounding in resonance with her heart. Her mouth was dry, and her bowels felt ready to release. She thought she heard a sound from the way she had come, and a gasp escaped her mouth—the sound seeming to echo down the hallway though it may only have been in her imagination.

Upstairs is death, a small voice told her. The voice of fear.

Stay down here. Hide in the dark. They cannot want you, will not look for you. Cause them no trouble and they will leave.

Mira whimpered softly, fighting back tears. Again she looked back the way she had come. Someone could already be down here, hunting her.

Or not.

She swallowed hard, steeling herself against her instincts. There would be a cleaning crew arriving in two hours. Maids and body-baggers she knew by name. If the killers were still here by then . . .

She broke cover before she completed the thought, heading quickly for the stairs.

Each step was covered in a kind of maroon-coloured rubberized non-slip coating. Her crepe-soled shoes squeaked on the surface, no matter how she placed her foot.

At the landing, she turned slowly, neck craning to look up the next flight. Daylight shone down from the loading bay above. She could feel cool air moving against her face. Slowly, so slowly she felt the strain in her thighs, she ascended the stairs, peering out into the room as she rose.

The sliding metal door was up; the rising sun hit her at eye level. Not good: she put a hand in front of her face, squinting out into the parking lot, but couldn't get past the glare.

She stepped cautiously into the cavernous room, smelling the industrial odors of the place. Casting her gaze around the various crates, machine parts, fuel barrels and tools, she saw a smear of blood on the floor: a body had been dragged some distance out of sight.

Her heart rate escalated and for a moment, her legs locked. *Move*, she told herself. She was standing on the top step of the stairway, in plain view. On camera for all she knew.

Move!

She broke into a run, and the second she did it, she knew it was a mistake. All her instincts fed off the running—the flight— and all the fight went out of her. Sniveling tears fell now as panic set in, her feet pounding concrete as they had never done in all her life. Blubbering, she bolted from the loading bay and sped into the parking lot.

Thank Christ she'd kept her phone! Their phones started the cars.

She came to a slamming halt against the car door—a later model Mitsubishi electric. Reefing up and down on the handle, she fought back a scream of frustration until she remembered the thing she had just thought of: her phone. Fumbling in her skirt, she retrieved the handset and froze.

She'd have to turn it on.

She stared at the shining black opacity of her view screen, her trembling features gazing back at her.

She'd have to turn her phone on, then initialize the driving app, then unlock the car, then start it.

The car had GPS and other electronics. She hadn't thought about that. The car was like a gigantic phone from the standpoint of tracking Mira Dhaliwal. If she started it, they would know. She didn't know that for certain, but deep in her heart, she felt it.

SHE NEVER HEARD the shot that killed her because it was supersonic. It took her in the base of the neck as she was fretting, standing up straight like a target on a range. Her body rag dolled into the car, then slumped onto the pavement, dead eyes staring into the sky.

"Did you see that?" Clarke said on the open tac-lens line, lowering his Israeli-made Galil assault rifle. He'd taken up a position at the treeline, using a forked tree trunk as a gun platform. With the sun at his back and good sightlines over the parking lot at the access road, it made a perfect sniper's perch.

"Yeah," Miguel said, grinning as his image appeared. Clarke played back the shot with magnification so everyone could be certain of the kill.

"Parking lot secured," Clarke said.

JAMES SHOCKEY HAD been one of the first SEALs to go private, and one of the last to have been government trained. He had never regretted the decision on moral grounds. The truth was, military specialists had been defecting to private contractors for years prior to the big sell-off. All that World War Two human-rights rhetoric wore a little thin when you saw junior officers bringing down six figure salaries for escort duty while you were getting your ass shot up for love of country.

In the end, it had been an easy transition. Defending the constitution made more sense in a private context, because what were you defending if not individual rights and freedoms? James had always been a man who thought about such things; a man who had taken his oaths seriously. He hadn't felt like a traitor when he'd cashed his first big Global Con bonus cheque. He hadn't felt like a traitor, but that wasn't to say that he had walked away from government service without any reservations at all.

For the most part, government targeted the same people as the corporations did. A Somali pirate was on the shit-list regardless of who was giving the order. Muslim extremists: same deal. And it wasn't hard to see through the hypocrisy in a lot of assignments. Where government might target a "communist", consumers via corporate management targeted a "labour organizer". In the end, it often seemed like distinctions without differences. Somebody with power needed somebody taken out. Either way, James was a guy who had always gotten the job done.

But sometimes, working for Eric, you had jobs like this false flag against a StandardGen clinic. James hadn't been asked to be on the masking squad partially because he wasn't the man he once was. Still highly effective and lethal enough, but the clinic-strike was a job for quick reflexes and cold blood, and James no longer had sufficient quantities of either commodity. Years of performance-enhancing drugs had dulled his edge, left him with unreliable twitches and hitches in his movements. In truth, the only job for which he would've come out of retirement was being the Old Man's personal shadow on a mission like this. Eric had set James up for life, and if the Old Man needed support, James was there to provide it.

But James wouldn't have been a triggerman on that hospital job for any amount of money, and he figured both parties knew that going in. Even in his prime, that would've been a tough set of orders to process. It was a job for kids like Morrisey, and that Miguel. Jesus, Miguel. They sure didn't have anything like *that* boy in the old days. Not on the SEAL teams, they didn't.

He saw Sarah up ahead, standing on a wooden pier that stretched out into dark blue water. Sun was rising, creating twinkling motes on the tranquil surface of the lake. James was the perfect choice to manage Sarah: he'd been looking after her since she was a little girl. He'd been more babysitter than bodyguard at times. He was glad that it was he, and not one of the others, who had come across Sarah first. He knew she'd be a bundle of turbulent nerves and emotions in the aftermath of a Spawning Event, but deep down, she was his responsibility, and always had been. That would count, if things got dicey.

James holstered the Sig with its subsonic rounds and internal noise-suppression baffles. Gun was the proper choice for the mission, but this part was a talking job, not a shooting one. He didn't want Sarah spooked or threatened. Long as she saw it was him, long as she didn't feel pressured, there was no reason this couldn't go peacefully.

James approached the shallow steps that rose from the beach onto the pier, and Sarah must have seen him, for she turned and smiled. God, she had grown into some beautiful woman. Not a little girl anymore, that was for sure. She was dressed in hiking boots, jeans, and a light blue sweat-top; she looked like a model for one of those outdoor outfitting companies. She stood with her arms crossed against the chill of the early morning air, her pale blue eyes shining like dimes in the low-angle sunlight.

"Hey, Sarah," James offered, voice carrying easily out across the water.

"Hey, James."

"You're looking well. Good to see you came through okay."

"Dad here?"

"'fraid so."

"How is he?"

"Pissed."

Sarah chuckled and glanced away before returning her gaze to James. "He sort of comes pre-pissed," she said, wandering towards James at a gallery pace.

"That he does." He noted her approach, but sensed no necessary threat in it. They were talking: she was closing to talking distance. Still. He silently went to Def Con 3 just in case.

"I guess you're here to collect me," Sarah said from fifteen feet away, arms still crossed.

"Yes, ma'am."

"You know I'm pregnant, right?" Ten feet.

"Yes, ma'am. Congratulations." Five.

"Guess that means you need to take me alive."

James went for his shoulder-holstered gun, but she was on him in one lithe, springing pounce. Good Lord she was fast . . . not so fast that James wouldn't have cleared his holster on the best day of his prime perhaps, but plenty fast enough now. Her left hand pushed the gun back into the holster while her right foot stamped down hard and flat on the inside of James' right knee. He felt the pop of the ACL, grunting as he dropped down in pain.

Going to one knee actually helped him draw. He swung the gun up, but he needed to be careful: he couldn't risk any kind of torso shot. He'd have to knee cap her, and in the split second it took to make that calculation, Sarah's hands closed over his gun-grip, twisting the weapon around in the grasp, jamming the barrel into James' chest, and pulling the trigger with his own finger still on the mechanism. Three quick, muffled pumps from close-in and the career of James Shockey came to an end. He fell to his back in the sand, dead before he landed.

For a place called the "Spawning" Ground, Sarah reflected, there was a lot of killing going on. She watched as James closed his eyes in repose, his lips parting in grimace.

Sarah bent to retrieve the weapon from the dead man's hand. Pulling the gun away from the fingers, an indicator light alongside the barrel went from green to red, indicating the weapon was palm-coded for James and James alone. Sarah had suspected as much: such precautions were standard for domestic security arrangements these days. Attempting to change the protocol would have raised suspicions. She tossed the gun into the water, and gazed upon James Shockey one last time.

The man had been with her most of her life. Any random memory from her childhood almost always conjured his image in the background. It had given her no joy to end his life, but the hard truth was, he had been the easiest one to cut from the group. Sarah had pre-arranged with Kelly to task James with the retrieval sub-op if possible, because it put Sarah in the position of most advantage. James would have been the most reluctant of all of them to fire upon her. The most conflicted and hesitant. It had made too much sense to set him up.

As well, there was no way Eric could be directly confronted while James lived. The bodyguard's own devotion had killed him in the end, just as he must have known it always would.

Sarah stooped again to retrieve James' phone. Tapping the screen, she brought up the tactical maps she herself had made of the terrain—the very maps Eric's team would be using, thanks to Kelly. She indicated that the pier had been cleared, and showed "James" continuing to move up along the shoreline as per Kelly's instructions.

Sarah could see from the terrain diagnostic that the other two agents were moving into the kill-zone she had designated when she had first done the survey. There was no time to waste. Moving quickly to the tree line, Sarah left James lying in the sand, the sound of lapping lake water providing a gentle requiem.

The first virtue of a soldier, is endurance of fatigue.

— Napoleon Bonaparte

"SHIT," VANCE TELLER said as his dress-shoes slipped on dew-moistened leaves. The underbrush was fairly thick up here, and there was no defined footpath cut into the incline of the hill. *Seek and destroy mission, and I'm wearing a suit*, Teller thought. *Brilliant.*

Kelly Lee was supposed to be some hot-shot tactician, but so far, she'd been a fucking screw up. No tac-lenses. No long guns for Eric's detail—only for the masking squad. She hadn't anticipated an escape-attempt, so everyone tasked for the cabin was in standard business-dress. The search grid was a shit-show, though with three guys Teller supposed it made sense to be so dispersed. Still, this was tricky terrain. Obviously roaming pairs would have been better.

Teller ducked a branch and squinted up ahead. The forest was alive with early morning bird song, and smelled like a golf course, it was so fresh. Beat the shit out of the desert, Teller decided, but conditions were far from optimal. Tac-air for another thing: where the hell were the drones? Even given the false-flag aspect of the op, short-range hand-held units should have been on the asset-list.

If he didn't know better, Teller might have suspected some kind of deliberate set-up. But A.) Nobody in their right mind would try anything against the Old Man. And B.) He realized that Eric's own haste had condensed the planning envelope. Kelly Lee had only had a few hours to pull everything together. Truth was, you did the best you could, and when things went to hell, you improvised. All of them had been there.

Teller wondered about the target—the Executive Program stud who had won the Spawning Competition. Meant he was an Alpha male right there. Meant he knew his shit with his bare hands. But a SEAL was no joke when it came to unarmed combat, and besides . . . this wouldn't be unarmed combat. Most EP grads had basic anti-terrorist weapons training and survival skills, but that fell far short of SEAL standards. The kid had killed, obviously, but that was under the near trance-like state of a Spawning Surge: killing in cold blood was a whole different story.

True, the Program Victor was genetically enhanced, and there was no getting around that. He may have been injured during his Spawning Contest, or he may not have, but either way, he'd be above non-program norms in most combat-related biometrics. Enhanced didn't mean "super", however. Vance Teller was six feet two, two hundred pounds of battle-hardened meat, and although he hadn't opted for implant enhancement due to the certainty of carcinogenic and other side effects (not to mention the risk of third-party hacks), he *was* juiced on this fine spring day. His senses all seemed hyper alert, and he knew his reflexes were amped to hair-trigger efficiency. He had no intention of letting Mr. Warren Milner close distance, but if it happened, the kid might be shocked at what he found. Teller had never met an EP grad in the field, but he'd certainly dealt with all kinds of jacked and ramped-up individuals over his short and bloody career. This asshole wanted to go, Teller would go with him. May the best man win.

Teller steadied himself as his footing threatened to give way, and in the moment of re-balancing, he noticed something up ahead. Eyes narrowed, he verified the details: fingers; a human hand, lying behind a couple of intertwined, massive cottonwoods.

Interesting.

Teller brought his left hand in under the pommel of the gun to assume firing position and cautiously made his way to the tree. He flanked-out to his left a bit, getting a better angle on the hand, bringing the upraised forearm into view as well. For a brief moment, he hoped that the man was injured after all, and had collapsed during the night. Wouldn't it be nice to catch a break for a change?

Nearing the base of the tree however, Teller saw that the hand, the arm, and the body to which they belonged didn't fit the target description. For one thing, this was a woman, her skin oddly mottled and puffy against the soft loam of the ground—as though she'd been immersed in water for an extended period of time. Looked like she might have been a real beauty: long black hair and lashes; body that would have caused double-takes back in the world. Teller repressed a shudder, even though he'd seen much worse. There was something extra-special creepy about the Spawning Ground, and the stuff you could find just lying around out here.

Teller grunted as Warren's full weight came crashing down upon him from the boughs of the cottonwood. The agent went down hard, the gun springing from his hand as he rolled a few rotations down the incline.

Warren quickly retrieved the Sig, drew the slide back, squeezed off a shot . . . only to hear a faint whining noise and a mechanical click from the gun. "Fuck," he hissed, momentarily frustrated.

Teller scrambled to his feet, yanking off his tie and throwing his coat aside. Dropping into a wrestling crouch, he moved up-hill to close, hard lips pulled back in a willing grin. Warren made as if to throw the deadweight of the gun—thought better of potentially re-arming the agent—and in that moment of indecision missed his chance to avoid Teller's tackle. SEAL and Program grad hit the ground rolling as the gun bounced into the grass.

Warren grimaced, turning his head to the side as the agent attempted to claw his eyes. Bridging up with his hips, and rolling to his right, Warren managed to throw Teller off and both men scrambled to their feet. Warren assumed a loose-kneed stance, willing to let the other man initiate. Teller backed off a step, catching his breath, then smiling as he produced a short, thick-bladed knife from an ankle-sheath.

Warren swallowed hard and backed away. He was beginning to regret targeting the gun-hand when he'd had the drop on Teller. Something told him that might have been his best chance to get this over with.

Teller advanced with his left hand forward, the knife-hand

back. A strange thought emerged from the matrix of his fighting-concentration. *I'm only a couple of years older than this guy, tops.* Still, he couldn't help thinking of Warren as the "kid".

Teller feinted and noted the cobra-quick reflexes of Warren, but it was only a matter of time. Sooner or later, the SEAL would close and start pumping home the knife-strikes. So much for genetic superiority.

Teller jabbed the fingers of his open left hand at Warren's eyeline then lunged for his torso with the knife. Warren trap-blocked with both hands, neatly intercepting the knife hand, then securing it, ramming the cold metal up under the agent's chin. Teller's eyes bugged as he slammed into shock: Warren wrenched the knife violently sideways, slicing through the jugular and sidestepping to avoid the jet of blood that erupted from the wound.

Vance Teller buckled to the ground on his back, hands clutching at his neck. In moments, he was dead, his wide eyes staring blankly skyward in astonishment.

To his great relief, Warren felt sickened at the sight. He hadn't felt anything at the time of Terry's death—hadn't been present enough to feel—but at least here he'd felt a reassuring jolt of revulsion at what he'd been forced to do. Despite the nightmare his Spawning experience had become, Warren took some comfort in the fact that he hadn't been totally, fundamentally altered by it. He'd killed for Sarah and he'd killed in self-defence, but in the end, he hadn't felt any bloodlust, hadn't exulted in the moment. In the end, it was "murder", not "victory". He hoped he'd never lose sight of the distinction.

He was still staring at the dead agent when the first silenced bullet took him wide on the right shoulder, and the second clipped him better along the collar bone, shattering it and dropping him face-down in the dirt. He didn't immediately feel the white-hot blast of pain he should have, and wondered dimly if that were a good thing or a bad thing. These SEALs were expert marksmen—presumably if they had wanted to take him out, two shots would have done the trick. So it was a bad thing then. That meant there was more to come.

Cody Wallace straightened up from his crouch, lowered his gun and lifted his phone to his face. "I've secured the man," he said. "Closing for picture reference. Tell Eric I've got a full clip left. I'll make it last."

Wallace advanced on the stunned Program kid. Like Teller, he had suspected something was off about the op, though he couldn't figure exactly what the problem was. Unlike Teller, he'd acted on his instincts, indicating that he'd been following Kelly's instructions on the map while deciding instead to shadow Teller's position. It had been a good call: Teller had been drawn into an ambush, and that meant only one thing.

Kelly Lee was moving against the Old Man.

Nothing for it but to play along, circle back, and get the drop on her. Eric Wheeler could handle himself, of course, but the op was blown wide open: unknowns were everywhere. Lee had botched everything from the get go, but subtly enough to make it look more like incompetence than design. She was as good as advertised, but not good enough. This was not going to end well for her.

Wallace advanced on Warren and decided to start shooting at the feet and work his way up. "Use as many bullets as you can," Eric had said: *will do, chief.* Wallace raised the Sig . . .

And Sarah brought the rock down hard behind the man's right ear, landing with a bone-crunching thunk. Wallace's hand spasmed, putting a bullet into the ground mere inches from Warren's head, but as Wallace's torso sloshed to his left, Sarah hit him again with crashing force against his brain stem.

Wallace flopped onto his back, eyelashes fluttering as his eyes rolled back into their sockets, and Sarah slammed the brick-sized river stone into the man's mouth, shattering teeth. Straddling the agent, Sarah went to work on the remnants of the face—blood-spatter misting up onto her sweat top and neck as she pounded the man into putty.

She was lost in berserker fury at the sight of Warren down. The thought that he might be dead filled her with such inchoate rage and pain that she felt she herself might not survive the moment. Smashing away at Warren's assailant contained its own world of logic: a way of stopping time; a way of keeping Warren in stasis. When the battering stopped, Warren would have to be checked. If he was dead . . .

Sarah couldn't bear it, kept bashing away to banish the thought. But there was only so much skull to shatter.

Breathing hard, Sarah sat back on the dead agent's stomach and cut her eyes toward Warren. She blinked away sudden-onset tears as the thought of losing him overwhelmed her—or at least, overwhelmed her centres of emotion. The protective/reproductive imperative was over-powering: Warren had to survive because the child growing inside her was everything. Her body told her so. Her blood throbbed with rage and despair, her DNA howling in non-verbal angst.

Please . . . please . . .

Sarah pushed up off the unrecognizable corpse and rushed to Warren's side. Sniveling with fear, she rolled him over onto his back and sobbed aloud to see him draw breath. He groaned as pain began to push through mind-fog at last. Sarah could not control her tears. A near-total stranger had survived a shooting, and the relief Sarah felt was heart-breaking in its intensity.

"Hey . . . ," Warren muttered, licking dirt off his lips. "Nice . . . plan."

"Shut up," Sarah sputtered. She pushed up off her knees, rushing to recover Teller's coat, bringing it back to cover Warren's chest. There and back, she glimpsed Polly's pale body lying on the ground. The sight sent shockwaves of fresh, unguided emotion through Sarah's body.

"I'm okay . . . ," Warren mumbled.

"You're . . . fuck, you are not okay," Sarah hissed, assessing his wound. Warren's right arm lay numb at his side. His eyes had a waxen, rolling aspect to them.

"Finish it," Warren said, making rheumy eye contact. "Finish it, come back for me."

Sarah trembled at the thought of leaving, but knew it was the only course of action left. Right now, Eric was at the cabin; if she screwed around for too much longer, he wouldn't be.

"Go," Warren urged, wincing in pain.

Fresh tears fell as Sarah bent to kiss Warren's forehead. The tears felt alien even as they felt like the expression of her own heart. It was all she could do to leave his side.

Then she was up and running, setting a miler's pace for the lake, and destiny.

"Trickle-Down" is a measure of market inefficiency. We can fix that.

— Eric Wheeler

SARAH APPROACHED THE cabin from the lakeshore, using the footpath access through the underbrush. She emerged into the backyard, the morning sun cheerful upon her face, Eric and Kelly sitting together on the swinging porch-chair made for two.

Eric had his right arm around Kelly's slender shoulders. Eric's left hand was in his lap, holding his gun.

Kelly sat motionless—as rigid and still as any other prey-item would be. All she had left was hope.

Sarah approached slowly, eyes locked on her father's. She struggled to contain all her roiling emotions. It wasn't just the Spawning Aftermath, the Quickening . . . she hadn't seen her father in years, and despite the circumstances, part of her reacted as any daughter might.

Sarah came to the bottom of the porch steps, standing on one of the flat lawn-stones set in the grass. Eric was smiling grimly, looking ancient as a gargoyle with that black eyepatch and brooding bone structure.

"Sarah darlin'," Eric drawled. "You look like hell."

"Hey, Dad," Sarah said quietly.

"Kelly here's been bringing me up to speed on your various shenanigans. Seems as though my information hasn't been as accurate as I would've liked over the years."

"Sorry."

"Why don't you take a seat? We've got paperwork to sign."

Sarah climbed the steps, giving Kelly a quick once-over. The girl was petrified, but whole. On paper it was two against one, but Sarah didn't over-estimate Kelly's capability at this point. Whatever happened, it was down to Eric and Sarah alone.

Moving to a stool across from a small table, Sarah took a seat. Spread upon the table's surface, Sarah could plainly see the new Conlin/Wilhelm/Loughren/Wheeler brochure—her name now added to the title. A number of supporting documents on CWL letterhead laid out her contract-upgrade: she had no doubt the terms where generous. And atop the documents lay Kelly's gun. Kelly had thought of a lot, but Sarah doubted she would have had the foresight to give herself a dumb-weapon—one not coded for her own hand. A weapon Sarah might use in a hurry.

"So," Sarah said, resetting her eyes on her father's gaze. She might look like hell, but he didn't look much better. He looked half-again as old as the last time she'd seen him in real life. "This is what it takes for us to get together."

Eric nodded. "I know. Been a long time. Too long. Left you to do too much on your own; didn't give you enough hugs. But you know: world ain't gonna conquer itself."

Sarah couldn't help herself, reached forward to finger the gold leaf of the new brochure. A part of her stirred with pride at the accomplishment. Every professional success meant her baby was that much better situated. Her body rejoiced at the promotion.

"Congratulations, honey," Eric said. "Senior partner at twenty. Gotta be some kind of record."

"How'd Conlin take it?" Sarah asked. It was the first time she'd thought of Jacob and his loss.

"Deal's a deal," Eric shrugged. "He took it like a man. More than I can say for his son. In any event, once the grief passes, he'll see the fees you bring in will more than compensate for any loss."

"Thank you," Sarah said absurdly. And yet . . .

"You earned it. I've also negotiated maternity leave for you. After that you'll head up the legal team for Global Con as discussed. You're going to be the most powerful woman in North America—my right hand lady. Maybe we can make up for lost time."

"Maybe."

"I need you to sign that," Eric gestured with the gun to the

StandardGen optimization booklet for the child. "Speaks volumes that it's one of the last legal documents in the world that requires an actual live signature. Something fitting in that I suppose. Don't worry: I've already filled it out."

"You'll still raise the child?"

"That was the agreement."

"And if I've changed my mind?"

"Well, that wouldn't surprise me. You are one willful girl, that's for sure. But regardless, I'm taking you, and I'm taking the child, and you can give birth in a dungeon if you want, or you can stick to the plan. Kind of running out of patience for these little curveballs you keep throwing."

"What about Kelly?"

"Speaking of curveballs! I gotta admit—that one did surprise me. I'm truly impressed: really thought Kelly here was my asset. It's just getting so you can't trust anyone these days."

"I know the feeling."

"Touché. Listen, I get what I want, Kelly can go back to being your . . . whatever. No hard feelings. Sign those modifications. Let's get this train back on track. Nothing has changed. In five years, you'll be one of a hundred or so most powerful people on the planet. In fifteen years, you'll hand the reins of a truly global empire over to your son. Then you and I will sit back and marvel over all that we have wrought."

"They don't let you choose sex anymore."

"They don't let *you* choose. I'm pretty sure it'll be a boy. Call it a hunch."

Sarah dropped her gaze to the optimization booklet again, feeling her thoughts drift. Her emotions threatened to swamp her like high seas turbulence. "How'd you do it?" she murmured, only barely aware that she'd spoken aloud at all.

"I'm sorry?" Eric frowned.

"How could you send Mom away? And hurt me. How could you force yourself to do what you did with the Spawning upon you? I can't even imagine what that must have cost you."

Eric paused, smile gone. For the briefest of moments, he was Sarah's father again: just and only that. "I didn't undergo a second surge," he said at last. "Couldn't have survived the stress. I just had them put me back in the queue."

Sarah felt her jaw drop. "At forty years old? Against someone in full surge?" She was absolutely incredulous, a tsunami of fresh emotions threatening to engulf her. Half of her was in awe that the man could have won a Spawning Competition so far past his prime. The other half hated him for trying. He was her father biologically, but he wasn't Spawning Bonded to her. He had never felt the feelings for her that she already felt for her unborn child. He literally could not have.

It was how he'd kept his emotional distance. How he'd been able to do what he felt needed to be done, to her, and to her mother.

It was a terrible shock to Sarah, and a terrible betrayal.

A single tear pushed its way down her left cheek. Eric remained impassive at the sight of it, though not, Sarah imagined, completely unmoved.

"Do you ever not get your way, Dad?" Sarah whispered.

"Little glitches here and there," Eric said, smiling almost kindly. "What's that saying—'Often wrong, never in doubt'. I like to think I retain operational control during fluctuating circumstances. You know, everything I've done, in one way or another . . . it's all been for you. You're special, kiddo. Once-in-a-generation special."

Sarah made a noise that was an awful hybrid of disgust and laughter, the events of her life cascading past her mind's eye.

Everything done was for her.

As though that could make her feel better about things.

With a lurch, Sarah lunged across the table, sweeping Kelly's gun into the startled girl's lap and hurtling forward into Eric.

He'd been ready for it, anticipating it. He kicked a leg out to shunt Sarah straight back, sending her staggering down the porch steps.

Kelly fumbled with the gun, eyes wide as her fingers scrabbled for purchase. Too late: Eric shot Kelly twice in the stomach.

Standing, he shot her four more times, her body spasming on impact as her eyes rolled back. Putting the gun down, Eric removed his jacket and tie, turning to glare down at his seething daughter in the yard.

"You son of a bitch," Sarah gasped, trying not to look directly at Kelly Lee. It was only in that moment that Sarah realized Kelly hadn't been a fungible good after all. There really had been something there. And now there wasn't.

Eric descended the steps as he rolled up his sleeves. "You're angry," he said. "I get that."

Eric blocked Sarah's swinging right with a left hand so quick it seemed almost a blur to Sarah. *He's jacked,* Sarah realized. *That was faster than drugs. He's wired up.* Eric's check-jab with the left hand split Sarah's lower lip and knocked her back a step. He stepped-with, hooking her liver with the left hand, doubling his daughter up even as she continued to back away.

"Think how I feel," Eric deadpanned. "You fucking serpent's tooth."

Sarah lunged again with all the lithe power in her ballistic frame. Eric blocked shots with both arms raised, let her punch her way out of position, then stiff-jabbed her mouth again, knocking her head back, sending her reeling.

"I didn't kill Kelly," Eric continued, his voice as bruising as his fists. "You did. True, I guess I did kill Warren, but you should have."

Eric checked a leg kick, sending electric bolts of pain through Sarah's shin. He moved back in his stance, smiling now: Sarah circled to her right, his left, trying to get into Eric's blind spot. Eric nodded, turning southpaw by putting his right foot forward, rotating with his daughter, keeping her in front.

"Kids today," Eric rasped. "No gratitude."

Sarah cried out in loneliness and pain, in horror and fear, giving vent to all her pent up emotions. She kicked and she punched, trying to break the Old Man's defences down, but he was insanely, unnaturally efficient. Finally he snatched her left wrist out of the air, pivoted and worked her around with an Aikido grip, eventually pitching her head-over-heels to her back on the grass.

Sarah saw stars, the wind knocked out of her on impact.

"Get this out of your system," Eric growled down at her. She tried a desperate up-kick, hoping to catch him mid-soliloquy, but he easily stepped back from the attempt, allowing her to rise. "Once we're done here, that's it," Eric continued. "I want us both on the same page going forward."

Again she tried for him, trusting her body to unleash. If she could only hit him clean, he was a sixty-year-old man. For all the augmentation he'd subjected himself to—genetic and otherwise—he was still essentially human.

Eric bobbed on the spot as he stepped his right foot back into orthodox stance, rolled to his right with Sarah's swinging right roundhouse while simultaneously countering a left hook over the top. The punch crashed home over Sarah's right shoulder, impacting her temple, swiveling her head. She went out on her feet, twisting as she collapsed down and to her right, sprawling onto her back in a heap.

Sarah lay moaning in swoon, her eyelashes fluttering.

"Get up and give me what you've got," Eric commanded, inspecting the knuckles of his left hand. "If you're done, then that's it. Let's go home."

There was a whizzing, buzzing noise, and Eric grunted as blood bloomed in a crimson blossom on his crisp white shirt. Two more blood-blooms grew as silenced rounds punched into Eric's chest cavity. Perplexed, Eric staggered on the spot, then reeled backwards as vertigo set in, tripping over his feet to sprawl on his back.

He stared into an incandescent blue sky and frowned as thin cirrus clouds seemed to turn in a clockwise rotation around a pole. He heard his breathing as though magnified through a scuba apparatus, yet somehow coming from far away. Soon, the face of Sarah's mate came into view, indistinct and shadowy against the bright, bright sky. Then Sarah's face appeared, looking somber. All his family in one place, looking down in wonder, and concern. It was oddly comforting.

Warren held the gun of one of the operatives, the agent's hand still in place around the trigger, severed at the wrist by Teller's combat knife. Eventually, as if only now becoming disgusted by the gruesome appendage, Warren tossed the gun away onto the lawn.

Eric turned his head and made eye contact with his daughter. And in the moment before he died, Eric Wheeler smiled. It was a knowing, secret smile, the smile of triumph, and vindication.

As Sarah held that awful gaze, she gasped in what she thought was understanding. That dying smile froze her to the bone. *You bastard*, she thought.

Somehow, with just a look, the Old Man had done enough to haunt her for the rest of her days.

. . . you could now see, they said, what the world and mankind really looked like. They ran about everywhere with the glass, and at last there wasn't a country or person left who hadn't been distorted in it.

— Hans Christian Andersen "The Snow Queen"

WARREN COULD HEAR the helicopter—a big Sikorsky transport—thumping down the valley well before he saw it. It was a bright, cool morning. Gulls turned in the sky, their bodies reflecting the rising sun like sparks in the air. Sarah tried to spend at least one weekend a month out at the house. Said it hurt her to be away from Warren and Kelly for any longer than that. She always made the trip by helicopter, like a visiting head of state.

Kelly ran around the grass fields and rolling hills of the country estate with the endless reserves of any carefree five-year-old. Unlike most five-year-olds, however, her gait was eerily coordinated—the relaxed loping of an Ethiopian marathoner cruising to Olympic gold. Earlier, they'd been playing with a kite they'd built together from Warren's own design; had to bring it down when Sarah's escort drones had taken up orbiting positions over the house. The AI could recognize birds all right, but it wouldn't pay to deliberately confuse the sensors.

Five years, Warren reflected. A lot had changed. A good five years in some ways; a hard five in others. *All because of that fucking smile.*

That dying, death's head grin of Eric's had poisoned his daughter. It always reminded Warren of the "Snow Queen" fable: Eric's grin had been like the slivers of Troll-glass that had gotten into Kay's heart and eye in that story, changing him by changing his perceptions.

"He intended this to happen," Sarah would say soon afterwards. Once she'd had time to obsess over it. Once the thought had started to take on a life of its own.

"No way," Warren would assure her. "Nobody plays chess on that level."

She would fix him with that shining gaze of hers. "I do," she'd say. And he could hardly argue with that.

She had a point. There were moves Eric could have made at the Spawning Ground—obvious ones in retrospect. He had reserves at the clinic he could have called upon. He could have called his search party back once Kelly's treachery had been revealed. He hadn't done any of that. He'd let Sarah come to him, and let things play out. He'd devised the ultimate test of her mettle, and she had passed with flying colours. At least according to Sarah, that's what had happened.

As time went by, Sarah became convinced that Eric had known everything—all of it. He must have known about Kelly from the start. He must have known what Sarah had been up to, from the very inception of her planning envelope. Eric had known, and everything he'd done had been to shape Sarah into something special. He'd been a bastard, but he'd been a bastard with a purpose. In the end, Sarah would argue, hadn't the Old Man been right? The more time that passed, Eric Wheeler dead became more omnipotent that Eric Wheeler alive ever had been.

"Sometimes I can see ahead to endgames," Sarah would say when they talked about it, maybe lying in bed together, perhaps strolling the apple orchards, blossoms drifting down like snow. "I can get outside the market, see where it's going before the signals arrive. Prediction is control, Warren. My dad built me to lead markets, not follow them."

"Right," Warren would say, exasperated by her persistence on the theme. "Like a Napoleon."

"Or a Keynes."

She believed this shit. More and more, with every passing year, she believed she had some sort of extra-sensory intuition about potential equilibrium states. Believed she could bring them about through sheer force of will. *One fucking smile.*

Warren couldn't argue with the results. Sarah had been

confirmed as a director of GCM along with her partnership at CWLW, and it actually streamlined the flow-chart when you thought about it. Eric had been redundant at the end. The board at GCM had seen that right away, and Sarah fit into their plans like a long-lost puzzle piece.

And she'd wasted no time putting Eric's plans into final execution mode.

Atlas-class transports were leaving the ports of Vancouver and Los Angeles every twenty-one days, taking the North American middle class to their new pre-fab camps and fortunes. It was the beginning of the greatest migration of people since the nineteenth century: population distributed not by place of birth, but by market forces. A new gold rush, with millions of miners hurrying to get in, and people like Sarah selling them shovels at every stop.

Stubborn jurisdictions finally gave way to the inevitable in the face of Sarah's will, and the implacable might of comparative advantage. Structures that had seemed so solid just five years ago collapsed, shattered into shards, dissolved into smoke, and were changed utterly.

Governments the world over began breaking up, ceding the vestigial remains of their authority to ascendant markets. The money poured in—more money than Warren had ever dreamed of, or could even understand. And he had benefited directly as well, forming his own firm of consulting engineers, and feeding contracts from GCM into his own networks. He rarely needed to leave the house now, could manage his empire from his home-office. On top of that, he had all the time in the world for Kelly. In many ways, things had worked out better than he could have imagined they would, especially given the tenuous nature of the starting line.

"It's a new Reformation," Sarah would say, and Warren could hear Eric's voice somewhere behind the words. "Representative governments are like the medieval Catholic church. The internet's like the printing press." And so on. Warren didn't have the background to discuss matters on that level. He had the sense of massive, global movements taking place, but couldn't perceive it all the way Sarah did, or thought she did. Whatever energies were being released, Sarah was harnessing them, channeling them into profit, using the profit to reinforce the dynamic.

She was reaping a whirlwind, but was she shaping events, or were they shaping her? Warren could never tell.

He was in awe of her, at times. She had signed billion dollar trade deals and changed the fate of nations. She had over-ruled governments and authorized limited nuclear strikes on intransigent pirate bases. She would work forty-eight and seventy-two hour stretches as she crisscrossed the globe, relentlessly grinding out an already accelerated timetable. He had never seen anybody as driven or as capable as Sarah. She was huge. A leviathan of a human being.

His body still had a dreadful, yearning desire for her—the cellular connection between them as strong as it had ever been. But over the years, the idea of liking her seemed ever more remote. They weren't growing in that direction. His parents hated her, and failed the security-vetting process as a result. So much for Christmas dinner with the family.

Sarah and Warren fought often—sometimes almost on sight—but their dug-in positions were defeated when heated passions inevitably gave way to arousal. They had been conditioned for it. The sight of a curled lip, a blazing eye, a flared nostril, and that was it. They were irresistible to one another. Their lovemaking was "war by other means", as Sarah put it. The phrase came from Clausewitz, one of the military theorists upon whom she'd been raised.

But Kelly was the key. If they got Kelly right, then everything else could be negotiated. As the Sikorsky began hovering into position over the helipad, Kelly pulled on Warren's hand, tugging him towards the machine. "Wait'll it's set, honey," Warren murmured by rote. Kelly grinned up at him, emerald eyes sparkling. She knew the drill.

At first, Sarah had doted on Kelly, and that first year had been their best as a couple. But as the work took precedence, Warren could see Sarah distancing herself, hardening herself, convinced that "father knew best" about such matters. She'd taken to waking Kelly up at 3:00 A.M., and the increasingly limited mommy/daughter time had taken on the tone of a boot camp, or lecture circuit. The crazy thing was the toll it took on Sarah to be harsh with their child. Whenever Kelly cried, it was almost certain that Sarah would echo the tears later, out of sight of anyone except Warren.

All because of that smile.

The copter landed, the engines whining-down as the twin rotors continued to beat the air. A telescoping ladder-stair extended automatically from the fuselage, and Warren let go of Kelly's hand, allowing her to run towards the pad.

Warren knew the stakes, and he gave Sarah latitude where Kelly was concerned, but he was always ready to draw hard lines when necessary. "They can't be adults if they were never children," he'd say. "You can't program that kid to perform on one particular day." Sarah had never hurt Kelly, but as the child got older, Warren knew his wife was feeling a desperate pressure to harden the child. He felt the pressure himself, but he wouldn't give in to it. And he wasn't about to give in to Sarah either.

Eric Wheeler might have been a genius, but Mr. and Mrs. Milner knew a thing or two about life, and the Spawning, too. Warren was determined to see their point of view get equal time. He had to be determined, to set his will against Sarah's.

It wasn't Kelly's birthday, but it was close to being the day of conception: that brutal, majestic night at the cabin when Warren and Sarah had been at their best, and worst. It was nice that Sarah had made the effort to come home on the date. She wasn't all business, Warren reflected. Her arrival was downright sentimental, for her.

The helicopter door opened and a tall, slender man wearing a long coat emerged from the hull. Warren could see Kelly hopping up and down on the spot, clapping her hands. He couldn't hear her voice at that distance, but he could imagine it clear as a bell: "Miggy!" she'd be shouting. "Miggy! Miggy!"

Warren's skin crawled at the sight of the killer's lethal grin as Miguel descended the steps, ruffled Kelly's hair with one long-fingered hand. "He's almost like a brother," Sarah had explained, when Warren had initially refused to allow Miguel to step foot in the house. "You're the one who's so big on extended families."

"No fucking way," Warren had insisted.

"Find me someone else as effective. Find me someone else who could guard Kelly any better. You find it, I'll pay for it."

But he never had. Nobody was as good as Miguel at killing.

But Warren had never stopped believing that where that kid was concerned, they were using the wrong valuation metrics.

Sarah emerged next, and even then, after all the time that had passed, that first glimpse of her took Warren's breath away. His heart thumped in his chest, and he could feel the tumescence building down below. They'd built her to be a wonder for him, and vice versa. Every day was like the first day, their bodies forever enthralled, never complacent.

It wasn't Kelly's birthday, but Sarah carried a large box of some kind anyway, in recognition of the day. Warren smiled, feeling himself comforted by the gesture. Sarah rarely brought Kelly gifts these days, only lessons. The box looked to be big enough for a dog, which would be terrific. Kelly had been lobbying for a puppy for some time now, and was starting to be old enough to accept the responsibility.

Warren allowed himself a smile. As far as they'd grown apart, he'd never totally given up on Sarah. Perhaps this would be the day, this would be the gesture that started them on a better road together. *Dare to dream*, he thought, and headed down the hill to join his family.

ACKNOWLEDGMENTS

Having originally written "Spawning Ground" with no intention of finishing it – much less seeing it published – it is a profound pleasure to be now in a position of meaningful thanksgiving. To Margaret Curelas and Tyche Books, for reading, editing, and believing. To Tony King, for showing me what was theoretically possible and technically necessary, well before I was capable of writing useful fiction. To Diane Walton and the extraordinary collective at On Spec magazine, who published my first ever fiction sale. To Hayden Trenholm, who told me this manuscript was publishable: it matters who says such things to you. To Mariette Sluyter and Brian Padlewski, my intrepid beta-readers, either of whom could have killed the project in its infancy with little more than a raised eyebrow. A tip of the hat to John Maynard Keynes and FA Hayek for unwittingly preparing such fertile ground for sci-fi thrillers. And special thanks to film maker Michael Peterson, who along with the usual encouragements provided a singular example of how an artist can and should be in the world.

About the Author

A life-long Calgarian educated in Political Science and Critical Theory, with a professional background in Finance, it was perhaps only a matter of time before Kevin would slouch towards the writing of dark fiction. It has been a long, eclectic road en route to the "Spawning Ground." Wedding speeches, and comics-letters. Screenwriting and sports journalism (boxing). Aurora-nominated short fiction published in a variety of markets large and small. All of it was unintentional training for a seemingly random, yet utterly inevitable result.